# LADY HARTLEY'S INHERITANCE

When Clarissa Hartley discovers her late husband's estate has been left to his illegitimate son, she fears she has lost everything. Only her godmother's son, Luc, Lord Deverill, suspects fraud. Compelled to work closely with the rakish earl, of whom she disapproves, Clarissa catches glimpses of the compassionate man lurking beneath the indolent façade. But, denying any attraction between them and ignoring his autocratic attitude, she takes matters into her own hands. Plunged into a perilous situation by dint of Clarissa's stubbornness, Luc must race against time if he is to rescue her. But can he succeed?

WENDY SOLIMAN

# LADY HARTLEY'S INHERITANCE

*Complete and Unabridged*

**ULVERSCROFT**
*Leicester*

First published in Great Britain in 2006 by
Robert Hale Limited
London


First Large Print Edition
published 2007
by arrangement with
Robert Hale Limited
London

British Library CIP Data

Soliman, Wendy
    Lady Hartley's inheritance.—Large print ed.—
Ulverscroft large print series: historical romance
1. Inheritance and succession—Fiction
2. Love stories 3. Large type books
I. Title
823.9′2 [F]

ISBN 978–1–84617–636–4

Published by
F. A. Thorpe (Publishing)
Anstey, Leicestershire

Set by Words & Graphics Ltd.
Anstey, Leicestershire
Printed and bound in Great Britain by
T. J. International Ltd., Padstow, Cornwall

This book is printed on acid-free paper

*For André, with my love and gratitude*

# 1

**London 1820**

'Oh, how delightful!'

Lucien Deverill, The Fifth Earl of Newbury, looked up and smiled indulgently across the breakfast-table. 'And pray what news have you received that so delights you, Mother?'

'Why, dear Clarissa, of course.'

'Dear Clarissa?' Who in heaven's name was 'dear Clarissa'? Luc's head was pounding mercilessly, resulting in a deep ennui which caused his normally incisive powers of recall to desert him. Abandoning his less than enthusiastic attempts to identify the lady in question, he glanced helplessly at his mother, offering her a puerile smile of regret.

'Oh, Lucien, surely you must remember Clarissa? She is my god-daughter and at last she has accepted my invitation to come and stay with me. I could not be more pleased.'

'Ah yes, of course.'

Luc gave every impression of being absorbed by his mother's news but in reality he was uninterested and distracted, his mind occupied by the events of the night before.

1

Silently he vowed never again to attempt keeping pace with Felix Western when the mood for celebration came upon him. His lordship's brandy might be excellent but, when it came to imbibing, his friend had a head as hard as granite. In future Luc would not allow himself to be swept along by Felix's indefatigable enthusiasm, however great the temptation. Last night the inducement supplied in the form of Emily Stokes had been considerable, but Luc had a steady stream of attractive and compliant women readily available to him, and accommodating and inventive though Emily had been, she was not worth the debilitating headache with which his over-indulgence had left him to wrestle.

Luc needed to be alert at the best of times to follow his mother's disjointed monologues. She had the disconcerting habit of flitting from one subject to another without warning and today Luc was completely unequal to the task of keeping pace with her.

'Lucien dear, you do not remember at all, do you?'

'Of course I do, Mother. But just — uh — give me a moment?'

Marcia, Countess of Newbury, gave an exasperated little sigh before taking pity on her son and launching upon an explanation.

'Clarissa is Alexander Sneddon's daughter.'

'Of course she is, Mother. She is buried somewhere in deepest Cumberland, is she not?'

'Northumberland, dear. And anyway, Alexander died three years ago and so Clarissa married her neighbour, Michael Hartley.'

'Good God!' Luc was shocked out of his reverie and snapped up his head abruptly. He instantly regretted his untimely lack of deliberation and paused until the ensuing pain receded. 'I remember him. He was the famous Egyptologist and a contemporary of Sneddon's, was he not?'

'Yes, dear, they were of an age.'

'Then why did this Clarissa marry a man old enough to be her father?'

'Because they were business partners — the father and Hartley, that is. They have adjoining estates and were building up a prize herd of sheep of some sort — or was it cattle? I never can quite remember. Anyway, I know Clarissa was closely involved with it all and when her father died three years ago she could not just carry on flitting in and out of Hartley's home without a chaperon, could she? I mean, dear, people do gossip so.'

Luc's lips twitched. His mother's vague notions of propriety never failed to amuse him. 'It was a marriage of convenience then?'

'Possibly,' conceded Marcia, 'but I am sure there must have been some love, on Clarissa's part at least.'

'Oh, undoubtedly.' Luc knew his mother to be a hopeless romantic, who thought the best of everyone. 'And what age is *dear* Clarissa?'

'Oh, I am not sure. No more than five and twenty,' suggested Marcia vaguely.

'And I suppose we must expect your Clarissa to bring her decrepit husband with her on this visit?' Luc shuddered at the prospect.

Marcia sighed with exasperation. 'Lucien, I swear you never listen to a word I say.'

'On the contrary, Mother, I hang on your every word.'

'Well then, you will know that unfortunately dear Michael recently died also.'

'Oh God no, Mother! Not a drooping widow weeping and wailing all over the place? Spare us that, I beg of you.'

'Do not be so foolish,' remonstrated Marcia calmly, waving Clarissa's letter in her son's direction by way of explanation. 'Michael died more than fifteen months ago.'

'Ah good, then at least we will be spared the widow's weeds. I suppose we must be grateful for small mercies.'

'Show a little respect, dear.' Marcia's reproachful tone was mild. 'I have been begging Clarissa to come to town for months now and at last she is ready to oblige me. It seems she must call upon her man of business and thought to combine that necessity with a visit to me. How delightful. I must start making plans at once.'

The pleasure his mother took from her god-daughter's intended visit was almost sufficient to relieve Luc's headache and he offered her another indulgent smile. She was small in stature and at sixty her figure was still neat and trim. Her hair, now totally silver, was styled in an elegant chignon, revealing high cheekbones in what had once, undoubtedly, been a beautiful face. The countess's elevated position within the ton guaranteed that Clarissa Hartley would be welcomed everywhere and Luc did not doubt for a moment that his mother would enjoy introducing her into society. He also accepted that he would inevitably form part of her plans in that respect. Well, just so long as dear Clarissa did not intend to make her visit a lengthy one, then for his mother's sake, Luc would dutifully play his part without complaint. The prospect of squiring an unfashionable country widow about town did not exactly inspire him but he knew well enough that argument upon the subject would prove futile. Besides, it was quite beyond Luc to deny his mother anything. Her pleasure would just have to be his reward.

'And when can we expect to receive the pleasure of *dear* Clarissa's company?'

'Why next week. How nice! It means we will be able to take Clarissa to Lady Cowley's ball. It will be such fun.'

'As you say, Mother.'

Marcia continued to read her letter and munch upon a slice of toast simultaneously. 'Oh dear, that will not do at all.'

'What will not do, Mother?'

'Clarissa can only stay for two weeks. She will have to make it longer. I so wanted to take her on Mrs Cassidy's rout.'

'Perhaps the sheep cannot spare her, Mother?' suggested Luc helpfully.

'Do not be fatuous, Lucien!' Marcia sounded almost severe, which was quite out of character, and Luc regretted his flippancy. He would not for the world spoil her pleasure.

Rising from the table he stretched wearily, whilst reluctantly acknowledging that he was getting too old for all this carousing. Not so long ago he could have matched Felix Western drink for drink without feeling the effects, but now that he had reached the ancient age of thirty those days appeared to be behind him. He leaned over and kissed his mother's forehead affectionately. Straightening up again to his full six foot three and wincing from the pain that even this simple action occasioned, he excused himself and left the breakfast parlour.

Entering his library a short time later, Luc found Simms, his valet-come-secretary and general factotum, awaiting him.

'God, Simms, fetch me some water will you, my throat is parched.'

'At once, my lord.'

Luc threw himself into his chair and sighed dramatically. 'My mother is inflicting some country widow upon us next week.'

'Indeed, my lord, how tiresome.'

'My thoughts exactly, Simms. You must protect me from her.'

'Naturally, my lord.'

'Now, Simms,' continued Luc briskly, all thoughts of Clarissa's unwelcome visit already banished from his mind, 'what business do we have to attend to that cannot wait?'

'Just a few items, my lord.' Simms placed several letters in front of Luc.

'This can wait and so can this.' Luc cast the several items casually aside. 'Hello, what is this?' Luc picked up a thick cream parchment, penned in a lady's flowery hand. It exuded an overwhelmingly cloying perfume, causing Luc to be on his guard and study it suspiciously, absently taking in the unusual gold embossing, which formed a distinctive patterned border around the expensive paper.

'It was delivered by hand this morning, my lord.'

Luc broke the seal, read the letter rapidly, shrugged and consigned it to the fire.

'I take it you have no answer to send, my lord?'

'God no! Emily Stokes was accommodating enough last evening but I have no wish to repeat the experience. Anything else?'

'The Earl of Brabbington sent his man this morning with a reminder that you are engaged to take luncheon with his lordship at Whites today.'

'Oh heavens, I had forgotten. Can I not get out of it, Simms, I feel ghastly?'

'I think not, my lord. His lordship wished to discuss a joint investment with you, if you recall?'

Luc amused himself by investing in the bonds both on his own behalf and, on occasion, that of his acquaintances, but it was rapidly approaching the stage where his hobby was becoming too much like hard work. Even so, he would have to honour his engagement with Brabbington and conceded the point with a martyred sigh.

'Yes, all right, Simms, I suppose I must. Now, is there anything else? No? Good! Then I shall ride in the park and attempt to clear my head.'

★  ★  ★

Clarissa Hartley looked out of her carriage window for what seemed like the thousandth time that day, drummed her fingers impatiently against the worn velvet squabs and tried to hide her anxiety. Her maid and lifetime friend, Caroline Jennings, reached across the space that divided them, patted her mistress's hand and suggested she relax.

'How can I relax, Caroline? It is ridiculous that I must go to London at all but to leave Fairlands at this time of year is just too much. What can possibly be so pressing about Michael's estate that I must go to London and see Mr Twining in person?'

'These things are always more complicated that one imagines, my lady,' opined Caroline, attempting to sound worldly wise. 'But no doubt this visit will see an end to the legal matters and you will have full access to the estate's funds at last.'

'And not before time! But it is so unlike Mr Twining to procrastinate. My father and Michael both found Mr Twining Senior to be efficiency itself. That is why they left their business with the son when he removed to London after his father's death. Perhaps though, he just requires my signature to bring matters to a conclusion.' Clarissa brightened visibly at the prospect.

'You look so like your mother when you take on that expression.'

Caroline had been maid to Clarissa's mother, who had died giving birth to her only child. Alexander Sneddon had been bereft at the loss of his beloved wife and resisted any temptation he might subsequently have felt to remarry. Instead he devoted himself to Clarissa, treating her as an equal, almost from the time that she could walk. He was an intelligent man and gloried in the fact that his daughter demonstrated a quickness of wit and an intellect which almost equalled his own.

It was only Caroline who was able to persuade Sir Alexander of the need to bring some femininity into his daughter's life. She stood up to her formidable master, demonstrating a tenacious courage, and pointed out quite forcefully that Clarissa was not the son he had so desperately wanted but an attractive young lady who needed to be prepared for her eventual role as some gentleman's wife.

Caroline was the only mother Clarissa had ever known, as a result of which Clarissa simply adored her. She was the only person who could temper her excesses of enthusiasm, reason with her and persuade her to at least pay lip service to the dictates of society. Over the years Caroline had artfully steered her young charge in the direction of the many gentlemen who showed an interest in her but Clarissa, to Caroline's great chagrin, would have none of them. She loved her father, to the exclusion of every other man, and had no need for marriage.

When Sir Alexander died, Clarissa's grief was terrible to witness and for a long time Caroline seriously feared for her mistress's health. It was her fierce love of her lands, of the estates generally and of their herd of prize Cheviot sheep in particular, which she and her father had so painstakingly bred, that saved her sanity. But when Clarissa casually declared she had accepted Hartley's proposal, Caroline was disbelieving. A beautiful young girl would throw herself away on an old man, simply to save a herd of sheep? It was unthinkable! But Clarissa was obdurate. She liked older men — she liked Michael. He was kind to her, she felt comfortable in his familiar company, and if they married she would be free to continue her father's work on the two adjoining estates, unhindered by the disapproval of society. Her choice of husband was surely a secondary consideration when matched against the much greater need to continue with her life's work?

Clarissa was as good as her word. With the inconvenience of a hastily arranged marriage out of the way, she set to work with abandon and determination. Sir Michael was ailing himself by that time and, as well as caring for her new husband, Clarissa ran the two estates almost single-handedly, demonstrating a healthy, robust attitude towards the hard, physical work. She was indefatigable and appeared to thrive when pitting her wits against the myriad challenges thrown at her by the harsh conditions, airily dismissing any concerns raised about overtaxing herself.

Clarissa could feel Caroline's eyes upon her now as she twisted her hands anxiously in her lap, unable to sit still. Beneath her tattered gloves were hands that were blistered and torn, thanks to the continual demands placed upon her by her work. Clarissa offered up a silent prayer that this visit to Twining would indeed put an end to all of that. When the estates were legally transferred to her, she would have free access to the funds and would, at last, be able to leave the manual labour to those better suited physically to carrying it out. She would die rather than admit it to anyone, least of all Caroline, but the fact of the matter was that she was physically exhausted.

'I do so hope that Blazon will be all right without me.' Clarissa's respite from anxiety had been fleeting and her brow was again wrinkled with concern. 'I have never left him for so long before.'

'My lady, he is but a falcon. He will be right enough with Masters to look out for him.'

'Maybe so, but he is accustomed to me. I am sure he will pine for want of me.' Clarissa had rescued the injured young falcon from certain death and hand reared it. Caroline often voiced the opinion that the bird would give its life for Clarissa. Indeed, more tenacious than the fiercest of guard dogs, Blazon protected Clarissa with a single-minded, unwavering devotion, which had been described by some of her less generous (male) neighbours as obsessive and unnatural. 'And the lambing is not over yet. What if there are complications that Masters cannot handle?'

'Have you ever known Masters to find himself in a situation that he could not resolve?'

'N-no.' Clarissa gave the concession grudgingly. 'I suppose not, but still, my absence is causing me some unease.'

Clarissa fell silent for a moment. They were reaching the outskirts of London at last, and she could tell that she was losing her maid's attention as she gazed, with obviously increasing enthusiasm, out of the carriage window. Caroline had come originally from London and had only moved to the north when Clarissa's mother had married Sir Alexander. Clarissa did not think Caroline had returned to London once in all the intervening years and had delighted in her excitement when she learned of Clarissa's planned trip to stay with the Countess of Newbury. Indeed, her unbridled enthusiasm now they were reaching the capital was infectious and, with an indulgent smile, Clarissa asked Caroline to describe exactly where they were.

'I am so looking forward to seeing my godmother again,' remarked Clarissa. 'It has been an age. It is so kind of her to still take an interest in me.'

'Lady Deverill was always such a good friend to your mother. She promised her she would look after you.'

'Yes, indeed and she has been a most diligent correspondent over the years. But it is the thought of her son that concerns me. He has a terrible reputation as a rake, you know. That does not matter to me, of course, but I disapprove of a gentleman with so many advantages in life being so morally lax.'

'I hear he is very handsome,' remarked Caroline artfully.

'Humph, perhaps, but why should that be of any concern to me? I shall see as little of him as possible and spend my time — most agreeably, I have no doubt — with Aunt Marcia. I just hope though Aunt Marcia does not try and make his lordship accompany us when we venture out. That would be an agony for us both, I am sure. Anyway, doubtless he will have better things with which to occupy his time.' Clarissa spoke in a dismissive tone and turned her attention once again to the bustling streets through which they were now journeying.

'Now come, Caroline, tell me more about your time in London with my mother, before she married my father. Tell me again how beautiful she was and how fêted.'

Having noticed that their surroundings were rapidly improving as the carriage made steady progress through ever wider and grander streets, Clarissa realized for the first time that she would be spending the next two weeks in very august company. Delighted at the thought of being reunited with her godmother, she had not paused to consider it in that light before and, glancing down dubiously at her scruffy attire, she experienced a momentary lack of confidence.

'I feel the need for reassurance,' she added, almost to herself.

# 2

Luc strode home purposefully. The determination in his long stride, the grim expression marring his chiselled features, lent proof to his towering rage. The pleasantness of the mild spring afternoon went unnoticed by him as his black mood took a tighter hold.

Brabbington had invited him to luncheon for a second time. On this occasion they had dined at his residence in Sloane Street and Luc had supposed they would take their meal alone and agree the arrangements for their joint investment. Instead he had been compelled to endure Lady Brabbington alternately pushing her ridiculous daughter at him and then blatantly flirting with him herself. God, what a bore it had been! The singularly unattractive chit had looked at him through timidly adoring eyes: had simpered, blushed and proved herself incapable of stringing so much as one intelligible sentence together.

Did Brabbington really think that he, Luc Deverill, managed funds because he needed the blunt? That was just ridiculous! Surely he knew just how well placed he was and that he

17

looked upon his financial machinations purely as a sport — a challenge? But Luc could think of no other reason why Brabbington would expect him to show an interest in his mousy daughter.

Luc was handsome, rich, titled and highly eligible. He had been enduring the single-minded attentions of countless aspirants for his hand for years now. Indeed, scheming matrons took the opportunity to push their protégés into his path at every social occasion he attended. If his peers, or more likely their spouses, now contemplated using his business interests as a means of gaining his attention for their offspring then it was definitely time for him to reconsider his options.

Recently, Luc had been tiring of the artificial life within the *ton* anyway. Maybe now was the time to make good his half-formed plans and retire to his estate in Berkshire? His mother would naturally wish to remain in their town house for the remainder of the season: she enjoyed it all so much. But Luc had had enough. The endless round of balls, parties, masquerades and routs was becoming a bore. He supposed that he must have been at it for too long.

Cheered a little by this half formed decision, Luc rounded the corner into Grosvenor Square in time to see one of the scruffiest carriages he had ever encountered leaving his front door and disappearing into the mews behind. He cursed violently. That was all he needed! His mother's widowed friend was arriving today: he had completely forgotten. But surely she had not travelled all the way from Northumberland in that rattletrap? She would be black and blue all over if she had. And why would she anyway? The brief glimpse Luc managed of the horses harnessed to the damned vehicle was sufficient to tell him that they, at least, were good quality, well-cared for stock. But if this woman was as wealthy as his mother had led him to believe, why was she travelling in such squalor? It made no sense at all.

Luc entered the house to find the hallway deserted. Ever efficient, his staff had clearly already taken Lady Hartley's bags to her chamber and, from the sound of it, his mother had scooped 'dear' Clarissa up and taken her into the drawing-room for refreshments. Luc briefly contemplated taking the opportunity to escape unnoticed to the relative safety of his library. But he knew such action would be considered by his mother to be the height of bad manners. She would be aware of his return and he would not have her think that he was deliberately slighting her guest. Best get the introduction over with. He could then leave them to converse with a clear conscience.

Entering the drawing-room Luc barely suppressed a groan. An exceptionally tall lady turned to face him: or at least he assumed she was facing him. It was hard for him to be sure for she was clad from head to foot in the deepest of deep black. Her garments were threadbare and shapeless, making it impossible for Luc to make any judgement whatsoever about the condition of the body beneath them. As for her face, the lady wore a bonnet — black, of course — and her features were completely obscured behind a thick veil. Had his mother not said that her husband died more than fifteen months ago? Why still the deep mourning?

Showing none of his horror outwardly, Luc entered the room and smiled at both his mother and the apparition in black.

'Ah, Lucien, there you are!' exclaimed his mother brightly. 'Just in time to take tea with us. Now, Lucien dear, you remember Clarissa, of course? Clarissa, this is my dreadful son, Lucien. Lucien, allow me to introduce dear Clarissa, Lady Hartley.'

Luc made one of his effortlessly elegant bows to Clarissa, who in turn dropped a brief curtsy and offered a hand, now devoid of glove, to his lordship. Luc took it, noticing at

20

first that it was exceptionally large, with long fingers tapering to broken and neglected nails. He was accustomed to dealing with *tonnish* ladies who spent hours worrying about such trivialities. He thought absently that Clarissa could not appear in society with her nails in this state. His mother must find a way to mention the matter to her delicately. Then he noticed the blisters, the scratches and calluses. What on earth had happened to her? Had she been attacked during her journey? She looked as though she had been in a fight. Then realization dawned and Luc was able to cover his horrified reaction only by utilizing social skills born of many years' practice. These injuries had been caused by manual labour. Surely to God she did not care for her blasted sheep herself?

Showing none of the workings of his mind, Luc smiled at their guest and bade her a good afternoon.

'I trust I am not causing an inconvenience in your household, my lord, arriving at such short notice?'

Clarissa's voice was pitched low; its timbre melodic and easy on the ear. It was undeniably agreeable and Luc found himself wondering what other surprises she was concealing beneath that veil? Then he recalled the state of the hand, which he still held in his, and decided he could easily postpone the moment when he must look upon more of Lady Hartley's person. Releasing her hand he smiled once again.

'We are delighted to see you, Lady Hartley,' Luc assured their guest, as he fell automatically into the polished and faultlessly mannered role that was second nature to him, his socially correct smile masking his true feelings. 'My mother has been in alt since first receiving word of your coming.'

'Of course I have. Now come on, Clarissa dear, do sit down.' Marcia ushered her into a chair. 'And you too, Lucien. Ah good, here is tea now.'

Pouring tea and distributing cakes and sandwiches kept Marcia momentarily occupied. Luc was amused to see Clarissa help herself to a substantial portion of the food: something else that *tonnish* ladies never did. Perversely he found that he approved. She either did not realize her mistake, or simply did not care. Then again, perhaps she was just hungry. Whatever the reason, he liked women with healthy appetites — for all things. And if she really intended to eat then she would have to lift her veil and reveal her features, regardless of whether or not Luc was prepared for such an eventuality.

But Luc was to be disappointed. Clarissa

half lifted her veil and secured it to the top of her bonnet, thus revealing only her lips, chin and, he was pleasantly surprised to observe, an exceptionally long and elegant neck.

'Now, Clarissa dear, tell us all about your journey. Was it too tiresome? Did you encounter any difficulties? How long did it take?' Without waiting for answers, which was just as well since 'dear' Clarissa's mouth seemed to be constantly full, Marcia went on. 'I am so glad you brought Caroline along. She must be such a comfort to you. You know, I have not seen her above twice since your mother moved from London.'

'I do not know how I would have managed all these years without Caroline, Aunt.'

'Your mother used to say the same thing about her. She is such a treasure!'

Luc knew he should make some contribution to the conversation. 'Are you well acquainted with life in the *ton*, Lady Hartley?' he enquired languidly, his bad temper firmly back in place. If his manners lacked their customary gracious charm then he really could not summon the energy or will to do anything about it.

'This is my first visit, Lord Deverill.'

'Good heavens, is it really? Then you have missed much entertainment, being so far north all this time.'

'That, my lord, is a matter of opinion.'

The reply was succinct. She did not even look in his direction and Luc found himself mentally applauding her backbone. Here she was at the end of a tiring journey, in surroundings undoubtedly far grander than anything she was accustomed to, and yet she refused to be intimidated. Well, good for her! Luc was used to women falling all over him and agreeing with his every word. Just for the hell of it he must discover if this one really did have any spirit, or whether she too would moderate her behaviour and become as boringly predictable as the rest.

'Indeed it is my opinion, Lady Hartley.' He treated her to his most charmingly correct smile, the one that could tame even the frostiest of matrons and had bailed him out of trouble on more occasions that he cared to recall. 'Pray, what opportunities do you have for good theatre in your part of the world?'

'I have little time for such frivolities, my lord. I have two estates to run.'

'But surely you have reliable staff to undertake those duties on your behalf?'

She hesitated slightly before replying, clearly annoyed at this turn in the conversation and reluctant to reveal too much about her domestic arrangements. 'There is still much that requires my attention,' she finally managed in a dismissive tone.

Luc persevered, enjoying provoking her and sensing that she was holding on to her temper with the greatest of difficulty. 'But everyone must relax at some time, Lady Hartley. Pray, do tell me how you manage it. Do you play or sing?'

'I do neither.'

Marcia intervened. 'Lucien dear, leave poor Clarissa alone and allow her to finish her tea in peace. The poor child has been travelling for days.'

'You are right, Mother, and I apologize, Lady Hartley, for my indelicate enquiries. Now, I have business to attend to myself and will leave you ladies to converse. Pray excuse me.'

He made another of his elegant bows to Clarissa and left the room.

★  ★  ★

'Of all the rude, arrogant, opinionated, self-centred . . . '

Caroline chuckled. 'You have met his lordship then, have you, my lady?'

'Yes, unfortunately.'

'I take it you did not like him?'

'And that surprises you?' Clarissa was pacing distractedly in front of the fire in her chamber, far too agitated to remain still. 'How dare he patronize me!'

'Is he as good-looking as they say?'

Clarissa hesitated, reviewing in her mind all she had seen. A tall man, far taller than she and that was unusual. A thick crop of long black hair, which seemed to constantly fall across his face. Chiselled features, a straight nose and strong square jaw, full lips and even white teeth. She was surprised to realize she had noticed the breadth of his shoulders, the wide expanse of his chest. His blue superfine coat had sat well upon those broad shoulders, she reluctantly conceded, but then she supposed it should given that it had doubtless cost a fortune. The blue and black stripes of his waistcoat had contrasted beautifully against the snowy whiteness of his shirt, and his neckcloth had been tied in a perfect Mathematical. No doubt he spent hours perfecting his appearance. Well, that was fine if one had nothing better to do with one's time.

Clarissa appeared determined to further blacken her mood by dwelling upon the subject of Luc Deverill. His buckskin breeches had clung to exceptionally strong looking, muscular thighs. She wondered that she had observed such a triviality but assured herself that anyone would have done so when sitting beside him for above half an hour. That was undoubtedly why she had also noticed that when he smiled at his mother, his whole expression changed from almost severe indifference to affectionate indulgence.

'Good-looking, Caroline? Humph, I suppose so, if you like the dandified type.'

'And his eyes, my lady, did you happen to notice their colour?'

'No, of course not!'

Caroline regarded her mistress sceptically but refrained from making any comment, content instead to allow the silence to stretch uncomfortably between them.

'Navy-blue, black — I do not know!' snapped Clarissa impatiently, unsettled by Caroline's knowingly superior smile. 'As black as his soul I should not wonder; if he has one, that is — which I doubt. They make him look like the Devil incarnate.'

Caroline maintained her silence, a highly unusual occurrence, guaranteed to convey her feelings more purposefully than words ever could and to infuriate her mistress further.

'What is it, Caroline? You did not really expect me to like someone as shallow as his lordship, surely? Someone who doubtless occupies his time with nothing more taxing than pleasures of the flesh.'

'Ah well, there is a lot to be said for

27

pleasures of the flesh, my lady.'

'Humph, not you too, Caroline? Anyway, I just cannot imagine how someone as sweet as Aunt Marcia could have bred such a brute.'

'Ah well, my love, there is no help for it. You will just have to make the best of it.'

Clarissa screamed with frustration at the banality of their conversation and threw a cushion at her maid in an infuriated attempt to prevent her from smiling.

★ ★ ★

Luc stood up as Clarissa entered the drawing-room that evening — and gaped in astonishment. She wore a similar shapeless black garment to that in which she had travelled, but this time she was hatless: her face was revealed to him for the first time.

Her hair was the colour of burnt corn, pulled back severely into a knot at her nape, not a curl in evidence. But her face engaged Luc's attention for the longest time. Completely devoid of the powder and paint that habitually adorned the faces of the ladies of his acquaintance, she was, nevertheless, spectacular. Her face was almond-shaped, her features perfectly proportioned: small upturned nose, lips a cupid's bow, high cheekbones, a firm chin leading to that long, swan-like neck he had glimpsed earlier, all paled into insignificance however, when compared to the most compelling eyes that Luc had ever encountered in a woman's face. They were enormous; mirrors to her soul flashed brown fire, hinting tantalizingly at closely guarded passions just waiting to be released. Whatever the rest of her was like, and he still could not even hazard a guess because of that God-awful gown, her face was one of the most beautiful Luc had ever seen. His reaction to her beauty was entirely predictable and extremely uncomfortable. He hoped she would not notice, but then again she had been a married woman, so seeing arousal in a man could hold no surprises for her and she did not look as though she were the type that swooned. Besides, she must be accustomed to the reaction she engendered in men.

'My God, Mother, she is beautiful!' he muttered *sotto* voce, his eyes not once having left her face.

'Well of course she is,' agreed Marcia equitably. 'I told you as much.'

'No, Mother, you did not. Had you done so I can assure you I would have remembered.'

'Oh well then,' hissed Marcia in a theatrical whisper, 'I must have assumed you already knew.'

Luc took his eyes off of Clarissa for the first

time since she had entered the room and, suspicions aroused, transferred his attention to his mother. Her expression was innocence itself but there was a smug satisfaction about her whole demeanour which instantly set Luc upon his guard. If he was not much mistaken, she was up to something. But there was no time to dwell upon that now. Clarissa had crossed the room and was almost upon them.

'Lady Hartley.' Luc stepped forward to meet her and offered her his arm and an engaging smile simultaneously. 'I trust you are feeling refreshed and recovered from your journey?'

'Perfectly so, I thank you, sir. I do not tire easily.' Ignoring the proffered arm, Clarissa pointedly seated herself as far away from Luc as possible and turned her attention from him with a rudeness to equal his of that afternoon. 'Good evening, Aunt Marcia.'

Clarissa's gentle smile as she addressed his mother was sufficient to excite Luc all over again, obliging him to turn away in an effort to conceal his very obvious arousal.

'Good evening, Clarissa dear. Dinner will be served shortly but first we must discuss our plans for tomorrow. I am so excited at the prospect.'

'I am greatly looking forward to looking at the sights. What do you have in mind, Aunt?'

'Oh, all manner of things. But, Clarissa dear,' probed Marcia delicately, 'did you bring no other coloured gowns with you?'

Clarissa hesitated. 'No, Aunt, I do not have any.'

'You do not have any?' Marcia repeated aghast. 'What nonsense! And, Clarissa dear, why still the deepest mourning? Michael's passing was well over a year ago now.'

'I have my work clothes at home; they are all I need.' Clarissa's tone was sharp, defensive and impatient all at the same time, making her discomfort with the subject matter all too apparent. 'I do not have the time for socializing and therefore have no need for other clothes.'

'But, my dear, I have such plans for your visit. We are to attend balls and parties and all manner of things. I am so looking forward to introducing you. But never mind, we can call upon my *modiste* tomorrow morning, before we do anything else. She can work wonders and will have you fitted out in no time.'

'I cannot attend balls and parties, Aunt.'

'Cannot attend? Of course you can. You will be a sensation!'

'Aunt Marcia, I mean no offence, but such gatherings are not for me. I only wish to see you and then my man of business. After that I shall return home.'

31

'Oh no, dear, surely not? You deserve to have some fun.'

'We must allow Lady Hartley to make up her own mind, Mother,' said Luc gently. He stood as the dinner gong sounded. 'Ladies.' He offered an arm to each of them.

'Pray escort your mother, Lord Deverill. I shall not faint for want of a strong arm to lean upon, I do assure you.'

Having said as much, Clarissa swept ahead of him into the dining parlour without a backward glance; thereby missing her aunt's knowing little smile as she observed her suave son's stunned reaction to this casual and unprecedented slight.

Throughout the meal Marcia kept up a constant stream of bright chatter. She did not seem to notice Clarissa's barely concealed hostility towards her son, or Luc's growing interest in their guest and his determination to draw more than a few reluctant words from her whenever he addressed her.

'Louisa and Suzanna are to dine with us tomorrow evening,' trilled Aunt Marcia, beaming. 'You will recall that they are Lucien's older sisters?'

'Indeed yes, Aunt,' replied Clarissa, when she realized some response was required from her.

'Now, let me see. Of course you know that

Louisa is my first born. She is three and thirty now and married to Lord Snaresbrooke. They are in town for the season of course. They have three little ones already and they are such dears! And Suzanna, who is not quite two and thirty, is married to Viscount Denby. They are blessed with just one delightful daughter as yet — but,' continued Marcia, in a conspiratorial tone and obviously enjoying herself thoroughly, 'we have high hopes of more.'

'I look forward to making their acquaintance,' said Clarissa, meaning it.

'Oh, Clarissa dear, they are so looking forward to meeting you as well. It will be such fun. But where was I? Oh yes, Claudia — my youngest but one — was only married last month and is still on her wedding journey.'

'Indeed, Aunt.'

Aunt Marcia chatted on blithely about her family and Clarissa, realizing that only the smallest responses were necessary on her part, allowed her attention to wander. Even so she enjoyed her aunt's descriptions and found it impossible not to be swept along by her enthusiasm. She studiously ignored Luc's brooding presence at the head of the table. Instead she listened indulgently to Aunt Marcia's tales of her second son, Simon — an officer in The Prince of Wales 12th Light

Dragoons and married to the delightful Francesca, ('two dear children already and a third on the way — so exciting, my dear!'), and of her 'baby', Anthony, in his final year at Oxford. Such a clever boy as, of course, were all her children.

★ ★ ★

It was Clarissa's habit to rise early and she saw no reason not to do so the following morning. Entering the breakfast-room she thought to have the place to herself but was annoyed to find Luc already halfway through breaking his fast. He rose courteously as Clarissa entered and pulled back a chair for her on his right-hand side. After a moment's hesitation she took it, attempting to hide her annoyance at having to endure his tiresome company at such an early hour.

'Good morning, Lady Hartley. I trust you slept well?'

'Thank you, yes but then I always sleep well, my lord.'

'I daresay. The sleep of the just, no doubt. But why so early this morning?'

'I am in the habit of rising early. My life is not one of idleness you know and I see no reason to change my habits simply because I am away from home.'

'Indeed, perish the thought!'

A footman poured coffee for Clarissa and she smiled her thanks. She felt Luc's eyes upon her back as she stood and helped herself to a large breakfast from the sideboard.

'What is it?' she asked, resuming her seat and waving Luc's offer of assistance aside. She could sense that he was amused about something.

'You have a very healthy appetite, ma'am.'

Clarissa put down her fork and glared at him. 'Lord Deverill, I work extremely hard and very long hours. It would be impossible for me to put in a full day without proper sustenance. But then,' she added, 'I suppose hard work is a subject upon which you are ill qualified to voice an opinion?'

'I wonder what caused you to reach that conclusion?' he replied, in a deceptively mild tone. 'After all, you barely know me.'

Clarissa's spirited response froze on her lips as the door opened once again and a shaggy black head appeared. The body that followed the head belonged to one of the largest and scruffiest dogs Clarissa had ever encountered. She was astonished. What on earth was a nondescript hound of that nature doing in a household such as this? She would have imagined that if there were any dogs in the house at all they would be of the finest pedigree. This one was charmingly anything but. It had impossibly long limbs and, as it entered the room, Clarissa noticed, with alarm, that it walked with a definite limp.

'Oh!' Clarissa smiled with delight and offered her hand for the dog's inspection.

'Be careful!' warned Luc sharply. 'Mulligan does not care for strangers.'

'He is yours?' Clarissa could not keep the surprise out of her voice.

'Yes.'

Ignoring Luc's astonished gaze and chuckling to herself as she realized that in all probability no guest would ever have behaved thus in his breakfast-room before, Clarissa fell to her knees, smiling gently and talking quietly to the dog. Mulligan demonstrated his dislike of strangers by rolling on his back and graciously allowing Clarissa to tickle his tummy. When she stopped for a moment, an impossibly large paw touched her arm, demanding more attention. Clarissa chanced a glance at Luc, ready to enjoy his disgusted expression at her lack of restraint in crawling about his floor. In this though he disappointed for she could detect only casual amusement in his visage.

Clarissa looked up again, her eyes shining

with pleasure. 'He is beautiful!'

'There I agree with you, Lady Hartley, but I suspect that few others would.'

'Well, that is their loss. What do we care for the opinion of others eh, Mulligan darling?' She looked up at Luc. 'Where did you get him, my lord?'

'He was found abandoned, half starved and almost dead in the East End.'

'And you took him in?'

Luc shrugged carelessly. 'What else could I do?'

Clarissa could imagine most gentlemen in Luc's elevated position not giving a second's thought for the welfare of an unfortunate dog and, against her will, found herself admiring his compassion.

'I see. And what happened to his leg?' Clarissa stroked his injured limb gently; unaware that no one, other than Luc, had previously been permitted by the fastidious Mulligan to do so. The dog was still nervous after his ordeal and trusted few people.

'It was broken. We think he had been tortured, his leg broken for sport,' said Luc, his jaw tightening in anger.

Clarissa gasped and stroked the dog more gently still. She placed a few delicate kisses on his shaggy head and was rewarded by having her hands thoroughly licked. 'You poor, poor boy.' She turned her head towards Luc. 'Can nothing more be done about his leg?'

'No, it will not set right, but he gets about well enough.' Luc smiled briefly and Clarissa thought it to be the first time he had not offered her his artificial, *tonnish*, smile. She warmed to him a fraction more. If he cared about a scruffy mongrel there must be some hope for him. 'You should see him lollop about on the estate in Berkshire. Anyway, we are convinced he no longer has any pain.'

'I am very pleased to hear it.' Clarissa reluctantly righted herself and returned to her breakfast, mindless of the fact that her hands had been thoroughly licked by the dog.

'Lady Hartley, I have a favour to ask of you.'

'By all means,' responded Clarissa absently, as she ate with one hand, whilst stroking the dog's head, now resting comfortably in her lap, with the other.

'My mother has greatly been looking forward to your visit. She does not often have female company now that my sisters are all married with households of their own. Would it be too much to ask of you to accompany her to a few balls and parties whilst you are here?'

The affection that Luc clearly felt for his mother was reflected in his words and

Clarissa was moved by his obvious concern for her enjoyment. 'I understand you desire to oblige your mother, my lord, and I applaud your motives but unfortunately it is not possible.'

'Why not?' Luc was looking at her intently. His eyes were soft and there was today a warmth about him that she had not detected previously. But Clarissa did not doubt it was a façade that he used often to get his own way and was not about to be taken in by it.

'I do not care for such activities, my lord.'

'And so you would deny my mother on so flimsy an excuse? As a distinguished guest surely you realized when coming to us during the season that some small effort might be required on your part?'

'No, it is not that, it is just that I am not accustomed to dancing and I . . . well, what I mean is, I . . . '

'Is it money, Lady Hartley?' Luc spoke so quietly that Clarissa at first thought she must have misheard him.

'What? No, of course not.' She squared her shoulders defiantly and glared at him.

'No?' Luc said the word quietly but managed to infuse a wealth of challenge into it.

'Oh, well, all right, I suppose there is no harm in your knowing. I do find myself temporarily short of funds, but that is not the point. Anyway, what made you suppose that my reluctance was in any way pecuniary?'

'Well, if you will permit me to speak freely and not take offence?' Clarissa nodded impatiently but could not meet his eye, too embarrassed by the turn their conversation had taken to find her voice. 'The condition of your carriage first alerted me to the possibility. That and the fact that you travelled only with your maid and coachman and, excuse me, but your clothing too and — well, your hands.' Luc picked one up and turned it over gently. 'No lady I have ever met has undertaken manual labour to the extent you appear to have done,' he remarked in a gentler tone than Clarissa had thus far heard him employ. 'Why would you do it, I wondered? The only conclusion I could draw was that it is financially necessary.'

'Yes, but not for much longer. I see my man of business next week and hope to be informed that my husband's affairs have been settled and I can have full access to the funds.'

'You have not had access to them in the interim?' Luc sounded surprised.

'No, unfortunately not. But Mr Twining informs me that is quite normal.'

This statement definitely gave Luc pause. 'But you assume that when you see this Twining person next week all will be successfully concluded?'

'Yes, I most sincerely hope so. I cannot imagine why else he would wish to see me.'

'Indeed. But in that case, Lady Hartley, there can be no harm in your obliging my mother by visiting her *modiste* and purchasing one or two suitable gowns?'

'There is a problem, my lord.'

'The gowns will, of course, be added to my mother's account and you can repay me when your affairs are settled,' he continued smoothly, ignoring her interruption.

'Oh no, my lord, I could not possibly!'

'You would be doing me the greatest of favours, I can assure you, and the pleasure you would give my mother must surely be worth the small sacrifice on your part?'

Clarissa narrowed her eyes at him. 'Well, since you put it like that I suppose I cannot refuse. But only one or two simple, practical gowns mind, which will be of service to me when I return home. You are right, I suppose, in that I should eschew black. But I am only doing this for your mother's sake and,' she added, wagging an admonishing finger at him, 'do not dare to smile at me.'

'Certainly not, ma'am! Such action would be entirely inappropriate.'

But it appeared to Clarissa that Luc was having the greatest possible difficulty in keeping his lips straight.

# 3

When Clarissa finally left the *modiste*'s the following morning, in company with a very animated Aunt Marcia, she was beginning to suspect that she had been thoroughly duped. In spite of Caroline's best efforts over the years, Clarissa had demonstrated little or no interest in lady-like apparel and was completely unprepared for the complications pursuant to being supplied with a few, supposedly, simple gowns: to say nothing of the expenditure, which had to be mounting alarmingly by the second. The problem was that no one would tell her exactly how much things cost and Aunt Marcia waved any objections she raised airily away. Clarissa could tell that she had not enjoyed herself so much for years and simply did not have the heart to disappoint her by constantly insisting she be kept informed of the amount she had spent.

Clarissa decided upon just one ball gown and nothing Aunt Marcia said on the subject could persuade her to order another. What need would she have for ballroom apparel when back in Northumberland? She did however succumb and order two beautiful evening gowns, four day dresses, (refusing to differentiate between morning and afternoon — they would just have to do for both), and a carriage dress.

What totally flummoxed Clarissa though was the need for so many accessories. It was necessary, apparently, to have different petticoats to complement each dress. When Clarissa innocently questioned why one or two would not suffice for all her new gowns, an incredulous silence fell over the salon, only to be broken when everyone laughed at once to cover their surprise, convinced that this elegant lady must be speaking in jest.

Furthermore, an array of different footwear was required, as were gloves and hats for every conceivable occasion. A never-ending list of undergarments and stockings was deemed to be indispensable: so too were ribbons, shawls and decorations for her hair. It was exhausting and at the end of it all Clarissa decided that she had been less tired after a long day in the saddle rounding up stray sheep.

'Now, dear,' said Marcia brightly, as they finally left the salon, 'was that not the greatest fun? I do so enjoy spending money.' The alarmed look on Clarissa's face alerted Marcia to her excessive tactlessness, for she was quick to correct herself. 'Not that it cost very much at all, of course, have no concerns on that score. But what did you think of your ball gown, darling, you looked so lovely in it?'

Clarissa recalled the cool, luxurious feel of the beautiful silk as it slithered invitingly against her naked skin. She had never owned anything half so extravagant before and reluctantly admitted that she had rather enjoyed herself.

'Of course you did, dear, and I can hardly wait to see you in it in two nights' time.'

'Are you sure it can be ready by then? It seems such a short time away.'

'Oh, have no fear, Nicole can work wonders. Now then, why do we not return home for luncheon and this afternoon I will have my maid trim your hair for you, and tidy your poor nails too.' Marcia beamed at Clarissa, making it impossible for her to object to her tactlessness.

'Why not, Aunt?' she responded with a resigned smile of her own.

Over the next two days Clarissa continued to wear her black and was surprised to discover that she was looking forward to the delivery of her new gowns and the opportunity to show them off. She put it down to the fact that she had never before been to London and was anxious to see the sights.

She acknowledged now that she had been naïve to consider that she could do so dressed as she was whilst in the company of a countess. She cared nothing for herself but knew it would reflect poorly upon Marcia if they were seen together. Grudgingly she admitted that Luc had been right to persuade her, for Marcia had been positively animated since Clarissa had agreed to a new wardrobe. She pushed her concerns about the cost resolutely to the back of her mind. Time enough to worry about that after she had seen Mr Twining.

The dinner party on Clarissa's second evening proved to be a great success. Clarissa, still wearing her shabby black, began to have concerns as the time approached that she might become the subject of Luc's sisters' derision. They were obviously very grand ladies and doubtless shared their brother's cynical and disdainful attitude towards life. But Clarissa could not have been more wrong. Both girls were mirror images of their mother: attractive, witty, full of fun and ceaseless chatter. Their husbands were, indeed, very elegant gentlemen but both appeared genuinely pleased to meet Clarissa and went out of their way to make her feel comfortable, appearing not to notice her shabby attire. They were interested in her farming methods and would have spoken to her on the subject at some length had not Marcia intervened. Dear Clarissa was having a well earned rest from her endeavours and they were not to tax her with bothersome questions.

What amazed Clarissa most of all was the way in which Luc's sisters treated him. There was none of the deference she would have expected them to demonstrate towards the head of their family. Instead they appeared to take pleasure in baiting Luc about his unmarried state, competing with one another to make helpful suggestions — delivered with disarming smiles — as to potential wives. More amazing still was the calm way in which Luc tolerated their high spirits and allowed them to run on. He clearly held his sisters in high regard and Clarissa frequently observed him smiling at them indulgently.

When the girls were not interrogating their brother about his matrimonial intentions they bombarded Clarissa with questions: many of them relating to her new wardrobe, which Marcia had already described to them in exacting detail. And their husbands, seemingly undeterred by Marcia's ban on the subject of sheep farming, continued to converse amiably with her as well, putting her more and more at her ease.

Only Luc seemed to have little to say to her. He looked in her direction frequently and appeared a little disturbed when his sisters' husbands engaged her in conversation for too long, but other than that, for the most part, a penetrating silence reigned between them. Whenever he did address a remark to her, demonstrating the languidly polite yet mildly derisive attitude which Clarissa now associated with the man whom she still considered to be no more than a wastrel and rake, the caustic sparring that was becoming the norm between them sprang up, seemingly of its own accord, and appeared to entertain his sisters hugely. Clarissa was not to know that they had never before heard a lady address their suave and highly eligible brother in such a dismissive manner. No more had they previously encountered one who felt such apparent disregard for his opinion of her.

★   ★   ★

It was the evening of the ball and a beaming Caroline, making no attempt to hide her pleasure, assisted her mistress into her beautiful gown. Securing the last of the laces she stood back to admire her handiwork.

'At last!' she sighed contentedly.

Clarissa looked at her reflection in the pier glass but could not recognize herself. The gown was of sea green silk: a colour that Nicole had been most insistent upon and which Clarissa acknowledged now had probably been right. It was simplicity itself; a sheath that clung invitingly to her form, showing a good deal of her *décolletage* — too much, surely? In the *modiste*'s, surrounded by smiling, approving faces, it had seemed fine but now she could feel the first tentacles of self-doubt worming their way tenaciously through her mind.

'Calm yourself, my love, it is perfectly fine!' Caroline's throaty chuckle was infectious and its familiarity helped to restore Clarissa's confidence. 'This is not Northumberland, remember. There will doubtless be many ladies in attendance this evening far less modestly attired, you just mark my words.'

Clarissa kissed her old maid's papery cheek, promised her a full account of the evening when she returned, squared her shoulders and left her chamber, already curious to see what absurdities lay in wait for her on this, her first evening out in the famous *ton*.

Luc was in the drawing-room, a glass of whisky in his hand, as he awaited the arrival of the ladies. Dressed entirely in black evening clothes, the severity of which was relieved only by the crisp whiteness of his shirt and the midnight blue silk of his waistcoat, he looked more mysteriously handsome and broodingly dangerous than ever. The black sheen on his superbly cut coat complemented his swarthy complexion to perfection and lent him a piratical air, which would undoubtedly cause more than one delicately disposed lady to reach for hartshorn before the evening came to a close.

But Luc was impervious to the fine figure he cut. Instead he was deep in contemplation: his mind preoccupied by the subject of Clarissa Hartley. He was at a loss to know what it was about her that so attracted and unsettled him and, in a perverse attempt to discover the answer, he mentally listed her faults.

She had no idea how to behave in society and would doubtless embarrass him; she crawled about the floor playing with his dog; her enormous appetite would draw attention to her; her hands were a mess and she was impertinent, spirited and far too ready to express her opinion. And as for her person, doubtless her body would be a terrible disappointment but, really, what else could he expect when she ate all that food?

Luc re-examined his list, attempting to be

fair. Were they really faults? Had he not been wondering of late if he was fed up with the artificiality of the *ton* himself and so was it not refreshing to find someone who was not even willing to pay lip service to its absurdities? As for Mulligan, he seemed to love her as much as she did him and Mulligan did not usually like anyone! Her appetite had appealed to him when he first observed it: he found it to be another amusing aspect of her individuality. Most women ate large meals before going to balls so as to appear in public as though they had the appetites of sparrows. He could not somehow imagine Clarissa condoning such ridiculous behaviour. And her hands were the result of what he had now discovered was her single-minded determination to keep her father and her husband's lifetimes' work intact until such time as funds were made available to her. Surely a cause for admiration? And as for her body, well — what did it matter? She would be gone from his life in another week.

The door opened, Clarissa walked in and Luc almost choked on his whisky. Putting his glass aside hastily he found himself openly gaping at her for the second time in as many days.

'Good God!'

'Good evening, my lord,' responded Clarissa evenly, her new-found confidence deserting her as swiftly as it arrived. Judging by Luc's horrified reaction she had obviously got it entirely wrong, her appearance was somehow amiss and she would be an object of derision. 'Is something wrong?' she asked him, unnerved by his exacting scrutiny.

'Wrong, Lady Hartley? Oh no!' He spoke with reverent awe as an appreciative smile spread slowly across his face, his black eyes rendered luminous with surprise and pleasure. 'You are incredibly beautiful!'

But it sounded more like an accusation than a compliment as, for once, Luc's poise and habitual grace deserted him, rendering him as clumsy and gauche as an awkward adolescent. Recovering himself quickly, his eyes ran the length of her slowly and his wolfish smile broadened wickedly. How could he have got it so wrong? Her figure was certainly not slight, as was the current fashion; it was, however, perfectly proportioned, curvaceous, inviting and entirely to his liking. Her breasts looked to be full and firm but disappointingly covered by too much fabric. The silk of her gown glided smoothly over her waist and displayed the outline of long, slender limbs that set his heart racing and his mind wandering in all sorts of forbidden directions. The gown was perfection itself. Nicole had obeyed his dictate and persuaded her to sea green silk. He had just known the colour would be right for her.

Her beautiful face was still unadorned by powder and paint, but her hair had been freshly trimmed, particularly around her face, serving to relieve the severity of her previous style. It now fell in simple, natural waves which shone in the candlelight as she moved her head and emphasized the extent of her devastating beauty. Luc reached for her gloved hand and raised it to his lips.

'May I hope that you will favour me with the first dance this evening, my lady?'

'Ah, well, that could be a problem.' Clarissa extracted her hand and looked embarrassed.

'You do not wish to dance with me?' Luc affected a hurt expression.

'It is not *only* that,' she said, blushing slightly but not, Luc was amused to notice, denying the fact that she found the prospect of dancing with him to be less than inspiring. 'It is more that, well . . . ' She hesitated, unsure for a moment how to go on. Finally, tilting her chin defiantly, she met his gaze boldly. 'You see, the thing is . . . well, what I am trying to say is that I cannot dance!' There. She had said it. She maintained her regal stance and sent him a challenging look, defying him to have a good laugh at her expense.

'My dear Lady Hartley, you do not know how sad that makes me feel.' Clarissa was astounded not to be able to detect any sarcasm in his tone. 'Why has such a simple pleasure been denied to you? Surely they dance in Northumberland?'

'Of course they do!' she responded irritably. 'I can manage country dances: we had those sometimes on the estate when my father was alive and I can waltz — after a fashion. My father taught me but I am rather out of practice and I should hate to step all over those shiny shoes of yours,' she added sweetly. 'But as for those cotillion things, I have to confess that they are quite beyond me. I always seem to move the wrong way. I do not see the point of them anyway, all that twirling and swaying. What a waste of energy. No, I shall just remain with your mother, well away from the dancing.'

Luc observed her in silence for a moment. She had about as much chance of staying away from the dance as he had of avoiding Emily Stokes. One look at her and half the bucks in the room would be surrounding her. Luc felt absurdly protective all of a sudden. He told himself that she knew nothing of society: would not know what to expect. It would be far better if she remained with him. He would keep her safe. After all, she was his mother's guest so it was his duty to protect her.

Luc's silence appeared to unnerve her and she spoke again. 'Besides, Lord Deverill, I am usually taller than the gentlemen I meet and that tends to make them uncomfortable.'

'You are not taller than me.' He had taken her hand again and was standing very close to her, dwarfing her with his size and powerful masculinity. He could detect panic in her eyes as she looked up into his face, now looming dangerously close to hers. He was wearing his predatory smile once again and was well aware of the lethal intent in his eyes. He pranced, catlike, around her, surrounding her with his restless, tensile energy. Still holding her hand he took in her appearance from every angle. Then he permitted his smile to broaden lazily. 'Well then, my lady,' he said quietly, 'it seems that I must curb my impatience and wait for the first waltz before we take to the floor together.'

'Are you sure you want to risk it?'

'Oh yes, m'dear, I am more than willing to risk a very great deal for your sake.' He raised her fingers and kissed them once again, just as the door opened and Marcia entered. She appeared to take the scene in at a glance and beamed delightedly.

'Ah yes, Clarissa, my dear, just so, just so!' She gave a sigh of pleasure before clapping her hands briskly. 'Now, come along, my dears, I do so want to beat the rush.'

In spite of Marcia's best intentions they were not amongst the first to arrive. By the time their carriage had beaten its slow path to Lady Cowley's door, the ballroom was almost full. Clarissa descended the stairs on Luc's arm, her posture elegant and erect, an expression of polite interest gracing her beautiful features. But as they progressed she gradually became aware of a decided lessening in the conversations around them. Many people turned to stare at them; others moved a little closer, blatantly raising quizzing glasses as they attempted to gain a better view of the newcomers.

Clarissa had never been to a society ball and did not know what to expect. Furthermore she was distracted. The scene in the drawing-room with Luc had unsettled her. She recalled the strange emotions she had felt when he stood so close to her and grazed her hand with his lips. She felt his presence looming above her, drawing her in. He appeared to swamp her with the breadth of his shoulders, with the sheer force of his masculinity. She shuddered and tried to rid herself of the feeling, pleasant though it was. She was far too level headed as a rule to be given to fits of fancy and would not permit her imagination to run riot now just because she was in strange surroundings.

'Why are so many people looking at us?'

'They are not looking at us, Lady Hartley, they are looking at you.'

'But why? Have I committed some sort of *faux pas* already?'

'Not at all. They are simply looking at you because you are new and everyone wants to know who you are. The ladies are all insanely jealous because you are so beautiful and all the gentlemen wish to dance with you — and more.'

'But that is ridiculous! I am not beautiful.'

Luc chuckled wickedly. 'Allow me, and the rest of this throng, to be the judge of that.'

No sooner had they reached the bottom of the stairs than they were accosted by Luc's friend, Felix Western.

'Good gad, Luc, who do we have here? Who is this charming creature?'

Luc sighed resignedly, knowing the rest of the evening would continue in the same vein. 'Lord Western, allow me to present Lady Hartley. My mother's god-daughter,' he added, in answer to Felix's unspoken question.

Felix bowed elegantly, causing Clarissa to wonder if all gentlemen were required to practise the movement for hours in front of a mirror before being permitted to enter society. The notion amused her and she was smiling broadly as Felix raised her from her curtsy.

'See, Luc, I am making the lady smile already. Perhaps you should entrust her to my care? Speaking of which, Lady Hartley, the first dance is about to form up. Can I persuade you to stand up with me?'

'Lady Hartley is saving herself for the first waltz, Felix,' said Luc, affecting a studied nonchalance he did not feel, 'and,' he added laconically, 'it is promised to me.'

'Ah well, I can but — '

'Luc, you naughty boy!'

Their conversation was interrupted by one of the most elegant ladies that Clarissa had ever seen. She was small, with a profusion of white blond curls and an engaging face. Her ball gown was superb and she wore it with a casual familiarity, causing Clarissa to suppose that such garments had adorned her person for her entire life. The bodice was cut scandalously low, which amused Clarissa when she recalled Caroline's opinion upon the subject of necklines.

'Where have you been and why have you

not answered my notes?'

''Evening, Emily,' responded Luc, with another sigh. He had deliberately avoided the places where he knew Emily was likely to be since his tryst with her at Felix's last party. He had hoped that by so doing, and by not answering her daily notes to him, she would realize he had no serious interest in her, thereby saving herself any form of public humiliation. Obviously not! 'Lady Hartley, may I present Mrs Stokes.'

Emily offered Clarissa an appraising glance and dismissive nod before focusing all of her attention upon Luc once again. 'Come along, Luc, I am sure Felix and Lady Hartley will excuse us. You must dance with me.'

'On the contrary, Emily, I must do no such thing.' Luc's tone bore all the hallmarks of his usual languidness, but even the determined Emily must have been able to detect the intended slight. 'Now, if you and Felix will excuse us there is someone I would have Lady Hartley meet.'

Luc placed Clarissa's hand on his arm and led her casually away, leaving Emily and Felix to observe the elegance of their retreating figures.

'What was that all about?' asked Clarissa.

'Nothing of importance. Now come on, I

will introduce you to some of the leading lights.'

'With pleasure, but I did promise I would seek out your sisters.'

'Never fear,' predicted Luc, resignation in his voice. 'They will find us soon enough.'

And, of course, they did. Both girls swept upon Clarissa, kissed her expansively and declared themselves delighted with her gown. They flooded her with questions: wanting to know how she was enjoying the ball, with whom she had thus far spoken and so much more. Their husbands were scarcely less verbose with their compliments, causing Luc to frown at them and his sisters to dissolve into a fit of inexplicable giggling.

After a further exhausting half-hour the first waltz struck up. Luc bowed before Clarissa. 'I believe the pleasure is mine, Lady Hartley?' he said, with a disarming smile and, offering her his arm, led her to the floor and swept her into his arms. As he did so she observed his sisters exchanging a conspiratorial smile, causing her to wonder idly what mischief they could be plotting now.

After an unsteady start, when Clarissa almost made several wrong moves that were elegantly covered by Luc, they settled down. Luc danced well, held her tightly and led her firmly into the steps.

'Relax, Lady Hartley, you are doing well. Enjoy it!'

'Shh, I'm counting.'

Luc chuckled. 'Just follow my feet. I will not let you go wrong.'

'Why is everyone looking at us again?'

'For the same reason as when we entered the room. How many requests for your hand have you turned down?'

'I am unsure.'

'At least a dozen, probably more and now here you are dancing with me. Besides, people are curious and it is the first opportunity that *they* have had to get a good look at you.' Luc motioned towards a cluster of matrons seated near the dance floor, all of whom were observing them with differing degrees of interest and finding much that required discussion between them. 'And anyway, I dare say we make a very handsome couple.'

Clarissa snorted and put up her chin. Luc grinned smugly and held her a little closer. The dance ended and Clarissa was surprised to find she had rather enjoyed it.

'Are you all right, Lady Hartley?' asked Luc with concern, as he raised her from her curtsy. 'You look a little flustered.'

'Well no, not really, to be honest. It is so crowded in here and so hot. Is there

61

anywhere in this house where I might find a little quiet? A brief respite is all that I require.'

'Of course; come with me.'

Cutting a path through the throng with practised ease, Luc led Clarissa onto the terrace. As soon as she was outside she lifted her arms above her head and greedily took in huge gulps of fresh air.

'Thank you, that is better. I am not used to crowds, to the constant press of bodies. And all that perfume too. I found it a little overwhelming. Give me a recalcitrant herd of sheep to deal with any day.'

Luc appeared highly amused. 'Some pundits might observe that drawing similarities between a ball and a herd of sheep shows remarkable insight.'

'Actually, I am not really in a position to judge because I have never been to a ball before.' Clarissa was surprised that she admitted as much to him and wondered what had made her do so. She had not intended to leave herself open to his derision.

'What never? Not even in the country?'

'No, and I have never owned a ball gown before either.'

'Well that one looks delightful on you. I trust I will have the privilege of seeing you wearing others before long.'

'I doubt that. I return home next week.'

'Are you enjoying this ball, Lady Hartley?'

'Well — y-yes.'

'Do I detect a 'but' in there somewhere?'

'Well, since you ask, all those elegant ladies in there disturb me. They are so delicate and appear to be completely helpless and unable to do anything for themselves. They make me feel uncomfortable. I must appear as a clumsy elephant by comparison.'

Luc roared with laughter. 'Clarissa, m'dear, you underestimate yourself.'

'I do not think so. And also, no one seems to talk about anything. It is all so shallow! Oh, I am sorry, sir, I did not intend to criticize.'

'Not at all, your views are more than refreshing.'

'Well, then, perhaps you can explain what I did wrong earlier. Lord Sterling asked how I was enjoying my stay in town and what I thought of it and so I told him. He seemed very much surprised. Why should that be?'

'M'dear, you are a breath of fresh air. You see, no one here actually answers a question honestly.' He paused reflectively. 'Come to think of it, hardly anyone ever answers a question at all.'

'But why not? What is wrong with that? And why ask a question if you do not wish to know the answer?'

Luc gave another of his throaty chuckles. '*Tonnish* people giving honest answers? Now that is a thought!'

Confused, Clarissa moved to lean on the balustrade. It was a balmy, mild night and she looked up at the clear velvety sky, which was speckled with bright stars.

'I tried to count them once, you know, when I was a child. My father caught me at it and for nights on end we tried together to manage it but he warned me that we would not succeed; that they stretched into infinity. I wonder if he is amongst them now?'

'You loved your father very much?'

'Oh yes, above everyone. My mother died giving birth to me and my father took responsibility for me almost single-handedly. I never had a governess, you know. He taught me everything himself. I could read proficiently by the time I was six. At ten we had political discussions and spent our evenings playing chess. But most of all he taught me to love and respect the land: to put back as well as take out. He persuaded me that I could be anything I wanted to be. He was convinced that the only thing which stops people achieving their dreams is the limit of their respective imaginations.'

'But he did not think to supply you with feminine things?'

'Huh, what need did I have of them? I was more than content. Caroline, my maid, often used to say the same thing to him though.' Clarissa smiled at the memory. 'She used to get quite cross and say that I needed to be introduced into society, to go dancing and meet young gentlemen. But I did not have any desire to and so my father let me be.'

Clarissa was still observing the sky. 'My father also taught me to recognize the constellations. Look.' She pointed upwards. 'There is the Bear. And the Plough is yonder.'

Luc stepped up behind her and, standing very close, he caused a strange shudder to rock her body as he pointed upwards also, his hand skimming gently over her bare shoulder. 'And there, I believe, is Orion, the Hunter. I can just make out his belt and sword and can you see the hounds at his feet?'

'You know about the stars too?'

'I have a little knowledge of many subjects,' he responded with a smile.

Clarissa shuddered again and moved away from him, distancing herself from the distracting feelings of danger and excitement he seemed to engender within her whenever he stood too close: whenever those black eyes of his raked slowly over her face, leaving her with the distinct impression that he could see into her head and read her thoughts.

'Tell me about your Northumberland, Clarissa.'

'Oh, Northumberland.' Clarissa whirled round dreamily. 'Where to start? Have you never been there?'

'I have passed through Newcastle on my way to Scotland but that is all.'

'Well, it is England's most northerly county, as you must know. It is wild, rugged and mostly untamed. Some of our coastline is outstandingly beautiful and the countryside is home to a variety of unusual wildlife. We have red squirrels, roe deer, badgers, feral goats and eider ducks, to name but a few. We have white cattle too that roam free and, sensible creatures that they are, dislike the company of man. Besides that the rivers and coastal waters abound with salmon, sea trout, grey seals, otters and so much more.'

Clarissa paused to draw breath, unaware how animated her expression had become now that she was talking of something she loved so passionately. 'And then, of course, there is a wide variety of bird life. We have coastal, upland and lowland birds, all of whom enjoy the offshore islands and muddy estuaries. We have black curlew, red grouse, oyster catchers, sandpipers . . . ' Clarissa paused and, looking up at Luc, she smiled in embarrassment as she ticked the species off on her fingers. 'I am sorry,' she owned, 'am I getting carried away?'

'Not at all! You are making it sound most enticing.' He offered her an indulgent smile, ruthlessly quashing the desire to pull her into his arms and kiss her. 'Please continue.'

'All right, I am glad you said that because I am now getting to my favourites.'

'And they are?'

'Why, the majestic birds of prey, of course. There are sparrowhawks, eagles, falcons, merlins and, most importantly of all to me, Blazon.'

'Blazon?'

'My falcon. I rescued him when he was a fledgling and hand reared him.' Luc looked confused. 'He is a falcon and my friend,' she explained simply.

'What type of falcon is he?'

'You know something about birds of prey?' Clarissa did not try to hide her surprise.

'I have already told you that I know a little about many subjects.'

'Blazon is a magnificent long-winged falcon and I miss him terribly. I have never been apart from him for so long before.'

'I am sure he will be fine.' Luc smiled encouragement at her. 'But tell me, what made you and your father decide to breed sheep?'

'It was Michael and my father who made the decision when I was still young. Our estates adjoin but are both quite small — the two together do not extend to ten thousand acres — and with such poor pasture one requires at least that much land in order to succeed. Michael was a dedicated Egyptologist in his younger years and spent little time in England. He was delighted when my father suggested the scheme. It meant that his land would be properly managed during his absences.

'Anyway, the estates are ideally situated for our business. The Wansbeck River forms our southern boundary and affords us the advantage of being able to send our fleeces to the port of Newcastle directly via the river. Newcastle is but thirteen miles away and we have the market town of Morpeth on our western-most perimeter.'

'Doubtless the end of hostilities in France has opened up that lucrative market to you for your fleeces once again?'

'Indeed. But as to our reason for breeding Cheviot sheep, my father and Michael made that decision because they do well in our part of the world: they can survive the harsh winters and live on the sparse moorland. But they lack size and their wool yield was disappointing. My father experimented and I

68

have carried on with those experiments. A few years ago I introduced some merino rams in an attempt to improve the bloodlines.'

'And did you succeed?'

'Yes. There is a marked improvement in the size of the fore-quarters and last year my wool yield improved by almost twenty per cent.' Clarissa did not attempt to keep the note of pride out of her voice anymore than Luc attempted to hide his admiration.

'My compliments, Lady Hartley, that is a most impressive achievement.'

'You know something of sheep? No, you do not need to remind me!' Smiling, she held up her hands to prevent his response. 'You have a little knowledge of many subjects.'

They laughed together. 'Yes, but remember that I am a farmer too. I run a few sheep on my land in Berkshire.'

'But I thought you bred horses?'

'I do, but sheep are excellent for cleaning up the pasture. They happily eat anything that my fastidious thoroughbreds will not deign to wrap their dainty muzzles around.'

'Yes,' agreed Clarissa, with a soft, enticing smile that sent Luc's senses reeling, 'sheep will do that for you right enough.'

'Do you manage everything on your estate as well as helping with the manual work?'

'At the moment I do, but I hope after next

week things will get better. And I have Masters, my manager who was appointed by my father, and who is excellent. I would not have left Blazon, or the dogs either, if it were not for Masters.'

'Dogs,' said Luc with another indulgent smile. 'Why does that not surprise me?'

'I have four — all waifs and strays, like Mulligan, and all of whom I love to distraction.'

'Lucky dogs!' muttered Luc under his breath.

'Oh, you would not understand!'

Clarissa whirled away from him, hurt and disappointed beyond endurance. During her description of Northumberland she had formed the distinct impression that Luc understood her fierce determination: that he could empathize with her need to carry on her father's work. But with one careless aside he reminded her he was just a dandified, idle aristocrat who had never done an honest day's work in his life. For some reason she did not comprehend she had spoken to him of things that she had never discussed with another living soul and all he could do was mock. She paced the terrace, attempting to bring her temper back under control.

'Lady Hartley.'

Clarissa turned her head impatiently. 'What

is it you want of me now?'

'Why do you dislike me so much? You hardly know me.'

'You have just warned me of the dangers of speaking my mind whilst in society, my lord. In view of that do you still consider it wise to ask such a question, knowing that you will get an honest answer?'

'That was precisely why I asked.'

'Very well, you asked for it!' She rounded upon him. 'I have known you for less than a week, my lord, but that is sufficient for me to be able to deduce that you are idle, dissipated, scathing and fatuous. You never appear to do anything unless it is likely to reflect upon your own pleasure. With the exception of rescuing Mulligan I cannot find that you have done anything with your privileged position in life, other than to please yourself.' She stood facing him, hands on hips, brown eyes blazing.

'I see,' he responded evenly. 'And that is your opinion of me?'

'You did ask. And do not imagine that I did not see the hordes of those ... those ridiculous butterflies in there trying to single you out. It seems that Mrs Stokes is not the only one with whom you are intimately acquainted and you are only turning the others away because you promised your

71

mother that you would attend me. Well, it might surprise you to learn, my lord, that not every woman in attendance this evening is wilting for want of your company. This one certainly is not and you can feel free to leave me at any time you wish. Doubtless you are anxious to search out more congenial company?'

Luc remained annoyingly calm and raised a brow at her in mock amusement. 'My, my, Lady Hartley, do I detect a note of jealousy?'

'No, of course not!' But the fight appeared to have gone out of her and she turned away from him, shivering with cold.

'Come, Lady Hartley, you are cold. Let us return to the ballroom, if you can tolerate mixing with my indolent friends again, that is. And I believe,' he continued, cocking his head on one side, 'that the music has ceased. That can only mean that supper is being served. No doubt you are hungry?'

'Famished!'

Their eyes locked and in spite of their recent spat they simultaneously burst into a spontaneous laughter that eased the tension between them.

# 4

Arriving home late and fatigued, Clarissa promised Caroline, who was bursting with curiosity, a full account of the proceedings on the morrow. But the morning had now arrived and Caroline was not to be denied.

'And how many gentlemen asked you to favour them?'

'Oh I do not recall, Caroline, one or two perhaps?'

'And how many dances did you dance?'

'Just three waltzes.'

'Waltzes, ah? And with whom, my lady?'

'Oh, one with Lord Western.'

'And the others?' persevered Caroline doggedly.

'With Lord Deverill,' conceded Clarissa reluctantly.

'What, both of them? My, my, his lordship must be quite taken with you.'

'Not at all, Caroline, he was merely doing his mother's bidding.'

'Was he indeed?' Clarissa scowled at her maid's disbelieving attitude. 'Well, if you say so, ma'am.' But Caroline sounded less than convinced. 'And what did you do with the rest of the evening? Did you stay with Lady Deverill?'

'Well no, actually Lord Deverill squired me for the evening.'

'Did he indeed! Was that really necessary, do you suppose? After all, his sisters were in attendance and could well have looked out for you. His lordship must surely be a most devoted son to take so much trouble over his mother's guest?'

Clarissa swung round abruptly and faced her maid. 'Yes, Caroline,' she concurred slowly, 'I believe that despite everything he very probably is and I was uncommonly rude to him. I must apologize at once!'

So saying, she swept from the room, her expression grim yet determined, and left a dumbfounded Caroline staring after her, hairbrush still in hand.

Her maid's words had only served to confirm the increasingly uncomfortable feeling that Clarissa had been attempting to ignore throughout a largely restless night. There had been no need for Luc to remain by her side so constantly. He could easily have left her with his mother and gone off in search of more congenial company. Instead he had been steadfast in his attentions: resolute in his determination to make the evening enjoyable for her and she had repaid his kindness by pouring scorn on all the activities that he held most dear.

She did not regret having given her opinion so freely about his own character. He had, after all, asked her to voice it and she had warned him that she would be honest. She had not changed her mind on that score and would not apologize for her words. She did, however, need to inform him of her regret at the attack she had made upon *tonnish* society. She had no right to speak so freely after such a short time in the capital, and having reached that conclusion Clarissa knew she would find no peace until she had made her humiliating apology.

Gathering up her courage, Clarissa knocked on the library door, squaring her shoulders and taking several deep, fortifying breaths whilst she awaited Luc's invitation to enter. He looked up from his desk when she did so, appeared surprised to find it was her seeking him out and rose gracefully to his feet. For some irrational reason it annoyed Clarissa that all of his movements were all so effortlessly elegant. It also stiffened her resolve to get this interview over with as quickly as possible.

Mulligan, asleep in front of the fire, opened one eye lazily. Upon recognizing Clarissa he rose stiffly to his feet and trotted awkwardly across the room to offer her his own welcome. Clarissa stroked his scruffy head, grateful for any excuse to avert her gaze from Luc's inquisitively polite expression. Obviously, his guests did not make a habit of disturbing him in his private domain and, having no wish to needlessly antagonize him, Clarissa decided to say her piece without procrastination and make her escape from his less than welcome presence.

'Good morning, Lady Hartley. You look exceedingly well today.' Luc's expression was full of approval as his eyes travelled the length of her in his usual impudent manner. She was wearing one of her new gowns and Luc clearly approved of the sight of her in blue striped muslin. 'That colour suits you, m'dear. Now pray do sit and tell me what can I do for you?'

'There is no necessity for me to sit, this will take but a moment. I simply came to apologize for abusing your friends, and society in particular, in the manner that I did last night. I had no right to behave thus and I ask your forgiveness. You showed much kindness in remaining by my side and introducing me to your acquaintances and all I did to repay you was to pour scorn upon the proceedings. You have my apology.'

The words poured from Clarissa's lips in a rush, tumbling over one another in their anxiety to be spoken. Luc stood on the other side of his desk, unable to resume his seat since she had expressed her disinclination for a chair, and regarded her steadily as she made her clumsy apology.

'Thank you, Lady Hartley,' he said, with only the slightest suspicion of a lazy and most disconcerting smile. The arrogance and condescension she had expected from him were, astonishingly, nowhere in sight. 'I think it cost you a great deal to apologize, but as for the necessity to do so, well, that is altogether another matter. Much of what you said in respect of my friends and customs in general was, I fear, uncannily accurate.'

Clarissa glared at him. 'Are you making sport of me, my lord?'

'Perish the thought, my lady.'

'Humph, well in that case I think this interview is at an end, for,' she added imperiously, 'there is nothing else I said that requires an apology.' She turned to leave the room, annoyed that he had somehow managed to irritate and discomfort her, even though his manners and attitude had remained faultlessly correct.

'Please stay, my lady.' The quiet command couched as a polite request gave Clarissa pause and she turned to face him once again. 'As you are here there is something I would ask of you. Please take a seat. I need to sit even if you do not!'

Clarissa's curiosity was piqued. What could he possibly want of her now? 'Very well.' She inclined her head in gracious acquiescence and perched herself on the edge of the proffered chair, suspicious still as to his motives. 'But do not think to persuade me to more fancy clothing,' she warned him.

Luc shrugged. 'Not at all, I merely wanted to ask you if — '

The door burst open and Simms bustled in, his face flushed, his demeanour full of self-importance.

'Forgive me, my lord, I was unaware that you were engaged.'

'What is it, Simms?'

'I merely wished to remind your lordship that we have several matters to attend to this morning.' Simms indicated the pile of papers in his hand.

'Do we indeed!' Luc struggled to hide his amusement.

'Indeed, yes, my lord. You will recall that you specifically asked for my intervention in these matters.' He cast a significant glance in Clarissa's direction and fell silent.

Luc was finding it increasingly difficult to maintain his composure. Simms had obviously recalled Luc's flippant request for protection from Clarissa, had been made aware that they were alone in the library and had loyally rushed to his master's aid.

'Thank you, Simms, we will deal with my business affairs later.'

'But, your lordship — '

'I require a private conversation with Lady Hartley first. I will summon you when I have a mind to deal with business matters.' Luc's amusement was turning to irritation now, as Simms continued to stand beside him at military-like attention. 'That will be all, Simms,' he pronounced irascibly.

'Well, my lord, if you are entirely certain.' Simms headed towards the door reluctantly, looking entirely miserable.

Luc barked a laugh as the door closed behind Simms, before smiling an apology at Clarissa. 'I regret the intrusion. Simms can be a mite over-protective at times.'

'Think nothing of it. I know exactly what you mean. Perhaps I should introduce him to Caroline?' Clarissa smiled at the notion. 'Now, perhaps you had better tell me what it is you want of me, before Simms invents another excuse to interrupt us.'

'Well, my mother will not be about for hours yet. She always sleeps late on the morning following a ball. Can I persuade you to accompany me on a short journey?' Luc essayed his most winsome smile. 'There is something I would have you see.'

'What is it?'

'Ah well, it is to be a surprise. Besides, if I told you, you would never believe me.'

Clarissa had been planning to spend the morning with her aunt. She had hoped to persuade her to take in some sights. Being informed that she would be abed for hours yet was a disappointment. She was restless, unused to idleness. Any diversion would be welcome. 'Well, all right. It seems I have nothing else to engage my attention this morning anyway.'

'Excellent!' Luc rose to his feet. 'Shall we meet in half an hour in the hallway?'

'Do you not wish to leave immediately? Before Simms finds a reason to return?'

Luc's smile was stoic. 'Yes, but you will naturally wish to change your attire.'

Clarissa tossed her head impatiently. She was not yet sufficiently imbued in society ways to require half an hour simply to change from one gown to another. 'Ten minutes will more than suffice for that purpose.'

'Excellent!'

True to her word, Clarissa descended the stairs less than ten minutes later, clad in her new carriage gown of fine lavender wool. There was a jaunty bonnet to match and soft leather gloves too. Unbeknown to Clarissa, the boots that fastened to conceal her slender ankles became visible to Luc as she continued with her descent. This brief glimpse of her ankle, albeit completely concealed by leather, was enough to send his imagination spiralling uncontrollably in directions it had no business taking. It took a monumental effort on his part to do no more than offer her an appreciative look and, simultaneously, his arm.

Luc's curricle was pulled up at the front door. The magnificent and evidently restless pair of matched grey geldings harnessed to the conveyance was being held by a groom. Luc assisted Clarissa to her seat and, leaping up himself, encouraged the horses forward with a sharp crack of the ribbons.

They journeyed for some distance in silence: Clarissa taking in her surroundings with interest. They travelled in an easterly direction and, as they did so, the streets became progressively narrower, the houses smaller and closer together until, eventually, it seemed as though they were driving through some sort of slum area. Urchins ran everywhere, avoiding carriage wheels with a skill born of experience. Costermongers called their wares in lack-lustre voices; lines of grimy washing flapped in the breeze, barely leaving room for traffic to pass beneath, and everywhere there was the all-pervading smell of rotting vegetables and an undeniable sense of desolation and hopelessness.

In spite of the bright morning sunshine, none of which was able to fully penetrate the close packed streets, an air of despondency dominated. Most of the people they passed trudged about their business, not bothering to even raise their eyes to the smart curricle as it bowled past them, knowing it could do nothing to improve their lot, and seemed intent only upon surviving yet another harsh day. Clarissa noticed that many of them lacked the requisite number of limbs and employed ingenious methods of replacing them: peg legs, hooks and roughly hewn crutches being the most common. The children's faces, at first glance, appeared to be full of health. It was only as she observed them more closely that Clarissa realized the colour she had mistaken for rosy good health was, in fact, attributable to illness and disease: their severely undernourished bodies and sluggish movements told her at least that much.

Clarissa surveyed it all with horror, unable to understand why Luc should bring her to such a place. Was it an attempt to exact revenge for her rudeness of the evening before? Surely not? His faults were myriad but she had never before considered him to be spiteful.

'Where are we?' she asked him.

'We are approaching Whitechapel. The wharf is just ahead.'

'It is another world,' muttered Clarissa, her awed expression not doing justice to her feelings of horror.

Luc indicated the twenty or more narrow avenues they passed as they journeyed along Whitechapel Road. 'There are thousands of closely packed nests amongst those streets,' he told her in a voice unusually devoid of expression. 'All full to overflowing. Inkhorn Court on your left there houses several Irish families to each room and Tewkesbury Buildings yonder houses a colony of Dutch Jews.'

'What do the people hereabouts do to survive?'

'Those that can obtain employment are mostly dock labourers. The rest are costermongers, as you saw back there, or stall keepers. Either that or professional beggars, thieves or prostitutes.' He offered a protracted pause before speaking again. 'Here, we have reached our destination now.'

Luc turned the curricle into a side street and pulled up in front of a large, ugly stone building with small windows and an undeniably institutional look. As Clarissa looked more closely though she noticed, with astonishment, that the front step was spotlessly clean and all the windows were sparkling. She gaped in amazement when she heard children's voices raised in song from behind the door and, when they stopped singing, loud chatter and actual laughter. The door opened then and children of all ages and sizes spilled into the street and fell upon the curricle, shouting delighted greetings.

'Be careful!' cautioned Clarissa. 'They might try to rob you.'

'I doubt that.' Luc descended to the ground and scooped the youngest child into his arms. The other children swarmed around him, clamouring for his attention. Laughing, Luc patted heads and tried to restore some kind of order. The job was eventually done for him when a simply dressed middle-aged lady appeared from the building and, clapping her hands, smilingly managed to organize the children into lopsided rows.

Still with the little girl in his arms, Luc turned to Clarissa and then spoke to his audience. 'Children, I have brought a special visitor to meet you. This is Lady Hartley.'

'What do you say to Lady Hartley, children?' asked the lady in their midst.

'Good morning, Lady Hartley,' chorused the children. The girls managed curtsies with varying degrees of success. The boys made slightly more elegant bows.

'Good morning, children.' Clarissa found her voice with difficulty and accepted Luc's hand as he assisted her from the curricle.

Shooing the children before her, the lady encouraged her charges back into the building. Luc introduced her to Clarissa as Mrs Fielding.

'Now, Eleanor,' he suggested, 'perhaps we can show Lady Hartley around?'

'With pleasure, my lord.'

'What is this place?' asked Clarissa.

'It is an orphanage, ma'am. All of these children were discovered living on the streets. The boys were destined for undoubted lives of crime, the girls for prostitution. Without our intervention, almost all of them would not have lived to reach maturity.'

'And you have saved them?' Clarissa could not keep the admiration out of her voice.

'I live and work here, with a few other volunteers, and do what I can, but I do not provide the funds to make the venture possible.'

Luc interrupted hastily. 'There are about a hundred children here at the moment. Mrs Fielding tries to ensure that they all get a rudimentary education: that they can all read and write at the very least.' They stopped at the door to a classroom where about thirty children were dutifully writing on slates. A man in a threadbare coat was teaching them. His tone was firm but gentle and the children were paying him close attention.

Eleanor Fielding took up the narrative. 'They stay here until they are twelve: we cannot keep them after that, but we usually manage to find some sort of gainful employment, even for the dullest witted. The girls mostly go into service: and some of the boys, too. Those that show more aptitude are apprenticed: others are sent to work on the land. It is all we can do for them and we can only pray that the opportunity we offer them for a decent start in life will be enough to keep them honest.'

Clarissa could not hide her astonishment. 'How do you manage all this, Mrs Fielding?'

A reply was rendered impossible as they had now reached another classroom, occupied by the smallest children. The lady teaching them was unable to maintain control when they observed Luc smiling from the doorway and they ran, *en masse*, in his direction. He hastily took a chair before the approaching horde could knock him over. Clarissa could not hide her astounded reaction. The fastidious Lord Deverill was allowing these urchins to clamber all over him! Sticky fingers adhered to his impeccable coat, hands pulled at his hair, tiny feet trampled on his shiny boots, but all Luc seemed able to do was laugh and talk to them gently.

'Will you tell us a story, Uncle Luc?'

Uncle Luc? What in heaven's name was going on?

'Now, children,' said the teacher, striving to regain control of her charges. 'Uncle Luc has brought a visitor with him today. Shall we show Lady Hartley how clever we are?'

The children, the oldest of whom could not be more than five, stood in a crooked line and recited their alphabet. Crouching down, Clarissa smiled at them, told them they were indeed very clever and allowed the little girl who had previously clung to Luc to climb shyly into her arms. Emboldened, others stepped forward and fingered her clothing; touched her hair.

'Please forgive them, Lady Hartley,' said Mrs Fielding. 'These little ones have not seen such a grand lady as you at close quarters before. Naturally, they are curious.'

'Pray do not concern yourself,' said Clarissa, preoccupied as she endeavoured to regain her wits. 'They are charming and are causing me no inconvenience.'

'That is Rosie,' said Luc, ruffling the hair

of the little girl in Clarissa's arms. 'She has only been here for a few months.'

'But I will not have to go away again, will I, Uncle Luc?' The little girl trembled at the prospect and her bottom lip wobbled alarmingly.

'No, sweetheart,' said Luc, taking her from Clarissa and holding her tightly. 'No one will ever harm you again.' Apparently reassured, Rosie would still not allow Luc to put her down.

'Shall we continue with our tour, Lady Hartley?' asked Mrs Fielding with a smile. 'Lord Deverill appears to be somewhat occupied at present.'

'With pleasure.'

They moved on and looked at the children in the remaining two rooms. Everywhere the mood of laughter and warmth pervaded.

'How did you manage to start this institution?' Clarissa asked.

'I did not: it was Lord Deverill's doing.'

'What?'

'Yes. I myself lived on the streets as a child. My mother was a prostitute, as the mothers of many of these poor mites were. Lord Deverill came across me begging on the streets one day. For some reason I shall never understand, his lordship took it upon himself to save me and put me into service in his house. I met and married my husband there. You saw him in one of the classrooms just now.

'Subsequently, Lord Deverill informed me that he wanted to do more to help the underprivileged and had the idea to start this institution. I jumped at the chance to be of assistance and the result you see before you today.'

'I am overwhelmed,' said Clarissa truthfully.

'We pride ourselves on making a little difference, but really we are only scratching at the surface. Lord Deverill is more than generous and his mother and sisters enthusiastically raise funds for us. Many society ladies donate clothing, others are persuaded to provide work for the children when they leave us — either in their London homes or on their country estates — but still, we are woefully short of staff and resources.'

They were in a dormitory now and Clarissa remarked upon the neatly made beds.

'Each child is responsible for making his or her own bed. Each child also has specific chores to carry out during the day. The younger ones are helped and supervised by their elders but no one is exempt. And they are fiercely loyal to one another. We are often the only family they have ever known and they are naturally anxious that it remains intact. Whatever anyone has is shared with everyone else — that is a golden rule and they all adhere to it without question.'

'Mrs Fielding, I congratulate you! I think your work is admirable. If only there were more people like you willing to make a difference.'

'I could not do it without Lord Deverill.'

'No doubt his society friends are impressed by his work when they observe it.'

'Lord Deverill has never before brought a visitor here, Lady Hartley.'

'What! Surely that cannot be right? What of his friends who help with raising funds?'

'I know not how he organizes that, my lady, but I can tell you that apart from his mother, sisters and Lord Western, who is also closely involved, no other society person has ever set foot in this institution.'

'I cannot believe it!'

Clarissa was disgusted with herself. The notion that Luc could only have started this institution in order to impress his peers had been her first thought. She disliked the fact that she could, however fleetingly, have entertained such a cynical and very obviously erroneous view.

After an hour, Mrs Fielding and Clarissa returned to the classroom in search of Luc.

He was still seated in the same chair, Rosie firmly ensconced on his lap. The other children were playing some sort of complicated game that appeared to involve tying a rope around Luc, whooping and hollering and generally causing mayhem. Their teacher had given up trying to maintain order and simply watched the game in progress indulgently. Luc himself seemed perfectly comfortable with the situation: in fact he was directing operations, Clarissa now realized. She could see that there were two teams involved in the game and some sort of elementary point scoring system. She was watching in wonder, a delighted smile on her face, when a small boy fell at her feet. She picked him up and whispered to him. The child responded with a victorious shout: overjoyed to find that Clarissa had pointed out a shortcut by which he could ensure his team won the game.

Placing Rosie gently back on the floor Luc rose and joined Clarissa again.

'Thank goodness you have returned!' he exclaimed, mopping his brow in mock relief. 'I thought I was about to be consigned to the river.'

Clarissa was not in the slightest bit deceived by his apparent concerns but was still too astounded by all she had seen and heard to make her usual spirited response. She was, quite simply, incredulous. How could she have read Luc Deverill so wrong? She was mortified and ashamed when she thought of her words to him the previous evening. How could she even begin to make amends for such ill-founded censure?

When they were finally back in the curricle, the children lining the street to wave an enthusiastic goodbye, Clarissa turned to face him.

'What form would you like my apology to take this time? I am prepared to grovel, beg, throw myself prostrate at your feet or simply plead your forgiveness.'

'Pray, do not concern yourself. I did not bring you here to extract an apology.'

*Then why did you bring me?* enquired a small voice inside her head. She dismissed the thought and, instead, contradicted him. 'I pride myself on being fair minded, Lord Deverill, but I immediately jumped to conclusions when I first met you, basing my views solely on your manners and *sang-froid* attitude. I was not being fair. I should have looked beyond those traits. I hate myself for being so forcefully judgemental. Mind you, my father always did say it was my worst fault.'

Luc covered one of her hands with his. 'Do

not be so unfair on yourself. Besides,' he added, slipping into his *tonnish* mantle once again with practised ease, 'I should have been furious if you had been able to see past the façade that I have spent years perfecting for the benefit of the others.' His feigned air of arrogant disdain made her giggle.

'Stop it!' she said, but she made no attempt to remove her hand from beneath his. 'Tell me more about the orphanage. When did you start it?'

'About ten years ago, with Eleanor's assistance. I discovered she felt as strongly as me that something should be done for the unfortunate children. We found the building and started out with just a dozen of the neediest. Before we knew it we were inundated.'

'And you finance it all?'

'No, society does.'

'What! How can that be?'

'I manage investments for a large number of my peers. I enjoy juggling with money and am quite successful at it. I naturally extract a percentage for my trouble and I plough it into this place. Felix Western and I found the building and purchased it outright and made it as suitable as possible for the tribe you met today. My mother and sisters, somehow, persuade the ladies they know to loosen their purse strings.'

'Yes, I can easily imagine them doing so. It is a project I suspect they undertake with indefatigable enthusiasm and, somehow, I cannot see them taking 'no' for an answer.'

'That is exactly why they are so suited for the work. They enjoy it enormously and it gives them something meaningful to do with their time.'

'Yes, I can see that, but your peers must also be proud of your achievements.'

'They know nothing of them.' He made a tutting noise. 'That would not do at all! As you so perceptively observed last evening, people do not talk about anything that matters and if they were aware of what Felix and I have achieved here our reputations would never recover.'

Clarissa snorted with laughter. 'Do all of the children lead successful lives when they leave you?' she asked him, as they retraced their earlier route through the grim streets.

'No, unfortunately not all, that would be too much to expect, but we do what we can to give them a decent start. Some though, especially those who come to us when they are older, inevitably fall back into their former ways; others have older siblings who persuade them to a life of crime; others again simply decide that honest work is not for them, but on the whole we do well. Some come back and help when they can, others bring children in need of help. Like Rosie.'

'What happened to her?'

Luc's expression hardened. 'She was found being kept in a tavern by a bullish landlord. She was half-starved, lice-ridden and made to work until she dropped with exhaustion.'

'My God!'

'Exactly. Another few weeks and it would have been too late for her. Thank the Lord that she was brought to us in time.'

'I had no idea people could be so cruel,' said Clarissa faintly.

'Believe me, m'dear, that is just the tip of the iceberg.'

'Is this the part of town where Mulligan was abandoned?'

'Yes. The children found him wandering outside the orphanage. The older ones have not forgotten and often ask after him. I would take him back to see them but somehow he seems to know when I am coming to this part of town and no matter what I do I am unable to persuade him into the carriage.'

'The poor chap probably thinks you are going to abandon him.'

'I never abandon the things I love,' he responded lightly.

His words made Clarissa feel uncharacteristically light headed and she hastened to turn away from his disarmingly intense gaze.

# 5

Clarissa presented herself at Mr Twining's office the following morning, relieved that at last her business could be concluded and she could plan her return home. She had been away for too long already and was anxious to get back to her old way of life, to her dogs and to Blazon. London had been interesting and held her attention for longer than she would have expected, but already she was tiring of the daily round of social nothingness. She needed the solitary comfort of the moors around her; the familiar sound of the wind howling in from the sea, biting at her face, penetrating her clothing and whipping her hair from the confines of her chignon; the squabbles and disputes which arose between her tenants with predictable regularity and which they expected her to resolve for them. But, most of all, she needed the daily demands placed upon her by her animals. Only then would she feel fully alive again.

Mr Twining bustled from his inner sanctum to greet Clarissa, his whole mien one of self-importance and pomposity. There was an arrogant assumption of contrived superiority about him as he offered his hand to her but there was no disguising his admiration as he took in the sight of his beautiful client in her elegant new attire.

'My dear Lady Hartley, how pleasant to see you here and how well you look. I trust you are not too fatigued after your long journey.'

'I thank you, sir, I am quite well and not at all tired. I have been in London for over a week already and have had ample time to rest.'

'Indeed, my dear, I regret I had no notion of your early arrival. Such a shame, I could have placed myself at your disposal before now.'

'But I understood you to be fully engaged? Are you implying I could have seen you earlier?'

'A misunderstanding obviously for I can always find the time for you, dear Lady Hartley.' Twining covered his error smoothly, smiling ingratiatingly at her once again. 'I would have taken pleasure in showing you about town: the theatres and so forth, what with you being alone in the world and everything. No matter,' he continued briskly, 'you are here now. Come into my office, dear lady, and make yourself comfortable. Simpson!' He snapped his podgy fingers at his clerk. 'Bring coffee at once.'

Twining was short in stature, his round head barely clearing Clarissa's shoulder, but his lack of inches was more than compensated for by his considerable girth. His moderately well tailored coat did little to conceal the bulk of his formidable body as he fussed needlessly about Clarissa, insisting that she settle herself in front of his sparse fire. His head was almost completely bald but he appeared to be compensating for that unfortunate circumstance too by sporting an abundance of whiskers on his face and chin. He had small, beady eyes which darted about constantly, an unfortunately bulbous nose and thin lips, which stretched into a beaming smile whenever he looked in Clarissa's direction.

Coffee had been taken but Twining appeared to be in no hurry to discuss business. Instead he questioned Clarissa closely about her plans for the future.

'You do not feel, now that you have sampled some of the delights of town, that you might wish to remove here permanently?'

'Indeed I do not, Mr Twining. I intend to continue with my father and Michael's work on the estates. I trust you have brought me here today to inform me that the legal necessities have at last been completed and that I can continue with that work unimpeded?'

Twining adopted a mournful expression, shaking his head sadly, which caused his flaccid jowls to wobble alarmingly. 'My dear Lady Hartley, I regret more than you will ever know the necessity to inform you of an unexpected difficulty that has arisen.'

'A difficulty?' Clarissa was confused and not a little alarmed. This was not what she had expected to hear at all. 'What difficulty?'

'It seems, my dear, that another contender for the right of succession to Sir Michael's estate has come forward.'

'Another contender? I do not begin to understand your meaning, Mr Twining. I am Michael's only heir. He had no children and no siblings. What can you possibly mean?'

Mr Twining rose from his chair and paced the length of his office, taking small, fastidious steps on his short, plump legs. 'I had really hoped there would be no need for you to know of these developments, dear lady, for I felt certain they could have no validity. But now that I am not quite so certain I realized I can no longer prevaricate. You see, ever since Sir Michael returned from his last extended period in Alexandria he had been sending a fairly substantial sum of money each quarter to an account in that town. I was however never privy to Sir Michael's reasons for this generosity.'

In response to Clarissa's obvious bewilderment Mr Twining resumed his seat, picked up her hand and gave it a gentle squeeze. 'I should have found a way to spare you!' he exclaimed, all concern.

Clarissa took back her hand, forcing herself not to snatch it away from his clammy palm. She squared her shoulders resolutely and begged him to continue relating the facts.

'Well, my dear, naturally when your husband died I immediately stopped making the payments to Alexandria. I received a communication from the advocate's office, to which they had been directed, asking why payment had ceased and I informed my correspondent of Sir Michael's sad demise. I thought no more of the matter until I received a letter several months later, purporting to be from Sir Michael's son, saying that he was coming to England to make a claim upon his father's estate.'

'Oh, dear Lord! I had absolutely no idea.'

Mr Twining was again given to fussing over Clarissa. 'My dear Lady Hartley, allow me to fetch you some more water. You look quite unwell.'

'No, no, Mr Twining, I am perfectly all

right, I do assure you. Please continue. I must know it all.'

'Very well, my dear, if you are quite sure.' In response to Clarissa's distracted nod he continued with his explanation. 'Well, as you can imagine, I was as surprised as you appear to be but still held the opinion that there could be no foundation to the story. That is why I did not trouble you before now with its details. You know, my dear, how concerned I have always been for your welfare and I had no wish to alarm you unnecessarily.' Mr Twining's solicitous look, which he had spent hours perfecting, went unobserved and unappreciated by a stunned Clarissa. Undeterred, Twining ploughed on ponderously. 'It was only when the person in question reached London about a month ago that I began to have concerns.

'A Mr Omar Salik presented himself to me, with a bundle of letters purportedly written by your husband, in Arabic, to Salik's mother. From the information he claims they contain, and Sir Michael's generous financial contributions over the years, I fear there can be little doubt that this man is, er . . . ' Mr Twining paused and coughed in embarrassment. 'These matters are really not for delicate ears such as yours.'

Clarissa was roused almost to anger by this

needless procrastination. 'Mr Twining, if you please!'

'Very well. It would appear that Mr Salik is Sir Michael's illegitimate son. I said I would arrange for translations of the letters but did not see how that would entitle your stepson, if indeed that is who he is, to any part of your late husband's estate.

'It was only then that I realized we had a potentially serious problem for Salik produced a will, again written in Arabic, which he claims names him as his father's sole heir in the event of no legitimate children being born to Sir Michael prior to his death.'

'Oh dear God, no!' Clarissa clapped her hand to her mouth in horror. A raw, gut-wrenching pain coursed through every inch of her body, causing her to feel physically sick. All the colour drained from her face and she found that she was shaking uncontrollably. 'Surely, Mr Twining, this must be some kind of falsehood? Michael would have told me of the existence of the will when he was dying, if not before. He knew what the land means to me and was definite in his desire for me to continue with our work.'

'Calm yourself, my dear Lady Hartley.' Twining took her hand and patted it in a proprietary manner. 'Again, I thought as you did, and still do, but this claim must be investigated: there is no avoiding that, I fear. But before we go any further I thought it best to discuss the matter with you. I could have come to Northumberland and saved you the trouble of travelling south, but I do have much work to hand and besides, Salik is in London. I think it would be wise for you to meet him and give me your impression.'

'Of course,' agreed Clarissa faintly, 'but what of the will itself? What can we do to authenticate that?'

'Well, first of all I have had a translation made into English. It is a simple document, saying just what Salik told me it did but that in itself means nothing. The next step is to get an expert to authenticate your husband's signature. To my eye it does, I am distressed to say, look genuine, but I am by no means an expert. Once we have cleared that hurdle we must then . . . ' Twining leapt up and danced anxiously around Clarissa. 'My dear Lady Hartley, you look most unwell. Pray allow me to call a cab to take you back to your hotel. We can continue this discussion when you have recovered from the shock of these terrible revelations.'

Clarissa took a sip of water, a deep breath and made a huge effort to control herself. This just could not be happening! There must be a simple explanation: some sort of mistake; a misunderstanding; something of that nature for surely God would not be cruel enough to deprive her of her land now? Not after all her hard work and just when she was starting, at last, to enjoy some success. Her heart was at that moment a leaden weight within her breast, too vulnerable to withstand the ramifications of such dreadful tidings.

'No, Mr Twining,' she said at last, in a voice that sounded as though it was coming from a long distance away, 'I must know it all. If this Mr Salik proves to be genuine what happens then?'

'Well, my lady, I fear he will be entitled to take possession of Fairlands and you will be beholden to him for a roof over your head.'

'No!' Clarissa's throat constricted and she was unable to utter more than that one agonized word. For the first time in her entire life she seriously thought that she might actually faint. As it was, she was only able to hold back the tears by the sheer force of her willpower. The feelings of anguish and devastation inside her were continuing to run riot: her supposedly irrepressible strength futile in the face of such a brutally remorseless reality. Her mind, frozen by blind panic, refused to cooperate with her attempts to make sense of all she had learned.

'Lady Hartley — Clarissa, I know this is

not a good time and I realize too that on the previous occasion when I opened my heart to you my timing could not have been worse. You must however allow me to assure you that my love for you has never once faltered. If you will consent to be my wife then I will relinquish my other duties here and devote every second of my time to finding a resolution to this problem. As it is . . . ' His words trailed off and he made do with helplessly shrugging and indicating the huge pile of papers sitting on his desk.

'Thank you, Mr Twining, but I do not intend to marry again.'

'Oh come, come, my dear!' Twining smiled at her ingratiatingly. 'A young and beautiful lady such as yourself, all alone in the world: that cannot be. You need a gentleman to protect you, my dear. You cannot be expected to find your own way through this mess. It would be enough to overset the most robust constitution and, in any event, no lady should be expected to trouble her head with such a business: it is not at all fitting. Only a man could be expected to fully comprehend its complexities.' If Twining was aware that he was being excessively patronizing he gave no sign. Clarissa herself was, perhaps fortunately for him, too preoccupied to properly hear what he was saying and therefore unable to take exception to his tone.

'Who better than me to look after you?' he continued, encouraged by her silence. 'I have after all known you for most of your life and pride myself on understanding your character. No, I will not accept your answer now. I can well see that you are too overset to think straight. I beg you only to consider the matter when you are feeling calmer and we will talk of it again.' He beamed at her, seemingly confident that she would eventually come to see the matter from his point of view. He attempted to reclaim her hand but this time she was ready for him and removed it from his reach.

'I will not change my mind, Mr Twining, but I am indebted to you for your kindness.'

'You do not know your own mind at present. You will see things differently when you have had time for quiet contemplation. I could be of great assistance to you my dear.'

'What happens about this supposed will now, Mr Twining?' asked Clarissa, anxious to deflect his attention away from his marital aspirations.

'Well, my dear, as I said, I am arranging for the signature to be authenticated. I will advise you when that has been done and we will discuss the matter further in the light of our expert's findings. In the meantime, I would suggest that we move Salik to more comfortable lodgings. He has limited funds and at present is residing in a very seedy boarding-house. I would suggest that we move him to an hotel: Brown's perhaps? It is modest but respectable and the estate can easily afford it. In the unlikely event that this will does prove to be genuine I have no doubt Salik will look kindly upon your willingness to offer him reasonable lodgings in the interim.'

'Yes, of course, Mr Twining, if you think it for the best. Perhaps you will be kind enough to make the necessary arrangements.'

Twining offered her a slight bow in confirmation.

'Now, my dear, at which hotel are you residing? I will call a cab for you.'

'I am not in an hotel, Mr Twining, I am staying with my godmother.'

'Indeed!' Twining appeared very surprised at this intelligence and not a little taken aback. 'I was not aware that you had relatives in London — or indeed anywhere. No matter.' He recovered himself quickly. 'I am sure it is comforting for you to have female companionship, especially at this most distressing time. Now, about that cab?'

'Do not concern yourself, Mr Twining, I have my carriage and my coachman awaits.'

* ★ ★

Concern for her mistress winning out over her natural hesitation to disturb the master, Caroline rapped sharply on the library door. Luc's irritated voice bade an instruction to enter. Seeing Caroline hovering on the threshold and knowing well enough who she was he experienced an inexplicable sense of foreboding. There must surely be something seriously amiss if she had the temerity to interrupt him?

'Excuse me, my lord.' She bobbed a curtsy. 'I am Caroline, Lady Hartley's maid. I wondered if you might know when Lady Deverill is likely to return home?'

'Not for an hour or so, Caroline. Is there some difficulty?'

'Well yes, my lord, I fear there is.'

Luc looked at Caroline properly for the first time and realized that her old face was creased at least as much with concern as it was with age. 'What is it?'

'Well, my lord, it is Lady Hartley. I am most concerned about her. She returned from seeing her legal man above half an hour ago but since she got back she has just sat in a chair staring into space. She has not uttered a single word and appears ghostlike in her pallor. She will not even respond to me! I confess that I know not what to do and thought her ladyship might have some ideas.'

Luc was already halfway out of his seat. 'Let me see if I can do anything.'

Luc took the stairs two at a time, Caroline scurrying at his heels as she attempted to keep pace. He entered Clarissa's chamber to find her just as Caroline had described: sitting bolt upright and staring straight ahead through dry, unseeing eyes. Luc sat beside her and took one of her hands in both of his. It was as cold as the grave, in spite of the relative warmth in the room. He rubbed it briskly between his palms in an effort to infuse some warmth into her.

'What is it, Clarissa?' he asked her gently. 'What has happened?'

Taking her hand appeared to draw Clarissa out of her introspection. She blinked at him, as though seeing him for the first time. 'It has all gone,' she said flatly. 'Everything I have worked for is gone.'

At first Luc thought that she would elucidate but she simply continued to stare at him and repeat the same phrase over and over again.

'Run back down to the library, Caroline, and bring back the brandy decanter and a glass. Lady Hartley is in shock.'

Caroline did as he asked and returned a

very short time later, out of breath, decanter and glass in hand. Luc poured a strong measure and placed his arm around Clarissa's shoulders, the glass to her lips.

'Drink this, Clarissa, it will make you feel better.'

'Nothing will make me feel better.' But she took a sip anyway — and choked on it. Luc patted her back and made her take a taste more. Slowly the colour returned to her face and she appeared to be conscious of her surroundings for the first time.

'Oh, my lady, you gave me such a turn! Are you all right? What happened?'

'No, Caroline, I am not all right. I will never be all right again.'

'Tell us what happened, Clarissa? Tell me what can I do to be of service to you?'

'No one can do anything. I have lost it all.'

And she told them everything that Twining had said to her, using the same emotionless monotone that she had employed since regaining her voice.

'Oh, God above, no!' Caroline's hand flew to her face in alarm. She looked as though she could do with a shot of brandy herself. 'This cannot be.'

'I am afraid that it can, Caroline,' responded Clarissa, her voice resonating with desolation, 'and God, it would seem, has very little to do with it. Everything I have worked for has been for nought.'

The relating of her meeting with Twining unlocked the floodgates and tears poured unchecked down her face. Luc's arm was still around her shoulders. He pulled her head against his chest and simply allowed her to cry. She did so — uninhibitedly — thoroughly soaking his shirt in the process. Her wretched sobs, the depth of her misery, demonstrated to Luc the extent to which her heart had been broken, rendering her tumultuous emotions uncontrollable. He felt helpless and superfluous, not feelings he was accustomed to, but discovered that half-baked suspicions were already working their way into his brain. There must be a way out of this mess and he intended to do his damnedest to find it.

Eventually Clarissa's tears dried up and Luc offered her his handkerchief.

'Thank you,' she said, offering him a watery smile as she mopped her face dry. 'More brandy please!'

Luc poured her a measure and she knocked it back in one mouthful.

'She never could take strong drink,' warned Caroline.

'Well, I think today qualifies as an exception,' said Luc, offering the once again replenished glass to an unprotesting Clarissa.

'What will you do now, my lady?' asked Caroline, ignoring Luc's warning glare.

'Until this is sorted out you mean? What I have always done, I suppose, Caroline. I will work: hard and long. That way I do not have to think — or feel. And if I work hard enough I can fall into bed and sleep at night without dreaming. It works . . . hic . . . I should know, I have done it for long enough.'

Luc felt an excoriating anger course through him as he observed Clarissa valiantly trying to regain her senses and strength for her maid's sake. His anger was directed towards the perpetrators of this outrage: people whose acquaintance he now resolved to make for himself in the very near future.

'Come on, m'dear,' he urged gently. 'Have another sip, if you will. It will make you feel better.'

'Are you . . . hic . . . trying to get me intoxicated, my lord? Whoops!' She giggled.

'Perhaps she should lie down for a little rest, my lord?' suggested Caroline pointedly.

'Indeed!'

'Do not want to lie down . . . hic . . . oops! Want to be a flutter . . . blutter . . . a flutterby. Can I be your butterfly, Lukie Wukie?'

'You can be anything you want to be,

m'dear, remember? It just takes imagination. Come along now, allow me to be of assistance.'

Clarissa was giggling uncontrollably, babbling incoherently about being a butterfly, and was incapable of standing up. Wordlessly Luc swept her into his arms and headed for the huge tester bed.

'You cannot . . . hic . . . pick me up. I am too heavy.'

'Not for me you are not.' He carried her effortlessly, as if to prove his point, and sitting her unsteadily on the bed reached for the pins in her hair.

'I can manage her now, my lord.'

'I do not think so, Caroline,' said Luc, with a sad shake of his head. 'She is very unsteady.' Clarissa obliged him at that moment by almost sliding off the bed.

Swiftly Luc unwound Clarissa's golden hair and brushed his fingers through its lush thickness. Then, ignoring Caroline's outraged expression, he loosened her pelisse and removed it. With a speed and skill born of many years' experience, he loosened the ties to her gown as well and slipped it from her shoulders. He lifted her from the bed once again whilst Caroline, rigid with disapproval, pulled the garment away from her mistress's legs. Clarissa was humming a sad little lament, clearly unaware of what was happening to her. She reached up and wrapped her arms around Luc's neck, giggling.

'You're very handsome, Lukie,' she slurred. 'I want to be handsome, too.'

'Oh you are, m'dear, you most certainly are!'

'Can I be a flutterby as well?'

Clarissa was reduced to her chemise, petticoats and stockings. Caroline pointedly stated that her ladyship could rest dressed as she was and determinedly pulled the covers over her. In spite of the seriousness of the situation, Luc was unable to suppress a lupine smile. He lifted Clarissa into bed, surprising himself by taking no more than a fleeting look at her delectable body in its state of semi-undress. He dropped a light kiss on her brow and straightened himself up.

'You ... hic ... are no gentleman,' complained Clarissa, before closing her eyes and promptly falling into an intoxicated sleep, interspersed with light snores.

Luc's smile, when it came, lit up his ruggedly handsome features and softened the austere expression in his angry eyes. He turned to address Caroline. 'Stay with her, she should not be left alone at all. When my mother returns I will ask her to share the burden with you.'

'It is no burden, my lord, she is my life.'

'I applaud your dedication, Caroline. It is as it should be. When she awakens make sure she takes some water and try to persuade her to eat something.'

'That should not be difficult to achieve.' They shared a brief smile.

'In the morning I will come to see her again,' said Luc. 'By then she will have recovered from the shock and we can discuss ways to resolve this wretched situation.'

'You are of the opinion that it can be resolved then, my lord?' There was no mistaking the spark of hope in both Caroline's voice and expression.

'It is a little convenient, do you not think, Caroline, this supposed son of Sir Michael's suddenly appearing just at a time when Twining supposed your mistress to be alone and unprotected in this world?'

'Well, my lord, since you put it like that I suppose you could be right. Mind you, I never did like that Twining myself and could not comprehend why the gentlemen trusted him so implicitly. He has shifty eyes.'

Luc grinned, suspecting that Caroline's means of assessing character was not far off the mark in this instance. 'Call me at once if she gives you any more concerns. I will cancel my plans and dine at home this evening.'

'You would do that for her, my lord?'

Luc could see suspicion forming in the old lady's eyes but ignored the obvious implication. 'Of course! She is a guest in my house and whilst she is here I am responsible for her.'

'Naturally, my lord. You know,' she continued reflectively, 'she loves that land and those sheep above everything. Today is only the second time in her entire adult life that I have seen her cry. The first time was when her father died and I thought then that she would never stop.'

'She did not shed a tear at the passing of her husband then?'

'No, my lord. Oh, she was sad but composed and she carried on for the sake of the rest of us with her usual quiet efficiency.'

'I see.' Luc absorbed this information without further comment and stored it away for examination at a more appropriate time. 'All right, Caroline, I shall be in my library if you have need of me.'

# 6

As Luc made his way to Clarissa's chamber the next morning he encountered Caroline heading away from it, an untouched breakfast tray in her hands, a grim expression on her old face.

'She has not eaten a thing since she returned to the house yesterday morning, my lord.'

'That bad, ah?'

'I am afraid so, sir.'

'I will see what I can do.'

Luc discovered Clarissa clad in her striped blue muslin and sitting in front of the fire, an abstracted expression on her tormented face.

'Good morning,' he said quietly. 'I have brought you some company.'

Mulligan followed his master into the room. With the uncanny sixth sense peculiar to dogs he seemed to know some sort of crisis had occurred and settled himself at Clarissa's feet, resting his head on her lap and looking up at her through devoted eyes.

'Oh, thank you! Good morning, Mulligan darling.' She stroked his head absently.

'And how are you feeling today, my lady?'

'A little wobbly but ashamed of myself for falling apart as I did.' She sighed and offered him a brief smile. 'I trust I did not make too much of a widgeon of myself?'

'Think no more about it. Anyone receiving the sort of calamitous news you had would have reacted in the same way.'

'Be that as it may I believe I owe you yet another apology.' She shrugged. 'You know, I seldom have reason to apologize to anyone but find that I must apologize to you for the third time in as many days.'

Standing behind her Luc leaned down and smiled into her eyes. 'Once again apologies are quite unnecessary.'

The door opened at that moment and both Marcia and Caroline entered.

'Oh, you poor lamb, how are you today?' asked Marcia, kissing Clarissa.

'Better thank you, Aunt, and resigned to my fate.'

'What do you mean, my dear?'

'Well, if this Mr Salik really is Michael's son and if Michael did wish him to inherit then I will not attempt to stand in his way. If it is proven to be so then I will surrender Fairlands to him and retire to Greenacres. Who knows,' she added, in a falsely optimistic tone, 'perhaps Mr Salik will share my interest in the herd and will co-operate by allowing

119

me to continue using his land?'

Luc and Marcia shared an anguished glance.

'Clarissa,' said Luc gently, 'you do realize that if Salik proves to be genuine then you cannot reside at Greenacres any more than you could at Fairlands?'

'Why ever not? It was my father's estate, my childhood home. It is mine now. I have always been happy there and could easily be so again.'

'No, my dear.' Luc's voice was gentler still, full of regret. 'Greenacres became yours when your father died but when you married Hartley it reverted to him and became part of his estate. I thought you would realize that.'

The look of abject desolation, which she was briefly unable to conceal as she digested this latest intelligence, moved Luc's heart. 'In that case,' she eventually managed to say, 'I really have lost everything.'

Luc adopted a brisk, businesslike tone. 'Not necessarily. We have yet to prove that this Salik person is who he claims to be. Now then, let us go over in detail what Twining said to you yesterday. Apart from gaining translations from the Arabic and attempting to authenticate your husband's signature, what other steps did he say he was taking to get to the truth?'

'Well, he did say that I should meet Mr Salik.'

'What good does he think that will accomplish, for the love of God, other than upsetting dear Clarissa, that is?' enquired Marcia indignantly.

'Perhaps he thinks I might notice some resemblance to Michael?'

'Perhaps,' agreed Luc, making no comment about the wisdom of such a meeting. 'And what else has he done?'

Clarissa appeared to be lost in thought. 'I cannot recall that he mentioned anything else specifically. He said we had to take one step at a time.'

'Did the document carry any official seals?'

'I think so,' said Clarissa, wrinkling her brow in an effort to recall, 'but I am not entirely sure. I was completely shocked at the time and he only waved it in front of me for a second or two.'

'Has he attempted to contact the offices of the attorneys who drew it up?'

'He did not say.' Clarissa paused. 'I have been rather dense, have I not? I should have thought to ask these questions myself.'

'Not at all.' Luc placed a reassuring hand on her shoulder.

'I think I shall make a call upon Twining myself,' mused Luc. 'Will you allow me to act for you in any way I see fit, Lady Hartley?'

'Oh, I could not possibly ask it of you.'

'Nonsense, dear,' said Marcia brightly. 'Lucien is very good at this sort of thing. I am sure it is all a huge misunderstanding and he will be able to sort it out in no time at all.'

'We must not give Clarissa false hopes, Mother, but I do believe further investigations are called for. Would you sign this for me?' Luc produced a parchment from his coat pocket and placed it in front of her.

'What is it?'

'Simply a document authorizing me to act for you in all aspects of your affairs and giving me full and complete access to any records held by Twining.'

Clarissa moved to the handsome escritoire in the corner of the room, signed without hesitation, sanded her signature and handed the paper back to Luc. 'Thank you,' she said. 'But I fear Mr Twining will be distressed to discover I doubt his competence.'

'He will get over it. This is too important to worry about the feelings of one insignificant attorney. Now then, where are his offices? I think I shall call upon him right away.'

Clarissa gave him the direction. 'But he is too busy to see people without appointments. Perhaps you should arrange it with his clerk beforehand?'

'Oh no, I think, in the circumstances, a surprise is called for and, make no mistake about it, he will see me!'

It was an oddly reassuring promise which served to hearten Clarissa. 'Thank you, Lord Deverill, I appreciate your help. Is there anything I can do to be of assistance whilst you are gone?'

'Yes, my lady, you can eat your breakfast. You will be no good to me if you are wilting for want of sustenance.'

His words were persuasively convincing, causing Clarissa to actually smile briefly for the first time in what seemed like forever. 'But I thought you were of the opinion that I eat too much?'

'I am getting used to the idea,' he responded, matching her smile with a beguiling one of his own, 'and find that it rather appeals to me.'

'I will go to the kitchen and see if I can arrange something special for you, my lady,' said Caroline. She opened the door for Luc, her face wreathed in smiles, and honoured him with the lowest curtsy her arthritic legs would permit: the one she saved exclusively for people of whom she most approved.

★ ★ ★

123

Luc arrived at Twining's offices and presented his card to an overawed clerk who disappeared, with deferential bows, in the direction of Twining's own room. He returned a short time later. He regretted that Mr Twining was too busy to see anyone without an appointment, but if his lordship would care to state the nature of his business and make an appointment then Mr Twining would be delighted to place himself at his lordship's disposal at a later time.

This response was all wrong and caused Luc's suspicions to multiply tenfold. Any attorney of Twining's comparatively lowly status would give their right hand for the opportunity to be of service to an aristocrat of Luc's standing, if only for the benefit that the ensuing kudos would bestow upon his business. His casual dismissal of Luc's application for an interview, his disinclination to present himself and voice his apologies in person at the very least, simply did not ring true.

'In here, is he?' asked Luc, heading for the room at the back.

'Yes, my lord, but you cannot . . .'

Luc threw open the door and discovered a rotund person, presumably Twining, sitting behind a pristine and paperless desk, feet up, cigar clamped between his lips and Luc's card, which he was studying with interest, resting between his splayed fingers. Twining staggered to his feet, outrage at this unprecedented intrusion written clearly on his face. Luc was pleased to discover that he instinctively disliked the obnoxious little man on sight.

'What is the meaning of this invasion, sir?'

'I am The Earl of Newbury and am so sorry to disrupt your busy morning.' Luc's voice dripped sarcasm, whilst his upper-crust accent created an impression of rarefied snobbery and powerful command, guaranteed to subdue any thoughts of rebellion on Twining's part. 'However, I have urgent business that cannot wait.'

'I am expecting a client at any minute,' blustered Twining defensively. 'I regret therefore that I can only spare your lordship a few minutes. It would, perhaps, be more expedient if your lordship were to arrange an alternative appointment, at a time when I would be honoured to give my full and complete attention to your lordship's business.'

'Rubbish! Your client, if he exists, can wait: I, however, cannot.'

Luc chose to deliver his *coup de foudre* by throwing Clarissa's authority casually in front of Twining.

'What is the meaning of this, my lord?'

'I presume it is a basic necessity for any attorney to be able to read plain English?'

'Lady Hartley? Pray, my lord, what connection does she have to you?'

'She is my mother's god-daughter and a guest in my house.'

'Lady Deverill is Clarissa's godmother?' Luc enjoyed the satisfaction of watching Twining pale as he absorbed the enormity of this revelation. Clearly astounded, he recovered himself quickly and his whole attitude changed to one of snivelling obsequiousness. 'My apologies, my lord, she did not mention the fact. However, if you would kindly be seated, I shall be glad to know what service I can offer you?'

Luc remained standing and towered over Twining, dominating him with his formidable musculature, controlling the situation in a manner that was second nature to him. He was not accustomed to being challenged and would not permit this callow jackanapes to persist with his attitude of wilful precocity.

'Lady Hartley was too distressed to recall precisely what steps you have taken to disprove Salik's outrageous claim upon her late husband's estate. Perhaps you would enlighten me?'

'Well, my lord, I have arranged for

translations of the letters and the will and I am also arranging for the signature on the will to be authenticated.'

'Nothing else?' Luc frowned, feigning disbelief. 'How long have you had this document in your possession, Twining?'

'A little over a month, my lord.'

'And you have done nothing else in that time, knowing what a blow the intelligence was likely to be to Lady Hartley? What is your explanation for such procrastination, man?'

'One must proceed cautiously with legal matters,' declared Twining pedantically, pacing the length of his office, hands clutching tightly at the lapels of his coat, rather as if he bore it a grudge. 'Besides, if the signature is deemed to be genuine, I do not actually see what more can be done.'

Luc pulled himself up to his full height and glowered at Twining in a manner designed to be both menacing and intimidating. 'Do you not? How extraordinary! Have you made any attempt to contact the firm of advocates in Alexandria that handled the monetary payments and presumably drew up the will as well? What information were they able to yield?'

Twining looked uneasy. 'Well, no, strangely they are not the same establishment.'

'What? That surely cannot be correct? Sir

Michael trusted the same people to handle his monetary matters for more than twenty years but did not use them to draw up the will? Does that not strike you as odd, Twining?'

'Not really, my lord. In my experience people often like to keep these matters separate.'

'Indeed?' Luc raised a brow in mock disbelief. 'And so am I to understand it that you have not contacted either establishment?'

'Not as yet, my lord, no.'

Twining was sounding increasingly defensive, his voice reduced to an irritating whine, underscored with petulance. He seemed anxious to appease Luc but clearly disliked having his actions questioned. This was borne out as his answers became more sullen, his manner even more pompous and deliberating. Luc was feeling increasingly hostile; his irritation rose in direct proportion to his temperature as he observed Twining's increasingly clumsy attempts to cover his inefficiency. They were supposed to be on the same side, both fighting for Clarissa's rights. To observe Twining at that moment, one would never have guessed as much.

'I understand you have not made any funds available to Lady Hartley since her husband died. Why is that?'

'I offered to make an interim arrangement, but she declined and said she could manage,' he responded with a sleazy smile. 'I assumed she knew her own affairs and did not question her decision.'

'Really? Well, the situation has changed. She is now urgently in need of financial assistance and you are going to make it available. Draw up a fiscal plan for my approval immediately.'

Twining glowered but remained silent.

'Is there a problem with that?'

'No, my lord, not at all, but if . . . ' He paused, as though a point had just occurred to him. Luc waited him out in silence, already anticipating his response, which would confirm Twining's duplicity in this fraud beyond further doubt. It was not long in coming. 'It is just that . . . well, it has occurred to me that if Salik is proven to be the rightful heir to Sir Michael's estate then Lady Hartley is actually entitled to nothing.'

'Do not be ridiculous man! Just see to it. And I want full access to the estate's financial records too, going back to the time of Lady Hartley's father's death. See to that as well.'

'She should have accepted my offer,' muttered Twining mutinously to himself.

'What offer was that, Twining?'

'Oh, no, nothing at all.' And Luc was unable to get him to say more on the subject.

'I gather that you wish Lady Hartley to meet this Salik person?' said Luc icily, clearly relieving Twining by his sudden change of tack.

'Well, yes, I thought . . . '

'Splendid notion! I will escort Lady Hartley here tomorrow morning at eleven o'clock. Be sure to have Salik here: I do not care for her ladyship to be kept waiting.'

'But, my lord — '

'Good day, Twining,' said Luc briskly. 'I will not detain you further; your client must be getting impatient. Oh dear,' he said as he opened the door to the outer office, 'he does not appear to have arrived yet. I wonder what could have kept him?'

\* \* \*

Returning home, Luc found Marcia, Caroline and Mulligan still with Clarissa.

'What news?' asked Clarissa anxiously, half rising from her seat in her anxiety to be kept informed.

'Not so fast,' cautioned Luc with a smile. 'First, I need to know if you have kept your side of the bargain?'

'Two servings,' supplied Caroline helpfully.

'Once I started I found I had an appetite after all,' Clarissa informed him with a dignified toss of her head.

'Excellent!' Luc beamed at her. 'And you will be glad to hear your Mr Twining did not appear to be nearly so occupied today and was able to see me immediately.'

'Really? How strange. I could not detect the surface of his desk yesterday because of the profusion of papers upon it.'

'Indeed. Anyway, if you feel up to it we will go together tomorrow morning and meet this Salik person at his office.'

'Yes, I am prepared for it,' agreed Clarissa quietly.

Luc would tell her little more about his meeting with Twining, other than to say he had lines of enquiry he wished to follow on his own. She appeared to have a touching faith in his ability and accepted his explanation without question. It seemed to Luc that the effort of running two estates and making the decisions alone for so long had drained her of all her energies, leaving her depleted and ill-prepared to tackle the delicate intricacies pursuant to legal fraud. A surge of anger coursed through him as he realized Twining was probably aware of the fact and was taking shameless advantage of it. He vowed anew that he would not get away with it. But in the meantime he would continue to offer Clarissa any form of support she required and was more than willing to shoulder the burden of her problems in her stead. In fact, if it became necessary, he would insist upon doing so. No one would succeed in cheating her whilst he still had breath in his body.

'Upon your return you will have access to sufficient funds to carry on your work,' Luc told her gently.

'Thank you. How did you manage that?'

'It is quite normal to have access for running costs pending probate. In fact Twining says he offered you the opportunity but you declined. Is that right?'

Caroline could not hold her tongue. 'He muttered something but her ladyship's husband had just died and naturally she was preoccupied.'

'It is of no importance,' said Luc. 'But, Clarissa, did Twining make you some sort of other offer yesterday?'

It was Caroline who answered once more. 'Not again!'

'Mr Twining kindly offered to marry me.'

'Good God, you would not marry that weasel, surely?'

'I do not intend to marry anyone.' Clarissa sighed distractedly. 'But it was kind of Mr

Twining. He was only concerned for my welfare. He said if he were my husband he could devote all his time exclusively to my affairs. As it is, he is so busy he cannot give them as much attention as he would wish.'

'Humph! His first proposal came just after her father had died and she was prostrate with grief. Can you imagine the insensitivity of the man?' Caroline sniffed her disapproval.

The luncheon gong sounded. Marcia jumped up, suddenly recalling something that urgently required her attention, and ran off ahead of them.

'My lady?' Luc offered Clarissa his arm. 'What you need,' he informed her, in a voice that brooked no argument, 'is something to look forward to: a distraction. What say you to taking a ride in the park tomorrow before meeting the weasel?'

Clarissa brightened visibly. 'Oh, yes please, I would love that above all things!' She paused, seemingly deep in thought, then her face fell abruptly. 'Oh, but no. Thank you, my lord, but I must reluctantly decline.'

'Why?'

'I have nothing to wear. I do not possess a habit.'

'You mean you did not bring one?'

'No, my lord,' she countered with deliberation, 'I mean I do not own one.'

'But you told me you ride all the time in Northumberland. What do you wear?'

'I ride to work and can hardly do so perched demurely on a side saddle whilst rounding up sheep. I ride astride,' she said, flashing her eyes at him defiantly, 'and I wear breeches.'

'Now that,' said Luc, with one of his wolfish smiles, 'I would like to see. All right, Lady Hartley, we will have to ride a little earlier, that is all. How about it? You are an early riser. Meet me at the side door to the mews at six o'clock. I will supply you with appropriate clothing.' She looked at him dubiously, causing him to chuckle and issue a challenge he suspected she would be unable to resist. 'What, do not tell me you are not game?'

'No, it is not that. It is just that I would perhaps prefer not to ride at all if I can only trot about sedately. I prefer to ride hard and fast.'

'That is precisely why we will ride before anyone else is about.'

Luc was rewarded by a radiant smile that lit up her already beautiful face, reducing him to a state of concupiscence he had long since forgotten was possible.

'Agreed!' she said.

# 7

Luc waited at the side door the following morning, wondering if Clarissa would keep their engagement to ride or whether she would think better of it. His question was answered shortly thereafter when she appeared at the end of the corridor, wearing one of her drab black gowns, and walking silently in order not to disturb the still sleeping household.

'In here,' he whispered, opening the door to the boot room. 'I have brought you a pair of Anthony's breeches which I think might be adequate for your purpose.' Luc was incapable of wasting such an opportunity and held the unmentionables against her, an innocently helpful expression on his face, as he pretended to consider the question of their suitability. Clarissa snatched them from his hands, ignoring his mischievous grin.

'They will do!'

'And here is a shirt for you, and a jerkin and cap. Help yourself to whichever pair of boots fits you the best. Today,' he said, with a salacious smirk, 'you will pose as my groom.' Clarissa narrowed her eyes at him, her expression bordering on the malevolent. Luc had known her long enough now to recognize the danger signs in that look and beat a hasty retreat. 'I will await you without, my lady,' he volunteered, still unable to suppress a broad grin of anticipation.

Clarissa joined him again a commendably short time later and this time Luc was completely unable to hide his reaction. His brother's breeches fitted her like a second skin, graphically displaying the long, lean thighs which had occupied so many of his recent conscious thoughts. Luc was now able to confirm for himself that they were indeed toned to perfection from long hours in the saddle. They led to a small and delightfully rounded *derrière*: the stuff of his dreams. Luc could now also see that her stomach was perfectly flat, in spite of her insatiable appetite and that her waist, which he had considered to be large, was in fact far too small for his brother's breeches. She had tied them as securely as she was able but they appeared to be in permanent danger of sliding down. The cap was woefully inadequate for the purpose of restraining her magnificent hair and already long strands of it were making good their escape. Luc permitted a low whistle of appreciation escape his lips.

'Let us hope no one else is about, my lady,

for you would never pass muster as a groom if you were to be observed at close quarters by the gentry. I do hope I am not about to compromise your reputation.'

'Huh, what do I care for such stupidity,' she cried irascibly. 'Now, are we to ride or not?'

'Indeed we are.'

Luc led her into his stable yard where she found one of the grey geldings that had pulled his curricle the previous day saddled and waiting patiently. Clarissa went to him, stroked his muzzle gently and whispered to him. In response the horse dropped his nose and snorted softly into her hand.

'This is Albert,' said Luc. 'He is strong and lively but I have a feeling you will be able to handle him.'

'I am sure I shall,' agreed Clarissa, already preparing to mount.

'Here, allow me.' Luc took Clarissa's foot in his hand and helped her into the saddle. He watched for a moment as she settled herself, checked Albert's girth, adjusted her stirrups and gathered up her reins. She looked entirely at home and the expression of anticipated pleasure on her face sent a warm glow of pleasure coursing through his entire body, settling somewhere in the region of his heart.

'Who is this?' enquired Clarissa, turning her head and exclaiming at the sight of a fine-looking black thoroughbred being led from one of the stalls.

'That,' said Luc proudly, 'is Marius.' He needed to say nothing else: the look of pride in his eyes spoke volumes.

'Did you breed him?'

'No, he is an Irish stallion and responsible for many of the youngsters now eating their heads off in Berkshire.'

'He is magnificent!' Clarissa cast an expert eye over his conformation, 'but he also looks rather fresh. I think it would be better if we did not keep him waiting.'

They set off side by side and were in the park in a matter of minutes. As Luc had correctly surmised, they had it to themselves. It was only just light and even the most dedicated exponents of the sport were not yet about. As soon as the horses' hoofs hit the cinder track Marius in particular became impatient and fought Luc for his head.

'Shall we let them go?' he asked.

They did, galloping flat out the entire length of the track, Clarissa whooping with delight. Luc watched her with half an eye as he struggled to control Marius. He had been right: this was precisely the distraction she needed to take her mind off her troubles. He felt sure that after this she would be able to face their meeting with Salik with a far greater degree of equanimity. He needed her to ignore her emotions, if at all possible, and think dispassionately. If Salik really was Sir Michael's son then surely Clarissa must have had some inkling as to his existence? She needed to think hard about conversations she might have had with her husband over the years; particularly those pertinent to his time in Egypt. He might well have said something that in retrospect could prove to be decisive.

Luc found it impossible to believe that any man could have been married to this delicious creature and not ensured that he had made definite provision for her future: especially if he knew himself to be dying, which he understood to have been the case with Sir Michael. The fact that he did not appear to have made any such provision led Luc to suppose that he did not consider another person could have a legitimate claim upon his estate. Be that as it may Luc roundly cursed the academic's dilatory attitude towards such an important aspect of his affairs.

'Whew,' exclaimed Clarissa, drawing rein and smiling radiantly at Luc, 'that was exhilarating!' She patted Albert's neck solidly, clearly in her element.

Luc was momentarily unable to make any reply and instead simply devoured the sight of her with his eyes. Her face was flushed, her eyes sparkling and her breath coming in deep gasps as she recovered from her exertions. Her hair was now all over the place: the cap completely useless. Her breasts heaved invitingly against the confines of her shirt and altogether Luc felt he had never seen her looking lovelier.

The sound of other horses approaching brought Luc belatedly to his senses.

'I was right,' he said gently, 'no one would take you for a groom looking as you do now. Perhaps we should return home before we have awkward questions to answer.'

'Race you back!' laughed Clarissa, her heels already pressed into Albert's flanks.

Luc gave her a head start, glorying in the vision of her elegant bottom raised to the elements as she leaned over Albert's withers, encouraging him forward. Collecting himself, he allowed Marius his head and they reached the park gate simultaneously.

★   ★   ★

Luc awaited Clarissa in the hall. She joined him promptly and expressed surprise at seeing not his curricle but his barouche in

140

front of the door, Albert and Arthur resplendent between the shafts. It bore the earl's crest on the doors. Two liveried tigers were already up behind and a third held the door open for Clarissa and Luc.

'Rather grand for a short trip to Lincoln's Inn, is it not?'

'Appearance is everything,' responded Luc with a conspiratorial wink, taking her hand and assisting her into the carriage. 'Might as well make the most of the advantages at our disposal. After all, a little intimidation never hurt anyone.'

'You have a devious mind, my lord.' And much to her surprise Clarissa found she was actually laughing as they set off.

'Ready, m'dear?' he asked quietly, as they reached Twining's office. She nodded, her features grave but composed. 'Leave as much of the talking to me as you can and follow whatever lead I take.'

This time they were ushered straight into Twining's office, where Twining and another person rose to greet them.

'Good morning, Lady Hartley. Lord Deverill, your servant, sir.'

Twining attempted to take Clarissa's arm but she clung steadfastly to Luc. Not appearing to notice the slight he proceeded to introduce them to Salik. The stranger stepped forward and bowed elegantly to Clarissa. He was a little shorter than her and in possession of black hair that was already thinning; his colouring was swarthy and his bearded face deeply tanned. The sharpness of his features alone — his long, aquiline nose and thin lips stretched over uneven and yellowing teeth — prevented him from being truly handsome but he was, nevertheless, a striking figure. He was clothed in the style of an English gentleman but his garments were cheap and poorly tailored; especially when compared to Luc's impeccable attire.

As she observed him, a small gasp escaped Clarissa's lips, which Luc suspected no one else had heard. He also feared he knew what it meant. Clarissa could see a resemblance to her late husband in this strutting coxcomb before them.

'Lady Hartley,' said Salik, boldly taking her hand and smiling in a manner that Luc considered to be altogether inappropriate. 'I knew my father had married a younger lady but no one told me she was such a beauty.'

'Mind your manners, Salik!' barked Luc, more harshly than he had intended. 'There is a time and place for everything.'

Salik, unperturbed at receiving a dressing down from Luc, continued to concentrate his attention solely upon Clarissa. A dangerous

142

mistake, which would have been all too obvious to the Egyptian, had he troubled to observe the darkening of Luc's expression.

'Will you not sit down, my lady? Allow me to pour you some coffee.' All his attention was directed towards Clarissa still; he had eyes for no one else. Luc could cheerfully have taken a whip to him for his impudence.

'We are not here to socialize,' said Luc, his languid attitude once again firmly in place. As with Twining the previous day, his upper-class accent cut effortlessly through Salik's accented babble and served to return control of the situation to Luc. This became apparent when Salik turned to him for the first time and made a slight bow.

'As you say.' But his tone was still markedly lacking in the deference Luc was accustomed to. He made up his mind there and then that, no matter what, this impudent upstart would never take from Clarissa that which was rightfully hers.

Guiding Clarissa to a chair, Luc stood behind her, appearing to take up an inordinate amount of space in the small office, dominating proceedings and precluding either of the other men present from getting too close to her. 'What proof do you bring us of your parenthood, Salik?'

'Well, sir, my — '

'No, no, Salik, that will not do all! In this country we address the aristocracy by their correct titles.' Luc's tone was deliberately condescending. 'I am an earl and you therefore address me as 'my lord'. Have you got that? But being unused to polite society you would be unaware how to carry on, I suppose, and so on this occasion no offence is taken.'

Salik made a mock bow in Luc's direction but was obviously unsettled by his mistake, which was precisely Luc's intention. If he could intimidate Salik into dropping his guard, he was more likely to give himself away.

'You have my apologies, my lord,' said Salik, sounding entirely insincere.

'Your proof,' snapped Luc irascibly.

'Well, I have my father's letters and, of course, his will.'

'I have arranged for a calligrapher to examine the will tomorrow,' put in Twining, with an ingratiating smile for Clarissa.

'Whom do you intend to use?'

Twining gave him a name.

'What else do you bring to support your claim, Salik?'

'Memories of my beloved father,' he responded, his expression sad and, as far as Luc could detect, completely lacking in any

144

true regret. 'He took a great interest in my welfare, especially my education, and insisted that I learn to speak his language fluently. I did not realize at the time why he was so determined that I should do so.' He paused significantly, before adding in an undertone, 'Perhaps now I do.'

Luc ignored the implication and asked him his age.

'One and twenty, sir — my lord.'

Luc continued to fire questions rapidly at him, changing tack constantly in the hope of wrong footing Salik. 'When did you see Sir Michael last?'

'About five years ago. He always made a point of visiting my mother and me when he was in Alexandria, but he told us on that occasion he would be unlikely to call again. It made us all very sad, especially my father, since he loved my mother so much.'

A penetrating silence greeted this remark, leaving Luc with the uncomfortable feeling that it was the first truthful statement Salik had uttered.

'Then why did he not marry her all those years ago?'

Salik paced for a moment. When he turned to look at Luc his eyes blazed with suppressed resentment. 'An English baronet married to a simple Muslim girl? He could hardly have brought such a bride back to England, could he now? She would never have been accepted and my father's career would not have survived such a scandal.' The ferocity of Luc's glare was sufficient to curb the worst of Salik's sarcasm and he continued in a more moderate tone. 'Anyway, the same situation existed in reverse. My father would never have been accepted as my mother's husband in Egypt. He spoke excellent Arabic, my lady, as you must be aware and was also conversant with the Coptic tongue. He offered to convert to the Muslim faith, for my mother's sake,' he added proudly, 'but still that would have not been sufficient and my mother was the one who realized the impossibility of it all. She declined his repeated proposals, although it broke her heart to do so. His pleas were impassioned but she remained obdurate, knowing that it could never work and reasoning she would rather see him occasionally and be sure of his affection than lose him altogether.

'Finally, my father accepted the situation but he never stopped loving my mother and supported us financially until the end. He came to see us whenever he could and we lived for his visits. And now, in death, when it can no longer harm him, he has done what he always wished to do. He has acknowledged me publicly and rewarded me by bequeathing his estate to me.'

Clarissa tensed at his passionately spoken words and made to speak. Luc patted her shoulder and pre-empted her. 'We shall see,' he said dismissively.

'I do not understand the difficulty. Twining informs me that Lady Hartley understands the land well. She may rest assured there will always be a place for her in my home. And whatever else she desires,' he added, impudently raking his eyes over her body and almost earning the full force of Luc's clenched fist in the centre of his smirking face. 'I understand the property is vast and that there is more than enough room for us both.'

'We have seen enough,' said Luc, turning abruptly and assisting Clarissa to her feet. 'We will be in touch.'

Salik tried to take Clarissa's hand to wish her good day but Luc bustled her through the door and did not give him the opportunity.

Luc handed Clarissa into his carriage and, having told his coachman to drive around the park, took his seat beside her.

'You recognized him, I think.' He spoke gently and took her hand in his.

'Yes,' she responded bleakly. 'There can be no question that he is Michael's son. The resemblance around the eyes and mouth and in some of his mannerisms and expressions is too marked to leave any room for doubt.'

'I trust your Michael was less arrogant and better mannered?'

'Indeed, yes.' Clarissa managed the briefest of bleak smiles. 'He was kindness and gentleness itself.'

'Did you like Salik?'

'I wanted to as soon as I realized that he was who he said he was, but I found my anger and, yes, my disappointment got in the way. I was not so much angry with him: more with Michael for not telling me about him. But I think there can be no doubt that my husband loved his mother very much. It explains everything,' she added quietly.

'What do you mean?'

'Nothing.' With an obvious effort she roused herself from her reverie and focused luminous eyes on Luc. 'What happens now?'

'Well, just because Salik is your late husband's son it is by no means certain that he is also his heir. The will has yet to be validated.'

'But it will be.' Her tone was weary with resignation.

'We cannot know that. Clarissa, even if Twining's man says it is genuine I will still wish to have it verified by someone else. And there are many other steps to be taken yet before we even begin to consider the possibility of defeat.' He patted her hand. 'Try to be positive. There is much to be done yet and I find myself relying upon your courage and strength.'

'Why did Michael not tell me?' she muttered over and over. 'I, of all people, had a right to know.'

'Tell me more about your Michael,' requested Luc, in an effort to both divert her mind from her troubles and to gain a fuller picture of the man she had married. 'Tell me about his work.'

'His work?' The smile she offered him was not driven by humour. 'Oh, his work was his life. When he was engaged upon some new line, some new discovery, the rest of the world ceased to exist for him. He had knowledge of archaeology and took a great interest in trying to decode the hieroglyphics at the Pyramids of Giza — without too much success — and he eventually declared them to be 'scientifically insoluble'.

'He then moved on to Alexandria, fell in love with the city well before Napoleon was thrown out and became obsessed with discovering the location of the tomb of Alexander the Great. No argument, however well reasoned, could persuade him that it was elsewhere.

'Then it was the Lighthouse that held him in thrall. The Pharos used to guide sailors into the city harbour from it for well over fifteen hundred years. It was the last of the six lost wonders of the world.'

'I can see how his work must have absorbed him,' said Luc, intrigued even through Clarissa's second-hand account of it.

'Indeed, it mattered to him more than anything. And eventually it was the great debate about the Library of Alexandria that obsessed Michael. He became an expert upon the subject and knew all theories about its burning down. He brought the whole subject alive for me by describing how the original library must have looked with its lecture areas, gardens and zoo and Shrines for each of the Muses. But the place was doomed. Michael considered that it contained too much knowledge that offended too many different cultures and religions for it to be able to survive.'

'It sounds as though Michael infected you with his enthusiasm.'

'Oh yes, I could listen to him talk about Egypt for hours. He would tell me about the river traffic on the Nile. I could picture the dhows and feluccas with their colourful sails and mishmash of nationalities aboard. He made the cities and, now that I think about it, Alexandria in particular, come to life. I could smell the spices in the souks, see the crowds in the bustling streets and feel the heat of the unrelenting sun beating down. And his love of the Egyptian people was never in doubt.' She paused, before adding bitterly, 'Perhaps now I appreciate why. I could understand his obsession but sometimes I did become a little impatient with him for being so wrapped up in his academic world . . . '

'Leaving you to struggle with the reality of day-to-day living?'

'Yes.'

They had arrived back at Grosvenor Square. Luc was still holding Clarissa's gloved hand and he raised it to his lips and kissed it. He watched her confused expression, and a deep blush creeping across her features, with surprise. Surely she must be accustomed to gentlemen kissing her hand?

'We must try to forget all of this until tomorrow. What say you, shall we attend Lady Gillings' party this evening with my mother? Hopefully it will divert us.'

'Of course,' agreed Clarissa, trying and failing to raise enthusiasm for the scheme.

'I have business at the orphanage tomorrow. Would you care to accompany me?'

'Oh yes, please! I have a present for Rosie.'

'Do you indeed? She will be delighted, but take care not to get too involved with the children. It would be an act of unkindness to lead them to expect more from life than they are ever likely to achieve.'

'Yes,' conceded Clarissa, 'I can see that you are right. But I find it difficult to temper my enthusiasm, especially where Rosie is concerned. As you must appreciate by now, adopting waifs and strays is something of a weakness of mine.'

They smiled together as they entered the house and Luc went straight to his library, calling for Simms as he did so.

'Simms, send someone to Browns Hotel. Tip the clerk generously. I want to know which room is occupied by Omar Salik and how long he has been in residence.'

'I will arrange it at once, my lord.'

'Who is the best calligrapher in the capital, Simms?'

'I believe him to be a man named White who has premises in Bond Street, my lord.'

'Excellent, contact him on my behalf. I shall shortly have work for him.'

'I will so inform him, my lord. Doubtless he will be honoured.'

'Now then, Simms, see if you can answer me this one? Who in the capital is most likely to be able to make a realistic looking forgery of a will — in Arabic?'

'That, my lord, may require a little research on my part,' replied Simms sonorously. He looked as though he was prepared to undertake a week's penance for not being able to answer one of Luc's questions immediately, but Luc knew that, come what may, Simms would have an answer for him by the end of the day.

# 8

Luc and Clarissa kept their engagement at the orphanage the following morning. Once again the first sound to assault their ears was that of childish high spirits. As soon as their arrival became known all attempts by the adults to maintain discipline were reduced to an exercise in futility as children tumbled out of the door to shout excited greetings.

Rosie appeared in the midst of them all and was the first to rush forward and wrap her arms round Luc's legs, her expression one of total adoration. He swept her up and whispered to her. She listened with apparent incredulousness, her eyes gradually becoming as large as saucers. Only slowly could she be persuaded to turn a disbelieving look upon Clarissa.

Smiling, Clarissa handed Rosie a package but the little girl, mouth gaping with shock, was too stunned to open it. Eventually Clarissa did it for her and Rosie's suspicion rapidly gave way to stunned excitement when Clarissa handed her a handsome rag doll. Clarissa and Luc exchanged an indulgent smile as they watched a gambit of emotions cross the child's face.

'Is she really just for me?' Rosie was having difficulty believing her good fortune.

'Yes, darling,' Clarissa assured her. 'She is just for you. What shall you call her?'

'Annie,' she declared promptly. 'But I have to share her with the others.'

'Just this once,' said Luc, bending down to where Rosie now occupied the step of his curricle, Annie already cradled protectively in her arms, 'Mrs Fielding has said it will be all right if you keep her to yourself.'

'Really!' Rosie looked up at Mrs Fielding hopefully, who smiled her agreement.

'What do you say to Lady Hartley, Rosie?' asked Mrs Fielding.

'Thank you, Lady Hartley!' Rosie jumped up and wrapped her arms round the crouching Clarissa, all shyness forgotten. 'I will always love Annie.'

'Of course you will, darling. But come along now, we must go back inside with the others.'

Once again Mrs Fielding managed to restore order and shepherded her charges back within doors. Clarissa put Rosie down and held her hand as they made their way back to her classroom. Luc had preceded them and Clarissa found the other children already demanding that he tell them a story.

'I have business in the office today, children, but perhaps we can persuade Lady Hartley to tell you a story?'

'Please, Lady Hartley!' chorused thirty eager voices.

'Well now, let me see,' said Clarissa thoughtfully. She took a seat and was delighted when Rosie did not hesitate to climb into her lap. 'Have you ever heard the tale of Blazon the Falcon?'

The children, naturally, wanted to know what a falcon was. Most of them had never been outside of the London slums and birds of prey were a rare sight in that locality. Clarissa explained what they looked like, describing their hooked beaks, fierce talons, piercing eyes and extravagant plumage and drew a passable picture on a slate to illustrate her words. Her story told the spellbound children how Blazon was able to locate lost and lonely lambs on the bleak moors by soaring overhead and searching all the tiny areas where incautious lambs might accidentally become separated from the rest of the flock. The lambs were eventually restored, unharmed, to their anxious mothers, but only after suspense-filled delays created by Clarissa's lively imagination.

The children hung on her every word. When her tale came to a happy conclusion there was momentary silence in the classroom, soon broken by a barrage of noisy questions. As she answered them, Clarissa became aware of a presence behind her. Luc was leaning casually against the door jamb, watching her. She was unaware how long he had been there but blushed in confusion at the maelstrom of conflicting emotions which his mere presence and scrutinizing appraisal engendered within her. She was shocked to discover that she was noticing him in the way that a woman was supposed to look upon a man. It was something she had never consciously done in her life before: she was far too sensible, her head too full of more pressing matters, to find time for daydreaming. But now, somehow, she was unable to help it.

He looked so handsome, blast him, as he leaned there with an indulgent smile playing about his lips and his black hair flopping in silky disarray across his brow. She felt an overwhelming urge to brush it back, to run her fingers through its thickness, and just for a fleeting moment dared to wonder how it would feel to be kissed by him. But then she caught herself and common sense, always a reliable friend in the past, came belatedly to her aid.

Clarissa was a guest in Luc's house and he

was being kind to her for that reason alone. She had seen for herself that wherever they went women fell over themselves to gain his attention. He could, and clearly did, take his pick. He would have no interest in an unsophisticated, country-loving widow such as she, even had she wished it could be otherwise, which, of course, she most assuredly did not.

Luc stepped forward and smiled at the children. 'I must take Lady Hartley away from you now,' he said, raising his voice to make himself heard above the din.

'Will you come back soon, Lady Hartley?' asked several of them together.

'Yes indeed, if you wish it.'

'We want to know what happened to Blazon next.'

'Very well, I will tell you on my next visit.'

'Perhaps, children,' interposed their teacher, attempting to regain control of her charges, 'you could draw some pictures of Blazon for Lady Hartley and she can take a look at them, if she would be so kind, upon her next visit?'

Twenty-nine children clearly considered this to be an excellent idea and fell enthusiastically upon their slates: Rosie continued to cling tenaciously to Clarissa. Luc pulled her arms away gently, ruffled her hair and assured her that they would be back to see her again soon.

'You are very good with them,' remarked Luc as they drove away.

'How could anyone not be, the poor mites? And I do so enjoy their enthusiasm.'

'You have made a friend for life of Rosie now that she has Annie.'

'Good! I shall never forget the expression on her face when she realized the doll was just for her. I had one just like it when I was little girl and it went everywhere with me too.'

'I shall call upon the weasel this afternoon to find out how his calligrapher fared,' Luc informed her, deliberately offhand. 'I suggest you keep your luncheon engagement with my mother and I will let you know how the visit went later.'

'If you think it best.' Clarissa's voice was bleak: all the gaiety that had infused her tone when speaking of the children now a thing of the past.

Luc took one of his hands from the reins and placed it on top of hers. 'Do not worry! There are many bridges to be crossed before we allow Salik to put so much as one foot on your land.'

Clarissa paused before responding, choosing her words with deliberation. 'Why are you doing this for me, my lord?'

'Why?' He raised a brow in surprise.

159

'Yes, why? You are going to a vast amount of trouble on my behalf, which I appreciate enormously, but I cannot comprehend why you should wish to do so.'

'Well . . . ' It was Luc's turn to select his words with care. 'Because I believe my mother is your only relation in the world; because I can sense a wrong that needs to be righted; because I do not care to see a woman on her own being deliberately exploited and,' he added, after a further significant pause, 'because I want to.'

'I see.' But she did not really see at all and was no closer to detecting his motives. She did not doubt that he had spoken the truth but it still made no sense to her. 'Thank you,' she eventually managed to say but it sounded woefully inadequate, even to her own ears.

'What say you to another ride in the park tomorrow? Six o'clock again?'

'Gladly!' Clarissa brightened visibly. 'But this time, I think I should give you fair warning, my lord, that I intend to beat you.'

'Then I shall look forward to the challenge with great anticipation.'

★ ★ ★

Luc sat in his library later that day, having just informed Clarissa that Twining's calligrapher considered the signature on the will to be that of Sir Michael Hartley. He did not deem it necessary to add that the man was so confident he was prepared to stand by his opinion in a court of law.

Clarissa had heard Luc out in silence, appearing to stoically accept the news as a foregone conclusion. Luc hastened to assure her that it was only to be expected: after all, Twining could not be expected to select an expert who was unsympathetic to his cause. Luc would not even be surprised to discover that Twining had gone so far as to show him the will in advance of his formal examination of it in order to gauge his likely opinion. Clarissa demurred, still unwilling to believe the man she had relied upon and trusted for so long to be capable of such duplicity, but Luc brushed aside her objections and informed her it was their turn now. Tomorrow the most renowned and respected calligrapher in the capital would examine the will and Luc was hopeful that his findings would be very different. And even if they were not, they were by no means defeated. There were many more avenues for them to explore: many more facts still awaiting verification.

Luc was alarmed, both by Clarissa's resolutely cheerful demeanour and the fact that she asked no further questions of him.

She did not demand to know what other enquiries they could make, or how else they could prove Salik's claim to be false. It was almost as if she was calmly preparing herself for the worst: and from what Luc now comprehended in respect of her character he suspected that to be an attitude entirely alien to her.

He recalled, with admiration, her spirited defiance of his condescending attitude towards her when she first arrived in his house; her lively and robust denouncement of society at Lady Cowley's ball. He felt sure that she had revealed her true self to him then. But now that she was facing difficulties of a much graver nature she had withdrawn into herself, apparently giving in without fighting for all that she held most dear. Luc was frankly nonplussed by her attitude.

As Clarissa rose to leave his library, Luc reminded her that they were to attend Lady Beckendale's ridotto that evening. He did so hope that his recent revelations had not overset her to the point that she wished now to cry off. She offered him an economically efficient smile and told him that of course she would attend.

Luc continued to ponder the enigma that was Clarissa: something he had been doing a great deal of since her arrival in his

162

household. Every evening since she had come to the capital he had remained faithfully by her side at whatever function they attended. He knew his behaviour was giving rise to speculation. Clarissa had, unsurprisingly, generated much interest amongst his male acquaintances: not to mention suspicion and resentment amongst their female counterparts. She had a steadily growing band of admirers, headed by his old friend, Felix Western, but Luc was relieved to notice that she showed no particular interest in any of them. That helped to restore his wounded pride for he was uncomfortably aware that she was showing no particular interest in him either — and that was not a reaction he was accustomed to generating in the fairer sex.

Felix had broached the subject of Clarissa with him only the evening before. His friend pointed out that his behaviour had been quite out of character since Clarissa's arrival. Luc tried to dismiss Felix's suggestions offhandedly. Clarissa was his mother's guest and it was his tiresome duty to look after her. But Felix knew Luc too well to be deceived by his languid attitude and chuckled at his feeble protestations. He was dogged in his determination to give the subject a thorough airing though, reminding Luc that he had even absented himself from the most recent of

163

Felix's Gentlemen's Parties: a situation that hitherto would have been deemed unthinkable. And then there was the matter of his continued dismissal of Emily Stokes. The woman had been desperate to shed her widow's weeds and re-enter society. She was by far the most attractive of the women available to Felix, Luc and their contemporaries, but she had shunned them all, making it obvious all along that she wanted only Luc. What was wrong with him? He would not have foregone such an opportunity in the past.

Luc knew his friend spoke the truth. He certainly did not crave a long term future with Emily, he was not even sure if he liked her very much, but never before would he have declined her blatant invitation to satisfy the most extreme of his carnal desires. He knew from his one tryst with Emily that she was more than willing to accommodate him in any way that he dictated. She had taken every opportunity to remind him of the fact since then but Luc was simply no longer interested.

Could Felix be right? Was it Clarissa who had made him look more closely at the manner in which he lived his life and found it to be wanting, or was he, as he had told himself only last week, finally tiring of *tonnish* ways? Clarissa certainly fascinated him in a way that no lady had been able to manage in all his thirty years. What was more, she appeared to be doing so without even trying, for Luc was discomforted by the knowledge that she still considered him to be nothing more than an idle, aristocratic scapegrace.

What intrigued Luc most about Clarissa though was her skittish behaviour. She had been married to Michael Hartley for over two years: she must be well accustomed to the way of things between the sexes, but he had noticed, almost from the first, that she had an inexplicably naïve attitude towards such matters. If he so much as touched her arm she blushed scarlet, if he kissed her hand she started like a frightened rabbit, and if the mildest of risqué comments was made in her hearing he was certain that she had no comprehension as to its meaning. Something was amiss in that area of her life and Luc was determined to find out what it was.

Simms entered with his usual discreet knock and put an end to Luc's reverie.

'What is it, Simms?'

'I regret to inform you, my lord, that I have had no success at Brown's Hotel. No person by the name of Salik is occupying a room there.'

'It is all right, Simms, I suspected as much.'

'My lord?'

Luc had made Simms a party to Clarissa's troubles in the knowledge that, with his wide connections across all aspects of society in London, he would be of more assistance to their cause if he knew what they were trying to achieve.

'I should have been disappointed if you had found him there. It would have made it that much harder to prove the fraud that I am convinced is being perpetrated. But before we take that any further, what have you been able to discover about Arabic forgers for me, Simms?'

'There is only one person, I am given to understand, who could hope to carry out such a forgery and not be detected. I naturally went in search of him, my lord, but it seems that he left London about a week ago for a trip back to Egypt, with his entire family no less, and no one is able to advise me when he is likely to return.'

'I see. Wonder where he got the blunt for such a sudden journey? I assume it was an unexpected journey?'

'Indeed, my lord, I was able to ascertain that he took everyone he knows by complete surprise with his sudden departure.'

'Interesting.' Luc fell silent, deep in thought. 'All right, Simms, did you manage to find a person to carry out the translation that I require?'

'Yes, my lord, a person by the name of Al Sharmon is holding himself at our disposal.'

'Excellent. Now then, tomorrow we will take the will to the offices of White in Bond Street, together with samples of Sir Michael's signature, in order that he may give us his opinion. Twining is not willing to allow the document out of his sight, understandably I suppose, and so I have agreed with him that I will collect it. He was anxious to 'be of service to us', and deliver the will to the office of our calligrapher, obviously wanting to know in advance whom we are planning to use. Naturally I declined his offer. Instead, his clerk will accompany us to White's office and wait in the ante-room, taking the will back with him when White has completed his work.

'What I need you to arrange is for Al Sharmon to be secreted in the back room of White's office prior to our arrival. I do not wish Twining's clerk to know that he is there. He will make his own translation of the will, noting any discrepancies from the usual legal language in the Arabic tongue and also including the full name and direction of the advocates who drew it up.'

Luc paused to draw breath. 'In the

meantime you will arrange for Twining's office to be watched. I want him followed wherever he goes. Use three or four of our best men for the job, but for goodness' sake impress upon them that they must not, under any circumstances, allow themselves to be detected. They should lose him rather than have that happen. I have no doubt that Twining will eventually link up with Salik. When he does, have the men follow Salik. I wish to know where he is lodging. Are you clear on all of that, Simms?'

'I understand your requirements perfectly, my lord. Will there be anything further?'

'Not at this moment, Simms.'

★   ★   ★

Clarissa lay awake, pondering upon the events of the previous day, as she waited for the hands of the clock to make their slow progress round to the time she would ride with Luc. His behaviour was making her more and more confused. There was now no question that the attention he was bestowing upon her, both socially and more especially in respect of her legal problems, was way beyond that which could be reasonably expected from her godmother's son.

Why had he taken her to the orphanage, for

example? None of the explanations he had offered in that respect rang true. And why should he mind what her opinion of him was? She would be gone from his life soon and they were unlikely to ever meet again. More specifically though, why was he eschewing the company of the ladies who valiantly fought for his attention at every turn in favour of staying by her side? That certainly made no sense to Clarissa either.

He had, if nothing else, exemplary manners and was constantly telling her that she was beautiful and desirable. Huh, she knew well enough that was untrue. Had it been the case then why had Michael not . . . ?

But no, she would not dwell upon that subject. Suffice it to say that she knew Luc was merely being gallant when he paid her such extravagant compliments. Polished, experienced and full of confidence, Luc could effortlessly flatter a lady, making her feel as though she was the only creature in the entire universe who held his interest. But Clarissa was not deceived. She knew it all to be a gross exaggeration: nothing more than an amusing diversion for him. She was nothing like the elegant and sophisticated ladies that she had met; neither had she any wish to be. She only owned two evening gowns for goodness' sake! For some reason she was unable to name the thought made her smile. The frugality of her wardrobe gave her a perverse sort of pleasure.

Ever since her first ball, Clarissa had stubbornly turned herself out, night after night, wearing the same gown. She had seen the astonished looks on other ladies' faces: the horror that they were scarcely able to conceal. But their reaction amused Clarissa and only served to encourage her perverseness. She had noticed several ladies gesticulating in her direction when they thought her attention to be elsewhere. They sniggered behind fans and enjoyed themselves at her expense. The gentlemen though were, to a man, attentive and entertaining and she appeared never to be without the company of at least one of them. In the rare event that Luc needed to leave her for a moment or two, Felix Western appeared smoothly in his stead, along with several other now familiar faces: all of whom appeared to be competing for her attention. It was incomprehensible.

Last night Clarissa had decided to counter her depression at the news of the will by wearing her second evening gown. As she descended the stairs, clad in a simple sheath of silver and cream that floated about her legs like gossamer, she noticed at once the appreciation in Luc's eye. She noticed as well the extra warmth in his devilish smile and the lingering touch of his tongue as he gave her hand its now customary kiss.

Whenever he touched her it affected Clarissa strangely. Annoyingly, she knew she was blushing like a schoolgirl but was powerless to prevent it. Fortunately though, it was impossible for his lordship to detect the turmoil that his punctilious attentions created within her. She fervently hoped that her countenance did not give her away and how else would he find her out? She did not know how or why he was able to make her feel so giddy, so much like an awkward adolescent, maladroit and graceless, and she determined not to allow her thoughts to dwell upon the matter.

But sometimes, like now, in the early hours when sleep eluded her, her mind refused to listen to her resolution and she found herself plagued by images of those intense black eyes looking at her with such apparent pleasure; of that handsome face and curling smiling that crinkled the corners of his eyes and lit up his entire face when he was amused; the persuasive charm which she had not observed him employing with any of his horde of admirers. She was at a loss to understand it and even more annoyed with her treacherous body for responding to it with such vigorous enthusiasm.

This very night an even stranger incident had occurred. Emily Stokes had, as always, been in attendance and desirous of Luc's company. Luc had ignored her efforts, treating her almost as though she did not exist, and led Clarissa away to speak with others. Later in the evening Clarissa had been in the withdrawing room when Emily entered. She had stood behind Clarissa, glaring acrimoniously at her in the mirror. She made little pretence at the best of times to befriend Clarissa but now that they were alone she was openly hostile.

'He is mine you know,' she fumed mutinously. 'Do not deceive yourself or get carried away with fancy ideas. He is merely doing his mother's bidding by squiring you around but he will come back to me in time. Only I know how to truly satisfy him.'

'I do not understand your meaning,' said Clarissa evenly.

'Do not play that game with me. I can see through you, even if you have bewitched half the gentlemen here. Why do you not go back to the things you understand, rusticate in the country and leave society to those of us who belong here?'

Clarissa had looked at Emily in confusion, unprepared for her vitriol and even less able to understand what she had done to deserve such treatment. Unwilling to prolong such an unpleasant interlude she simply turned away from Emily and walked wordlessly from the room, leaving her adversary gaping at her retreating back. She did not understand the incident, the reason for Mrs Stokes' animosity towards her, or what she was supposed to say in response to it, so she had taken the dignified option and simply walked away, saying nothing at all.

It did not take a discerning eye to notice that Luc had not the slightest interest in Emily Stokes and the lady herself must surely realize it. So why the angry outburst aimed at Clarissa, and what did Emily imagine it would achieve? Clarissa had no experience of such nugatory activities and was therefore unable to recognize the traits inherent in a woman gripped by the fiercest of jealousies when they confronted her.

It was time to meet Luc. Clarissa rose silently from her bed and searched in her armoire for the breeches and shirt she had flung at the back, behind her gowns. She knew that if Caroline found the garments, explanations that she was not ready to make would be coaxed out of her. Clarissa was therefore astonished to find that her breeches had been sponged and neatly pressed and hung at the end of her row of gowns. The shirt and jerkin had been similarly washed and pressed: as had the bands she used to secure her breasts in place. Her boots had been polished; their shine easily equal to that which was customarily displayed on Luc's footwear.

Caroline! And the fact that she had made no comment could only mean that she approved. This was just awful! Notions that had no place to lodge there would now be fixed firmly in her old maid's mind and Clarissa knew if she had decided to promote these liaisons between her and Luc she would have a hard time persuading her as to their innocent nature. Clarissa sighed and smiled simultaneously as she dressed. Caroline's attempts at subtle encouragement were hardly dealt with a light hand.

Luc was waiting for her as she reached the side door. Wordlessly they headed for the mews. Albert was already saddled and soon they were in the deserted park. Three-quarters of an hour later, breathless and laughing comfortably together, they returned to the mews: neither of them noticing Caroline watching them from an attic window, a smile of approval creasing her features.

Clarissa dismounted and led Albert into his stall. She removed his bridle and replaced it with a halter, whispering softly to the gelding as she did so. She unfastened his girth and was just pulling the heavy saddle from his back when it was lifted from her hands as easily as if it was made of straw.

'Allow me,' said Luc.

'I can manage.'

'I have no doubt, but is it not pleasant to be relieved of the necessity for once?'

Luc placed the saddle on the cross beam behind him and Clarissa found herself trapped between him and the wall. The space was confined, emphasizing Luc's ominous presence as he loomed above her. Raw masculinity surrounded her, causing darts of danger and piercing excitement to take turns at attacking her body. She observed his predatory smile, the animal-like intent in his expression, and knew she had to get away. Ignoring the unfamiliar lurching feeling that now assailed her, she tried to back away from him — only to collide with the wall. There was nowhere for her to go.

'What is it, sweet Clarissa? Why are you so afraid of me?'

'I am not afraid,' she stammered, furious because she knew she was blushing, 'but it is getting light, we should return to the house before we are missed.'

'Umm, yes, indeed we should, but first I

believe I am going to kiss you.'

'Do not be ridiculous! Of course you are not.'

'Why ever not?' He took a step towards her, his eyes still devouring her features, and reached out a hand.

'No, I . . . ' She put her own hand out to ward him off but it made not the slightest difference to his intentions and she could see that he was not about to be denied. His arm slipped about her waist and he pulled her towards him.

'Come here!' His face was looming above her, mere inches from her own. His lips were smiling at her and she found her gaze fastened upon them in bemused fascination. Somehow she was unable to pull her eyes away. She watched with awe, trembling slightly, as his head descended slowly towards her own.

It was his breath feathering her face that finally snapped her out of her trance-like state. Coming belatedly to her senses she was reminded of the peril of the situation she found herself in: a situation which had only developed because of her crass stupidity in not preventing it earlier. He was trying to take advantage of her and she had not done a single thing to gainsay him. Trembling violently she attempted to push him away, desperate to escape, but her efforts had no effect whatsoever on his vicelike hold.

'Why are you so afraid of me, Clarissa?' he asked for a second time. His voice was husky; full of concern. 'You must, by now, have recognized my attraction towards you.'

Without giving her time to respond he dropped his lips to hers. Clarissa's eyes were locked wide open in fear, observing his horrified reaction as realization gradually dawned. If the situation had not been so mortifyingly degrading Clarissa would have laughed at his stupefied expression. She watched as he gauged her inability to respond to his kiss and the slow comprehension in his expression as he understood the reason why. He knew her secret, damn him. He knew that she had never been kissed before.

'Clarissa, what in God's name . . . ?'

'No!' She pulled away from him violently. 'Do not say anything.'

As she struggled to get away, the hand that had been holding the back of her head slipped down and brushed against her breasts. He made another startled exclamation and explored further, ignoring her futile struggles.

'Clarissa, what is this?' His hand slid inside her shirt and rested upon the bandages that held her breasts firm.

'I told you before,' she snapped, 'I do not have a habit.'

'Yes, but why the need for this agony? Do you have to bind yourself like this every day at home when you ride out?' His expression was one of tenderness but beneath that Clarissa could detect his horror and something else as well: shock perhaps, or even derision. Well, she thought bitterly, at least that should rid him of his desire to kiss me. She nodded, ashamed and unable to look him in the eye, but he placed a finger gently beneath her chin and tilted her head upwards, forcing her to meet his gaze.

'But why? I realize you cannot ride in a habit but you could easily have a jacket made that would support you.'

Clarissa, still too mortified to continue looking at him, attempted to move out of his grasp but he was not about to let her go. So gently she hardly realized what was happening, he loosened her shirt and pushed it from her shoulders. Slowly he unfastened the bandage that held her breasts. Clarissa momentarily closed her eyes and permitted the feelings he was generating — desires that she had long ago learned to ignore — to overwhelm her. A sensation of dizzying shock assailed her entire body. The temptation to surrender to his charm, to allow his skilled fingers to continue creating those wonderful, forbidden feelings, was almost seductive.

But it would not do. She was mortified and humiliated. It was impossible for her to stay here with him now: she had to get away. The shame that lurked could not be subdued for much longer and must be borne in solitude.

'Just leave me be!' She pulled away from him and holding her gaping shirt about her ducked beneath his arm and escaped in the direction of the house. Luc was left holding the bandages that had bound her so viciously, but Clarissa was too intent upon eluding him to notice the compassionate nature of his expression.

# 9

With a tormented sigh, Clarissa threw herself onto her bed. For possibly the first time in her life she allowed herself to wallow in her own misery: luxuriate in a solid bout of self-pity. The tears fell unbidden and were a welcome release for her confused and pent-up emotions. Luc had awakened in her feelings that had lain dormant for so long: incomprehensible longings that crept stealthily upon her in the middle of the night when she was powerless to prevent them from tantalizing her vulnerable and defenceless body. She had long ago disciplined herself to ignore such feelings, but now the need ripped through her with a hitherto unknown intensity, refusing to be denied. It once again taunted her in her frustration; enfolding her with an urgently acute sense of desperation, of futile longing; only to abruptly desert her again, leaving her feeling unfulfilled and more confused than ever.

Why, oh why had she allowed Luc to corner her in that damned stall? But once he had, why had she not simply insisted that he leave her be? *Perhaps because you did not wish him to?* suggested the voice of her conscience. She ignored the voice of reason, having no wish to examine too closely what it was trying to tell her, knowing that she had only made matters worse by demonstrating such an immature reaction. The situation between them would be untenable now. Two weeks ago she would have been delighted at the prospect of his avoiding her — but now? Well, now she was no longer sure what she wanted from him. She was becoming accustomed to his presence and found the prospect of losing the intimate friendship that had been building between them unsettling. But lose it she must for he had reason enough now to see her for what she really was: an inexperienced, unsophisticated widow who had no place within the *ton*: someone who would never be able to fit comfortably into his world.

But why should that matter? She had always known that she could not be happy leading the sort of shallow existence that appeared to satisfy him. For once in her life, Clarissa did not know her own mind. Every time she considered her relationship with Luc she was left feeling confused and uncertain. Every time she thought of that knowing, curling smile and the dark intensity in his eyes her heart missed a beat and she was plagued by feelings of loneliness and regret. Her fingers moved tentatively to her breast — the one against which he had so recently brushed his fingers. She could still feel his touch: her skin still burned where his fingers had rested upon it and a rushing sensation like hot, molten liquid assailed her. Powerless to resist reliving that brief, blissful moment, she allowed the memory to consume her.

Then she recalled how she had lost her nerve and fled from him like an outraged spinster and came back to reality with a resounding thump. He would be scornful of her now and would doubtless relate the incident for the amusement of his male acquaintance.

Clarissa did not know, when she paused to analyse it, just what she was crying about. Had she not achieved her end in ridding herself of him? She had just decided that she could never adapt to his sort of shallow life and neither would she wish to. Come what may she would shortly return to Northumberland and continue with her life there. Only when she had put all those miles between herself and Luc would she truly be able to find contentment again.

Clarissa pondered anew her difficulties with Salik. That he was Michael's son was not in question. But was he Michael's heir? In all honesty Clarissa did not think so, but she was still unable to share Luc's view that Mr Twining, whom she had known and trusted for years, could be involved in any attempt to defraud her. Why then was she sitting back and allowing Luc to pursue that line? Clarissa was ashamed of the debilitating lethargy that had settled upon her, rendering her incapable of taking any action to help herself. It was so unlike her to sit passively by but, in truth, she was exhausted. Bereavement and the unrelenting demands placed upon her by the hard, physical work on the estates had drained her of her usual determination to act on her own volition.

It could not continue thus, she realized that much now. Her position here in London was now untenable and reluctantly she came to a decision. Maybe the incident in the stables that morning had been the catalyst she had been unconsciously seeking to spur her into action. She admitted to herself that it had been very pleasant to lean on Luc for a while and allow him to shoulder her burdens: it was a luxury she had not experienced since the death of her father. But she could not permit it to continue. She must rediscover her customary strength, for her own sake as well for that of the people who depended upon her.

If Michael had wanted his son to have the estates then so be it. He had doubtless intended to tell her: possibly thought that he actually had, for he had been very confused during the latter months of his life, angry that the medicines muddled his mind and prevented him from continuing with his work. Clarissa tried to quell her resentment when she acknowledged that would have been his first concern: not the inconsequential matter of whether he had communicated his intentions regarding their property to her.

No matter, she would be true to his wishes. She would strike a deal with Mr Salik, do whatever was necessary to remain on the estates and carry on with her work. From the little she had seen of him he appeared keen to live the life of a gentleman and would doubtless wish to spend his time in London. Excellent! She could remain in Northumberland and ensure that the estates ran smoothly in his absence. She would be able to assure him that he would have no cause for concern with her overseeing matters.

And when she was safely returned to Northumberland her work would take all of her physical strength, and occupy her mental capacity to the full as well. She would be too busy, too tired to think about black, passionate eyes smiling at her and making her feel alive in a way that she had not previously realized was possible. And if thoughts of that mocking smile and seductive gaze had the temerity to invade her dreams, she would simply work harder still — until she was so exhausted that dreaming became an impossibility. The maelstrom of emotions created by the simple touch of his lips to her hand would eventually become entombed beneath her exhaustion and she would rediscover her precious peace of mind. It was the obvious answer.

Clarissa's tears dried up, leaving her feeling miserable but resolved. She rose from her bed, disrobed and crawled back beneath the sheets. This time, completely drained, she fell into a deep, exhausted and dreamless sleep.

⋆ ⋆ ⋆

Late in the afternoon Luc returned home, entered his library and shut the door with a resounding bang. The afternoon had seen his worst fears realized. White had been unable to say categorically that Hartley's signature was a forgery. It was the worst possible blow to Luc's expectations and he dreaded passing on the news to Clarissa. He had made light of it before, declaring it not to be their only course for redress, but he suspected she knew that to be a falsehood. White was the most respected man in his profession: his integrity beyond reproach. Had he been more sure than not that the signature was a forgery, Luc was confident that would have been sufficient to persuade any court of law. But as things now stood, they were no better off than they had been when Clarissa first learned of Salik's existence.

Luc knew his position in society and the influence he wielded would make it easy for him to persuade the courts to delay making a ruling until such time as further investigations could be made regarding the validity of the will in Egypt. The delay could easily be for several years, leaving Clarissa free to pursue her work in the meantime, but he knew that situation would be less than satisfactory. She would not be relieved of her worries and he only intended to go down that route as a last resort.

No, the area that still aroused Luc's suspicions was that of the separate firm of advocates who drew up the supposed will. Luc could not understand why a gentleman in Hartley's position would use two different concerns. If he trusted the one that handled his payments to Salik's mother for so long — a delicate situation in anyone's language — why use a completely separate concern to

186

draw up his will? And, more to the point, why tell no one about it, especially his wife? This was doubtless the area to investigate but it was a question of finding someone who knew Alexandria well and could advise whether the firm in question actually existed. Over the past two days an uncertainty in that respect had been frequently creeping into Luc's conscious thoughts. He had learned long ago to trust his instincts and anyway, he had precious few other avenues to explore.

Felix Western's family was in shipping. Luc would find an opportunity to speak privately with him at the ball they were to attend that evening. He might know if any ships were due from Egypt and whether they were likely to have on board any members of the crew who were natives of Alexandria. It was a long shot, but Luc was now too desperate to dismiss any possibility, however remote.

Luc's mind returned, unbidden, to the episode in the stables that morning and he cursed himself roundly for behaving in such a crass manner. He had acted like an unfeeling oaf, blundering and inept. He had known that she was timid and unsure of herself, her mind undoubtedly full of her troubles rather than with the type of licentious thoughts that occupied his whenever he was in her company. What in God's name had prompted him to act in such a way? Luc experienced again his horrified reaction at finding her breasts so savagely bound and felt absurdly angry that she had been forced to behave thus for so long. What had been wrong with her father? He must have realized what she had to endure, so why had he blithely permitted her to carry on in such a manner?

Thoughts of her breasts caused Luc's mind to take the inevitable detour. Giving in to the impulse he relived the exquisite feel of her soft flesh in his hands as he unwound those hateful bandages. She was a disarming mixture of supreme confidence and touching naïvety; spirited opinions bordering on disrespect vying against a mammoth portion of self-doubt. He also understood now that beneath that cool exterior lay a passion just waiting to be released: a desire to glory in all that she had been denied for so long.

Luc was now determined that he would be the one to awaken that passion. He was not about to let anyone else touch her in the meantime though and resolved to stand guard over her even more closely than she had thus far permitted. He would have to be patient, he knew that much, but the prize was well worth the winning and he was content to bide his time. Allowing his imagination to run riot, Luc smiled in slow anticipation.

A gentle knock on the library door preceded its opening and Clarissa herself entering.

Luc hastily brought his mind back to the present, rose to his feet and crossed the room in two strides.

'Clarissa, m'dear!' He took her hand and led her to the sofa next to the fire. 'It is my turn to offer you an apology. I acted like an unfeeling ape this morning.'

Clarissa smiled a sad little smile and told him there was nothing to apologize for, but Luc detected a gambit of emotions passing across her lovely face. Seeming to realize it, she averted her gaze on the pretext of greeting Mulligan. When she turned to look at Luc again she had her feelings under closer guard.

'I heard you come in. What news?'

Luc told her as gently as he could, watching her closely for her reaction.

'It is as I expected,' she said, in a tone that suggested resignation.

'You believe the will to be genuine?'

'I am not surprised to learn that it most probably is. I knew immediately that Mr Salik is Michael's son. I would not be surprised to learn that the will is valid as well.'

'I do not agree,' said Luc firmly, 'and there is still much we can do to disprove their case.

You must not give up hope, my lady.'

Luc told Clarissa of his suspicions regarding the advocates and his intended actions in that respect. He kept the explanation to a minimum, excluding Felix Western's possible role. She listened to him politely, her expression vague.

'What is it, Clarissa?' he asked her gently. 'What are you thinking?'

'My lord, I cannot allow you to spend any more time attempting to fight this matter on my behalf. You have been more than kind, as it is. I am coming to terms with Mr Salik's claim upon the estates and I have this afternoon decided to try and reach an agreement with him. Whatever I have to do I will, as long as he permits me to continue my work with the herd.' Luc was appalled and attempted to stop her from saying more but she waved away his objections and continued. 'I could move back to Greenacres and he could take up residence at Fairlands,' she said brightly. 'After all, we could hardly live with propriety under the same roof. Unless, of course . . . ' She paused, as though an idea had just occurred to her. 'Perhaps, like his father before him, he would be willing to make a marriage of convenience?'

This time Luc could not hold on to his temper and leapt from his seat. 'You cannot possibly mean that!'

'Why not?'

'Because the man is a snake, a charlatan, a fraudster.'

'Possibly, but we seem unable to prove it.'

'We are by no means giving up with our attempts to prove it: we have hardly begun in fact. No, m'dear, you must be patient; I promise you we will achieve our end. If necessary we will request a delay in the courts and I will send someone to Egypt, or even go myself, and make further investigations.'

Clarissa appeared touched by his willing-ness to undertake such a task but assured him she would not permit it.

'Rather that than I see you throw yourself away on that coxcomb,' said Luc bitterly.

'Me, throw myself away? It is a little late for concerns of that nature, is it not?' She turned away from him, attempting to hide her despondency and focused her gaze in apparent fascination upon the fire.

Luc pulled her to her feet and, standing behind her, turned her so that she was forced to look in the mirror above the fire. 'Oh, Clarissa, can you not see? Why do you not believe me? Why are you so impervious to the impression you have made upon half of the gentlemen of our acquaintance? Tell me what you observe when you look at yourself in the glass?'

Clarissa pulled away from him as though she had been scalded. 'Do not try telling me I am beautiful again!' Her voice cracked with emotion and Luc could see that she was maintaining control by the merest sliver. 'I know that to be a lie.'

'Clarissa, I do not understand you. Tell me why do you have so little confidence in yourself?'

Clarissa hesitated for some time before speaking. When she did so, her words were laced with a combination of anger and bitterness. 'Why? I should have thought, after your discovery this morning, that it would be obvious. If I am as beautiful and desirable as you keeping implying, why is it that I am still — well, that my husband did not agree with you?' Her eyes, suspiciously bright with unshed tears, belied her short-lived anger and it was only by exercising the most severe self-restraint that Luc stopped himself from pulling her into his arms and offering her the form of comfort she so richly deserved.

'Tell me,' he coaxed gently.

'There is very little to relate.'

She strode away from him, her every step followed not just by Luc but also by an adoring Mulligan. She seemed to be gathering her thoughts, deciding how much to reveal to him, and after a few moments she began to speak again in her low, melodic voice, her face displaying no emotion.

'My father had been dead for six months. I was just about managing to overcome my grief. It was the needs of the herd and the necessity to carry on with the work on the land that pulled me round. My father and I had always done those things together: Michael had never played an active role. At first he was abroad a lot and then his time was taken up with his academic activities. He was interested enough in what we did and seemed to be pleased that the best use was being made of his land but no more than that. He indulged my whims with regard to experimentation but I always had the impression that he was humouring me and did not think the subject sufficiently taxing to trouble his huge intellect. Anyway, by the time my father died, Michael was unwell himself, never having been physically strong and so everything was left to me.'

'He did not trouble himself to secure suitable assistance for you?' asked Luc, attempting to disguise his contempt.

'No, but I would not have accepted it anyway. I preferred to handle matters myself and in order to do so I was, at first, in and out of Fairlands all the time, just as I had been when Papa was alive. But it was pointed out to me, especially by Caroline,' she added, smiling properly for the first time since entering the library, 'that such behaviour would be frowned upon. The same thought must have occurred to Michael because he proposed to me. I could see at once that marrying him would solve all my problems and allow me to continue with my work and so I agreed immediately.'

'It was a marriage of convenience then, I take it? You did not love him, surely?'

'Well, yes, it is true I did not love him in the conventional way, but I was comfortable with him and thought the rest would follow. But I can see now that it was Michael's intention that it would be a marriage in name only. I had my own chamber at Fairlands already and often spent the night there when Papa was alive, if it was more expedient in terms of the work that I was undertaking at the time. I assumed that upon our marriage I would move into the master suite but Michael just smiled at me in that gentle way of his and said why did I not just stay where I was? After all, I was accustomed to my room and had all my things about me there.

'I still thought nothing of it. After all most

married couples have separate chambers, do they not? On our wedding night I fully expected Michael to come to me. I sat up in bed and waited for him, curious to know what would happen and willing to do whatever he asked of me. After all, I was now his wife. But' — she hesitated for the first time and sighed before continuing — 'I waited and waited, listening for the sound of him approaching my room. Three hours passed before I could bring myself to accept that he was not coming.'

Luc gave a snort of disapproval, hurt beyond measure at the desolation in her voice and outraged that anyone could so carelessly inflict such guilt and pain on one as gentle and sensitive as Clarissa. 'The fool!' he muttered, loud enough for her to hear. But she ignored his interruption and carried on. It appeared to Luc that having started to speak about the subject at last she was unable to stop the words from tumbling over one another. She needed to unburden herself, to expunge the guilt she unconsciously felt at her apparent inability to attract her husband.

'At breakfast the next morning he treated me as normal. He was kindness itself, enquiring if I had slept well and asking me what plans I had for the day. I could not make it out at first but knew he was still unwell. I assumed that when he recovered his health he would come to me and make our marriage complete. I wanted to ask him about it but did not know how to begin. And so I just waited. But he never did come and in the end I stopped expecting him.'

'And this is the evidence upon which you base your foundation that you are not beautiful or desirable?'

'Of course! He obviously did not feel that way about Mr Salik's mother. But I can see now that he probably still loved her and that is why he did not wish to treat me in the way that a husband should behave towards his wife.'

'Oh, Clarissa!'

Luc crossed the room to join her. Ignoring the fear that flared in her eyes he stood behind her once again, put his arms around her waist and pulled her gently until she rested against him. Just the simple contact of her body against his was sufficient to arouse him. Well, that was all to the good: she was bound to be able to detect it. He wanted her to. He wanted her to know just how much he desired her; how easily she could make him desperate for her.

'And so, sweet Clarissa,' he said, his voice low and gravelly; his breath peppering her neck; his tongue gently grazing her ear. 'You can round up a herd of sheep; recognize signs of any skin parasites they may have contracted; detect their foot lameness and respiratory diseases at a glance. You can man a falcon, ride better than most men I have met and work at least as hard as any of them. But' — he paused to brush his lips against the length of her long neck and tighten his grip on her waist — 'you have never enjoyed the comfort of a man to take on your burdens, never experienced the pleasure of his caresses; never received his protestations of admiration. Nor have you known the joy to be had when he makes love to you, claims you as his and fills you with his desire. I find that state of affairs to be inestimably sad.'

'Lucien, I do not — '

'Luc,' he whispered, as he nibbled gently at her earlobe, 'my friends call me Luc. Only my mother calls me Lucien.'

'Luc, I cannot, I — '

'Shush!'

He turned her slowly in his arms until she was facing him and gently lowered his lips to hers. This time she did not attempt to escape but froze in his arms instead, eyes wide open with fear, unable to respond to him at all.

'Just relax. Will you trust me and let me show you how?'

He pulled her close, towering above her, surrounding her with his protective strength. He forced her lips apart gently with his tongue and in so doing sensed a subtle change in her. With a sigh she relaxed slightly against him. It was as though someone had opened a door and released a thousand passions that had been held captive for far too long. Her eyes were still open and searching his face for a clue: she wanted to know what she was supposed to do and Luc was too experienced to misinterpret the signs. Triumph flooded through him as he felt her lips soften beneath his. It was all the invitation he needed. His tongue plundered her mouth, exploring its depths again and again in a desperate effort to relieve his frustrations. He kissed her harshly and crushed her against him, demonstrating by his actions just how desperate he was to possess her and make her his.

Horrified to realize that he had almost lost control, Luc abruptly broke the kiss. Just for a moment he had almost permitted his own needs to come first and was appalled at his selfishness. He had the inestimable privilege of teaching this gorgeous creature, of being the first man to pay homage to her in the way that she so richly deserved and he did not intend to rush matters. But his body had other ideas. It was burning with a raging desire he was hard pressed to ignore. Years of meaningless trysts with compliant, unchallenging women had dulled his senses and made the whole act seem trivial. But this was something else and he could never before recall experiencing such a sweet agony, such an urgent, overwhelming desire to possess a woman. It had never mattered to him more that he suppress his own needs and concentrate instead on hers.

An opportune knock at the door saved Luc from losing control. Clarissa pulled away from him like a scalded cat and retreated hastily to the sofa, her hand reaching out to seek the comfort of contact with Mulligan's shaggy head. Luc watched her as she averted her face, but she was not quick enough and he was able to take in her crimson blush, her expression of uncertainty and very obvious confusion. Standing by the fire, Luc cast her an apologetic smile before barking out an irritated instruction for his caller to enter. Whoever it was had better have a good reason for the interruption.

'What is it, Simms?'

Showing no reaction to his master's irritation Simms informed him calmly that he had come to report on the situation with Twining.

'What of Mr Twining?' asked Clarissa looking up, her expression once again guarded.

'Simms was carrying out my instructions.'

'Yes, I do not doubt it, but in what respect?'

Luc sighed. 'I did not want to trouble you with this until we know more.'

'I want to know everything that is happening.'

'Very well. I sent Simms to see Salik at Brown's Hotel. You are paying for his residence there, if you recall?'

'Yes, yes, but what of it?'

'Well, it would seem that at present you are paying for nothing since Salik has not registered there.'

'Perhaps he has not had the opportunity to remove there as yet? It has, after all, only been two days.'

'Indeed, my lady,' put in Simms. 'I came to inform his lordship that I checked again this afternoon and Mr Salik is now in residence.'

'There you are then.'

'More to the point, my lord, my lady, Salik has registered at the hotel, but no one has actually seen him there and, according to my information, his bed has not been slept in.'

Luc assimilated this information. 'Hm, interesting. But what of Twining?'

'He was followed to a house in Chelsea when he closed his office last night, my lord,' said Simms, passing Luc the direction, 'but as yet there has been no sign of his meeting with Salik.'

Clarissa was curious and peered at the address but it meant nothing to her.

'I see. Stay on it, Simms. Does he lodge in the house in Chelsea?'

'As I understand it, my lord, he occupies two rooms on the first floor.'

Clarissa stood and joined Luc at his desk. 'Why are you having Mr Twining followed? That implies you still consider some duplicity on his part.'

'Indeed!'

'I cannot accept that. He served my father and Michael faithfully. He was as surprised and upset as I was when he learned of Mr Salik's existence.'

'In that case our surveillance of him will doubtless prove to be fruitless. But as to his loyalty, look at this: these are the estate accounts for the last five years. Up until your husband's death they were perfectly correct but since then, well, look here.' Luc pointed to several entries. 'These are expenses and fees claimed by Twining. They are almost double those claimed over recent years. Why would that be, do you suppose?'

'Since Michael died I imagine there must have been a lot of extra work for Mr Twining to do with regard to settling the estates.'

'It is common practice not to take professional fees until those matters are settled: especially as he is continuing to claim his fee for overseeing the accounts.'

'Let me see for myself.'

Clarissa sat at Luc's desk and took a detailed look at the areas which were of concern to Luc. She was guiltily aware that she had not kept proper track of the accounts since her husband's death; quite simply she had not had the time or strength, but when her father had been alive the books had been her responsibility and she had been well acquainted with them. It did not take Clarissa five minutes to see the glaringly obvious errors and omissions which she should have detected for herself long before now.

Luc was watching her closely. The megrims, which had afflicted her since she first learned of Salik's existence, seemed to dissipate before his very eyes. She suddenly sat much straighter, inertia and lethargy going the same way as her blue devils. Her eyes were bright with a fulminating anger, flashing brown fire flecked with sparkling rays of gold. There was an unmistakable determination in her expression, purpose in her ramrod-straight posture as she stood up and faced Luc.

'I have been a blind fool! How could I have trusted him so implicitly?'

'Because you always have. He knew it and clearly relied upon the fact.'

'Well, in that case, my lord, he is in for a shock. Now, what can I do to help uncover his treachery?' Clarissa faced Luc, hands on hips, chin defiantly tilted, her recent expression of calm acceptance replaced by the unmistakable light of battle, which shone fervently from her lovely eyes.

'Well, at present I — '

She held up her hand in protest. 'Do not dare to tell me there is nothing: this is my battle and I refuse to be ignored any more. Now, why did you have Mr Twining followed?'

'To discover where he resided. I thought that if he and Salik are in league they might be residing together.'

'And that would prove their duplicity?'

'It would certainly help us in that respect. But we must be patient and allow Simms' men to do their work. They should be able to uncover the truth of the matter.'

'Oh, but of course,' agreed Clarissa sweetly, and far too readily.

Luc was so relieved that she was behaving more like her old self, so used to having his orders obeyed without question, that he failed to notice anything strange about her ready acquiescence.

# 10

Luc escorted Clarissa and his mother to the Duchess of Wiltshire's ball that evening: Clarissa once again clad in her sea-green ball gown. As the evening progressed Luc became uncomfortably aware he was not the only gentlemen in the room who thought she looked bewitching in it. Suspicious of the other men's motives Luc did not once leave her side for the first half of the ball. He claimed the first waltz with her, reluctantly surrendering her to Felix for the second but whisking her away from him again as soon as it came to an end.

Luc could see a great difference in her that evening. It was clear that she was still angry and disillusioned at the discovery of Twining's treachery and could hardly contain her impatience to denounce him for the fraud and liar that she now accepted him to be. But Luc knew that dwelling upon perceived injustices could create difficulties of another kind and did not hesitate to employ diversionary tactics in an attempt to bring her out of herself. He called upon his skills as a raconteur, shamelessly embellishing all the gossip he had recently heard, and was eventually rewarded when he sensed the tension draining out of her and she relaxed, responding to his banter in her mordacious attitude of old.

Initially encouraged by his success, Luc discovered there was a price to pay for it. Just the sight of her laughing up at him so spiritedly, blithely unaware of the enchanting image she created, was all it took for his frustration to return and leave him fighting the overwhelming temptation to whisk her away somewhere private, where he could have her all to himself and kiss her until she begged for mercy. Only the thought that he might not actually be able to remain in control prevented him from putting that plan into action.

Luc had other reasons, besides his growing attraction to her, to stand guard at Clarissa's side. Her band of admirers had steadily increased at every event they attended and Luc was well aware why that had happened. When a new person was introduced into society, rumours with regard to their circumstances quickly gathered pace. By now the whole room must be aware that Clarissa was recently widowed and the inheritor of two valuable estates. No one would yet be aware of Salik's insolent claim and so the fact that Clarissa was not only beautiful but also richly endowed with property was sufficient in itself to promote the interest of many a gentleman in need of a wealthy wife.

Indeed, some of the most impecunious gentlemen in the room were now making serious attempts to gain Clarissa's attention. He had been able to forestall their attempts to dance with her by informing them that Lady Hartley only cared to waltz and that the first and last of the evening were promised to him, as was the honour of escorting her into supper. He carefully orchestrated matters and ensured that the remainder of the evening's waltzes only went to people whom he could trust: Felix, Lord Denver and the like. But that did not prevent Clarissa's would-be suitors joining her and Luc at the side of the ballroom and attempting to gain her attention in any way that they could.

'I say, Lady Hartley, my mother is proposing a picnic in Kew Gardens later this week. Would you do me the inestimable honour . . . '

'My dear Lady Hartley, pray do tell me more about your fascinating work with your Cheviot sheep. I would be so interested . . . '

'My dear, may I offer you my services as an escort should you and Lady Deverill wish to see the new play at the Covent Garden

Theatre later this week?'

And so it went on. Clarissa did not seem to have a particular interest in any of them, but they persisted stoically and, in her present distracted state, Luc could not trust them to behave towards her as gentlemen should. They would consider her widowed status as *carte blanche* to proceed in any way they saw fit to gain the advantage. Clarissa was too naïve to recognize their stratagems and so could well be compromised.

One of Clarissa's suitors was especially persistent. He was Lord Eversham, heir to a vast estate not twenty miles distant from Clarissa's. He was also, Luc had reason to know, well below the hatches. He was infamous in the hells and rumour had it that he was having trouble honouring his latest vowels. But he was clever in his pursuit of Clarissa. He did not attempt to flatter her, but instead discussed with her in detail their native Northumberland and his own efforts with his livestock. No strategy could be guaranteed to work better for he was the only one Clarissa appeared to have any time for. It was also a subject upon which her other admirers were ill-qualified to pass comment, leaving the field clear for Eversham. He was handsome, personable, charming, and in Clarissa's presence careful to show no signs of being the imbiber that Luc knew him to be. His persistence worried Luc more than any of the other gentlemen's clumsy attempts to attract her.

After the supper interval, Luc passed Clarissa over to Lord Denver's care and the waltz she had promised him. He whispered to her that he needed a private word with Felix and would be back for her after the dance. If, for any reason, he was not, then Lord Denver would return her to his mother. Clarissa accepted his explanation wordlessly and smiled as Lord Denver offered her his arm.

Casting a final warning glance in Denver's direction, Luc motioned Felix to join him at the back of the ballroom. They left the room together and sought out the library, confident they could talk there uninterrupted, unaware that Emily Stokes was observing their departure from the edge of the room, a calculating look in her eye.

Upon gaining the library Luc did not hesitate to relate to Felix the whole of Clarissa's problem. Luc and Felix had been friends forever and there was no one he would trust more to both keep his confidence and offer whatever help it was within his means to provide.

Luc asked Felix if any ships were expected into London in the near future from Cairo, or better yet, Alexandria, and if any of their crew were likely to be able to assist. Felix promised to meet with Luc the following morning, as soon as he had been able to make the necessary enquiries.

The friends discussed Clarissa's predicament for a while longer, Felix agreeing with Luc that attempted fraud was the only possible explanation. Having exhausted the subject at last, Felix resolved to rejoin the dance but Luc told him to go ahead: he was in no hurry to return to the mêlée and would remain here to finish his cigar. Clarissa would be safe enough with Denver and he could be relied upon to return her to his mother when the dance ended. Luc simply craved a moment's solitude.

But it was not to be for the door opened again almost as soon as it had closed behind Felix.

'Luc, there you are! Were you waiting for me?'

'Emily, what in the name of Hades are you doing here?'

'Looking for you, of course. Luc, why have you been avoiding me?'

'I was not aware that I was doing any such thing,' replied Luc wearily, throwing his cigar into the fire and sensing that getting rid of the obdurate Emily would not be so easily achieved on this occasion.

'But of course you are! You do not answer my notes, you will not dance with me, you ignore me at parties and make no effort to single me out. What has changed between us? I thought we had an understanding,' she finished petulantly.

'Good God, why ever would you think that?'

Emily hesitated fractionally. Colour flooded her cheeks and her confidence slipped for the first time in the face of Luc's withering contempt. 'Oh, Luc, how can you ask that after what passed between us at Felix's the other week?'

Luc chuckled. 'Emily, that was simply one of Felix's 'parties'. You knew well enough what you were attending when you accepted his invitation. How could that form the basis of any sort of understanding between us?'

'Oh but, Luc, think how good we were together.'

'Emily,' said Luc with an emphatic sigh, 'there is absolutely nothing between us except a pleasant evening, which culminated in mutually requited lust, and we both know it. Why can you not just accept it and move on?'

Luc now heartily regretted his dalliance with Emily. Never would he have considered that she would cling so defiantly. She had indeed been well aware of what to expect at Felix's parties, for even before her husband's demise she had not been averse to attending them. Luc had been foxed and restless when she made herself available to him and, knowing the extent of her amatory history, he had not hesitated to take full advantage of all that she offered him, thinking that would be the end of the matter. He was not a vain man and had, in all honesty, not noticed what was plainly apparent to the rest of the *ton* in that she had been shamelessly pursuing him for months.

'You know you do not mean that, Luc. You liked this, darling, did you not?' She casually shrugged out of one of her shoulder straps. The neckline of her gown was impossibly low and her breasts now peeped invitingly above the lace of her corset. She took Luc's hand placed it upon her, forcing his fingers to close about her. 'You see, darling, you want me still. I just knew you would!' Her tone was triumphant and she wrapped her arms around his neck, attempting to kiss him.

Luc had not laid so much as a finger on any woman for almost two weeks and, just for a moment, he was tempted. God alone knew, he was no saint and no one need ever know. If he could just relieve his frustration might he be able to think more rationally about Clarissa's plight?

But no, if he gave Emily what she so obviously desired he would never be free of her. With renewed determination he removed his hands from her body and attempted to push her away from him.

'You see, I knew it!' Ignoring his futile protests, Emily smiled victoriously, convinced that she had persuaded him. 'Perhaps if you locked the door we could become reacquainted?' She smiled up at him, her heart reflected in her glowing eyes.

'No, Emily!'

'All right, darling, have it your way. I had forgotten how much you enjoy a little danger.' She tilted her head flirtatiously and pulled him against her.

Luc knew that if she so much as touched him, in his present heightened state of awareness, he would be unable to resist what was on offer. He tried more forcefully to push her away but Emily's desperation was giving her superhuman strength and she just laughed at him, lacing her fingers more tightly at the back of his head.

'Come on, Luc, where is the harm in it?' She attempted to lift herself up and wrap her legs around his waist. 'You know you want me. Why do we not have a little fun now and perhaps tomorrow you could call upon me and we could continue at our leisure?'

★ ★ ★

Clarissa, waltzing with the charming Lord Denver, struggled to make conversation. She had danced with him before and had found him to be a welcome exception to the predictability of the throng, but tonight her heart was not in it. She needed to think about all that had happened to her that day but thus far there had been no opportunity for solitude. Most of all though she needed to assure herself that Luc was not attempting more unilateral actions on her behalf. She was convinced that his requirement for a private conversation with Felix was somehow connected with her affairs. He had promised that he would take no further steps without consulting her, but she sensed he was still trying to shield her from the unpalatable truth and did not entirely trust him to keep his word. In his chivalrous but ridiculously misguided endeavour to protect her from the unpleasantness of her attorney's duplicity, she would not put it past him to try and gull her once again. That decided it for her. She would go in search of him now and confront him.

Excusing herself from Lord Denver on the pretext of visiting the withdrawing room and having no wish to be cornered by the hovering Mr Basnet and Lord Thomas, Clarissa slipped from the ballroom unobserved. She took the same door through which she had seen Luc and Felix disappearing, only to be confronted by a confusing corridor which branched off in different directions. She paused, wondering what to do now. Perhaps she was just being fanciful after all for surely Luc would not actually lie to her? She would return to the ballroom and await his return after all.

But no, vacillating still, she suspected there would be a posse of gentlemen awaiting her and she had no wish to spend the next half an hour fending them off. She did not enjoy balls very much and had no wish to dance again: at least, not with anyone but Luc, she reluctantly conceded. She could return to Aunt Marcia but suspected that would not deter her suitors either.

Changing her mind for the third time, she decided she would definitely seek Luc out. Conveniently, just at that moment, she observed Felix leave a room on the left and head back to the ballroom. She was standing in the shadows and he did not see her. Luc must still be in the room that Felix had vacated. She was about to approach but something made her hesitate. This was the first time that he had left her alone for any period of time. She would not have him think that she could not survive for five minutes without him. She would visit the withdrawing room after all and then return to the ballroom. Luc would doubtless reclaim her upon his return and need never know that she had been tempted to go in pursuit of him. God alone knew, his ego did not require any additional fuelling of that nature.

Upon returning to the edge of the dance some ten minutes later she observed some of her patient suitors anxiously scanning the crowd, presumably looking for her. She noticed Lord Eversham was amongst their number. She enjoyed his company more than most since she was able to counter her homesickness by discussing Northumberland with him. But even the prospect of his pleasant conversation was not sufficient inducement this evening.

Clarissa looked about her cautiously. Luc was still nowhere in sight. Retreating quickly before she was seen, she returned to the threshold of the room that she suspected Luc occupied and opened the door: only to stop dead in her tracks. Luc had Emily Stokes in his arms. Half of her gown was around her waist and she had one leg hitched over his hip. It was obvious, even to someone as naïve as Clarissa, what was about to happen.

Luc looked at Clarissa with something akin to horror: Emily turned and simply smiled triumphantly.

'Clarissa, I — '

'Excuse me,' Clarissa managed to say with dignity, before closing the door and walking away, tears of humiliation burning her eyes.

'Damn!' Luc threw Emily bodily aside and rushed after her.

Clarissa did not know where she was going. All she did know was that she could not return to the ballroom in this distracted state. She tore on blindly, opening several doors at random. Had she been less miserable she might have taken in what was happening in those rooms and laughed about it later with Luc. This thought brought her up short. Since when had she fallen into the habit of even mentally sharing experiences with her godmother's son?

Clarissa finally found the door she sought that led to the terrace, fresh air and solitude. Breathing deeply she tried to think more calmly about what Luc and Emily had been doing and why it should upset her so much. She had known, after all, that Luc had an understanding with Emily: Emily herself had told her as much. That they chose to indulge their passion at a ball was hardly her concern. Luc had looked after her faithfully throughout her time in London and could hardly have had much time left to spare for Emily. Could she blame them for snatching a few precious moments alone? Anyway, it was of no import. In spite of Luc's undoubted protestations she would find a way to work with Mr Salik and escape from this madness.

Clarissa sensed a presence behind her. Luc did not need to announce himself: she knew instinctively that it was him.

'There you are! I have been looking everywhere.'

'I am sorry to have interrupted you, my lord,' she said, in what she hoped was an even voice.

'You did not.'

'Do not be ridiculous. Even I could see what — '

Luc rested one hand on either side of the balustrade against which she was leaning, trapping her between his arms. 'Emily Stokes came looking for me.'

'Half dressed?' snapped Clarissa, more forcefully than she intended.

'That was her doing, not mine. Believe it or not I was trying to fight her off!'

'Oh please, credit me with a little intelligence!'

'No really.'

Clarissa turned and faced him. 'It is of no importance to me, my lord, what you do or with whom. And I know you have an understanding with Mrs Stokes, you need not trouble yourself to deny it.'

'Whatever gave you that idea?'

'She did.'

'When?'

Clarissa explained, noticing a marked darkening in Luc's expression as she did so.

'Damned woman!' he muttered.

'It does not matter.'

'Clarissa, it does matter. There is nothing whatsoever between Emily Stokes and me.'

'But what she said and what I witnessed a few moments ago?'

Luc was in difficulties now. He could hardly explain to the innocent Clarissa the exact nature of Felix's parties and what had so casually occurred there between him and Emily. He felt ashamed now that he had been so foxed as to permit it to happen. But, hell, no, who was he trying to fool? Until recently such actions had been second nature to him.

Sighing, he tried to set Clarissa's mind at rest by responding to her question lightly. 'Emily and I are old adversaries. She has been pursuing me quite determinedly of late. She obviously saw me leave the ballroom with Felix and followed me.'

Clarissa searched his face for the tell-tale signs that he was lying, but to her surprise and confusion could detect nothing but an earnest entreaty that she believe him. She was surprised to find how much she wanted to, and how hurt, how jealous even, she had felt when she saw him so intimately engaged with Emily. And why would he bother to lie if he really did have a *tendre* for Mrs Stokes? She nodded her head at him absently, unsure what to think.

'Thank you for telling me, but it was not necessary.'

'Yes, it was. I wanted you to know that I am not quite the heartless philanderer that you suppose.'

'Unless you happen to be Mrs Stokes,' said Clarissa with the merest suspicion of a capricious smile.

'Ah well, yes, that is regrettable.' He shrugged helplessly, managing to look so remorseful that Clarissa grinned in spite of herself. 'But, Clarissa,' he said slowly, 'why exactly did you come to the library?'

'I wanted to know what you were discussing with Felix. I suspected it was to do with my situation and you promised not to take further action without consulting me first.'

'Felix's family is in shipping. I simply wanted to know if a ship is expected from Egypt anytime soon. I hoped one of the crew might be able to enlighten us with regard to the advocates who drew up the supposed will. I had intended to tell you about his connections this afternoon but Simms interrupted us.'

'Yes, of course. Thank you for telling me now.'

'And talking of Simms, my lady,' said Luc, whose face was now sporting its most predatory grin, 'what else were we doing when he interrupted us?'

'I . . . I do not remember.' Clarissa found that she was trembling but knew it was not because she was cold.

'Liar!'

Luc pulled her into his arms and kissed her. Clarissa fought him indignantly. How dare he treat her thus, so soon after she had discovered him with Emily Stokes!

Her resistance lasted all of five seconds. Suddenly the sensation of his lips so gentle upon hers, the soft probing of his tongue, the feel of his arms encircling her waist so protectively was all she could think about. It took only another five seconds for her to lose the ability to think at all and, with a sigh, she surrendered helplessly to the sweetness of his embrace.

'What was that for?' she asked him, when he finally released her.

'Reassurance.' And he pulled her towards him again.

'I cannot, I do not think — '

'It is my opinion, my lady, that you do far too much thinking and not nearly enough feeling. Do not think anymore, Clarissa, just concentrate on how I make you feel.'

'I have not done — '

'Um, I know, but is it not time you did? Have you not wasted enough years?'

His eyes regarded her with a deep intensity and Clarissa understood it was no casual question that he had just posed. The rarefied atmosphere between them was palpable: his masculinity at such close proximity, a devastating distraction. Clarissa looked into those somnolent eyes for a long time before replying: confused at first and unsure.

But suddenly the blinkers were removed and she knew, with blinding certainty, that he spoke the truth. She wanted to know what it was that she had missed for so long. What it was that woke her at night with feelings of intense longing, before abruptly deserting her again, leaving her feeling empty and unfulfilled. This man in front of her could teach her everything she needed to know. He was standing here, effectively offering to do so, and she knew now that she would not decline that invitation.

The thought of the possible consequences briefly penetrated her passion-fuelled brain but were not sufficient to deter her. The thing she regretted most about the non-consummated state of her marriage to Michael was the lack of a child. How dearly she would have loved to be a mother, to have a child of her own to nurture, love and protect. Well, if that should happen as a result of her coupling with Luc then she would be truly delighted.

As it was, as soon as possible she planned to return to Northumberland and continue with her life, far away from Luc and his plutocratic peers. Most of her neighbours viewed her with varying degrees of envy and resentment anyway, caused partly by her dismissal of many requests for her hand: requests which were based, she suspected, purely upon the desire to obtain her lands. She had spoken the truth when she told her aunt that she had no time for socializing and so what would it matter if she was ostracized as a result of her disgrace? She lived a solitary existence anyway and would scarcely notice the difference.

Clarissa nodded slowly, a decisive response to Luc's question. 'Yes!'

'No,' screamed a voice inside her head. '*Do not be such a widgeon as to give yourself to such a man: a man who is a philanderer and rake and who will doubtless break your heart.*'

She dismissed this voice of reason, determined for the first time in her life to abandon caution, to live recklessly and simply follow her instincts, not to mention her heart. Attempting to resist a gentleman as compelling as Luc, when he made up his mind that he wanted something was, she now had reason to know, totally exhausting and in her present debilitated state she had no energy left for that particular fight. She now acknowledged that which she had known almost from the first: for the first time in her life she had met a man to whom she was attracted and whom she wished to know intimately. The attraction was too strong for her to fight against it and she would not even attempt to do so.

Without blushing she held his gaze quite brazenly. He had no feelings for her: she would be well advised to remember that. She would simply be another conquest for him to add to an ever growing list. But he wanted her, for some inexplicable reason, and she intended to take ruthless advantage of that fact. She had tried to live her life respectably, by the prescribed rules, and where had it got her? Her attorney was attempting to defraud her; her late husband, who had no feelings for her, had a family that she knew nothing about; her neighbours pursued her purely for her lands, and half the gentry she had met in the *ton* looked upon her with derision.

Well, she had had enough! She would grasp the opportunity to live a little with this beautiful *roué* — just once. Then she would return home satisfied, her education complete. But of one thing Clarissa was determined: Luc would never know that, against her wishes, against her most earnest resolve and much to her very great despair, she had developed a *tendre* for him.

Luc, smiling victoriously, placed his index finger beneath her chin and tilted her head up gently. His finger traced the line of the lips he had just kissed so thoroughly. He cupped her cheek in his hand and smiled again, this time so gently, so intimately, that a heady sense of anticipation gripped her as wave after wave of desire washed through her trembling body.

'Soon, sweet Clarissa,' he promised, as his lips descended slowly towards hers again. 'It is almost your time and I will come to you very, very soon.'

# 11

Clarissa awoke the following morning, wondering at first why she felt so different. Then she remembered the commitment she had made to Luc and waited for the flood of remorse, for the shameful feelings, which surely must be lurking close at hand, to consume her.

Nothing happened. Instead, the recollection of her brazen behaviour caused an allusive smile to grace her lips. She touched those lips with the tips of her fingers. They were delightfully bruised from his passionate kisses and she felt the now familiar glow in the pit of her stomach, which even the slightest contact with him — the touch of his hand, the memory of his provocative smile, a complicit look — could so effortlessly generate. Her warm feeling transmuted into a raging ache of longing as she recalled the gentleness of his caress and caused her to almost cry aloud as desire ripped through her.

She was still under no illusions about Luc's intentions, despite his tenderly spoken words and the passion reflected in his smouldering eyes. She did not take exception to the fact that she would be yet another of his conquests, knowing that if she was seeking a master in the art of seduction, she could hardly hope for a more experienced one. Smiling to herself, she wondered how much longer it would be before he deemed the time had come to commence her initiation.

Drifting restlessly through the downstairs rooms, Clarissa anticipated with pleasure the afternoon's activities, for Luc's mother had arranged for some of the ladies in her circle to spend the afternoon at the orphanage. They would see for themselves the efforts that were being made to save the poor unfortunate children and would, it was hoped, be moved into loosening their purse strings a little wider.

All was organized activity when they arrived there and only Rosie felt compelled to break away to briefly greet Clarissa before, bustling with self-importance, she resumed her task of painstakingly setting the cups in a straight line on the snowy white tablecloth. Clarissa, smiling at the sight of Annie tucked carefully under Rosie's arm, mentioned to Aunt Marcia that she had never seen the child looking happier.

'She is settling down, I think, and is less haunted now by the demons from her past.'

'Yes, it affords one great satisfaction to see the more troubled spirits amongst them finding solace in the security of routine.'

A commotion at the door indicated the arrival of the first guests. Clarissa looked up and sighed in frustration when she observed that Mrs Stokes was one of the first ladies to enter the orphanage. The woman made Clarissa feel uncomfortable at the best of times but after what she had observed last night she felt acute embarrassment; as much on Emily's behalf as her own.

'Hateful woman, I must say I really do not care for her at all!'

Clarissa stared at her aunt in disbelief, having never before heard her utter a single derogatory word about a living soul. 'Then why did you invite her?' asked Clarissa smiling.

'Oh, my dear, her husband was such a sweetie and he left her so well provided for. I have no doubt that desperation will cause her to give most generously.'

Clarissa stared at her aunt for a second time — disbelieving. She clearly knew exactly how Emily felt about Luc and was relying upon it to gain additional funding for the orphanage.

'Aunt Marcia,' declared Clarissa indignantly, trying not to grin broadly, 'I do believe you must be a witch!'

'Nonsense, my dear,' responded Marcia, patting Clarissa's hand and giving her a cheerful wink. 'It is not possible to reach my age and have six grown children of one's own without knowing something of the ways of the world, you know.'

Eventually all the guests had arrived and taken their seats to watch the little concert the children put on. Clarissa would have been delighted with it all but for the fact that she seemed destined to trip over Emily Stokes wherever she moved. Sitting beside Marcia in the front row she had thought that there, at least, she would be safe. But no, Emily and her companion sat directly behind them.

And there could be no doubting the fact that Emily was going out of her way to cultivate Marcia's friendship. Clarissa watched it all with amusement. Had her aunt not informed her beforehand of her opinion of Emily, Clarissa herself would have been completely taken in by Marcia's apparent pleasure at the younger woman's presence.

Clarissa could tell that Emily was put out to see her in attendance, but she hid it well enough and spoke to her in a friendly fashion in front of Marcia, clearly feeling none of the agonies of embarrassment that Clarissa was still enduring on her behalf. Clarissa was forced to acknowledge that Emily was single-minded and relentlessly determined in her pursuit of Luc. But if what he had told her last night of his total indifference towards her was true, then Emily must surely realize that her campaign was doomed to failure. If? Clarissa had not realized until that moment that she still entertained doubts.

The concert began and delighted its audience. With the commencement of the finale the whole orphanage lined the stage, the smallest children at the front — Rosie with Annie at the centre of it all — and sang their little hearts out. The applause was prolonged and Marcia cast a satisfied glance at Clarissa. The children had played their part to perfection and they could only hope now for generous donations.

'Thank the Lord that is over!' Clarissa heard Emily say *sotto voce* to her companion. 'What a pack of little monsters. How soon can we get out of here?'

'There is no rush,' countered her friend. 'You can do yourself much good here with his mother. Use your brain, Emily. You know very well that he holds her in the highest esteem. You must cultivate her friendship.'

'Huh, I suppose you are right, Mary. But really, it is too much to ask. I will make him pay for humiliating me thus when I have him safely back under my wing.'

'I dare say.'

'And what is that damned Hartley woman doing here? Am I never to be rid of her?'

'Shh, she will hear you.'

'I do not care if she does. Oh, Mary, what can he possibly see in her? She has no style, no clothes, no social graces and have you seen how much she eats? She does not seem to be able to dance and is far too tall to be fashionable, but the gentlemen are all falling at her far from dainty feet for the privilege of merely conversing with her. I just do not understand it.'

'Calm yourself, Emily. She is new and that always creates interest. And Luc will have no lasting interest in her. How could someone such as she hold his attention for more than five minutes? You know his exotic tastes as well as I. No, do not worry, my dear, she will be gone off again soon and then Luc will come scurrying back to you with his tail between his legs.'

'Huh, I will not have him.' Emily tossed her pretty head.

'Yes you will!'

Clarissa could detect a smile in Emily's satisfied tone as she responded. 'You are right, Mary, of course I will.' She dropped her voice to a conspiratorial whisper, but Clarissa, eavesdropping shamelessly now, was still able to make out her words. 'Oh Mary, I cannot wait. I have never met a gentleman who comes close to him. He is so handsome, charming. And as for his wicked demands! Well . . . ' Emily, dropping her voice even lower, went into some detail: Clarissa appalled but unable to prevent herself from listening in horrified fascination, blushed again and again. 'I cannot live without him,' declared Emily stoutly, as the ladies rose and headed for Rosie's arrangement of tea cups, 'and I am determined that I will win him back.'

Clarissa was devastated. Luc had assured her that Emily Stokes meant nothing to him, but it was obvious now that he had used her for his own gratification. Clarissa told herself she had known as much all along but still felt ridiculously hurt and moved with her tea as far away from Emily as possible, determined to hear no more.

Clarissa and Aunt Marcia left soon after that: Aunt Marcia having been assured by a gushing Emily Stokes that she would like to call upon her later in the week to make a substantial donation to the orphanage.

★   ★   ★

Luc conducted his business that morning with uncharacteristic haste. He was anxious to see Felix and discover what news he was able to supply with regard to the shipping register.

'You are in luck, as always,' said Felix, when they met a short time later. 'A clipper out of Cairo is already a week overdue. Doubtless either storms or the doldrums will be responsible for any delay at this time of year.'

'But Cairo, will that help us?'

'Yes, dear chap, because the first mate, it seems, is a native of Alexandria.'

'So, he could provide the information we seek?'

'Undoubtedly.'

'When can we expect the clipper to make port?'

'Anything up to a two-week delay is not unusual, I am afraid.'

'Hm.' Luc stood and rubbed his chin thoughtfully. 'So up to another week, at least. Well, I should be able to procrastinate for that amount of time. I have no doubt that we shall shortly receive a message from Twining, anxious to get on with things, but I shall become uncharacteristically dilatory.'

'In other words, you will stall for time?'

'Exactly!'

The friends laughed together, and Luc, already feeling the leaden weight of responsibility for Clarissa's troubles easing from his shoulders, suggested that they take luncheon together at Whites. During the course of the meal Felix listened with increasing interest to Luc's conversation and the frequent mention he made of Clarissa's name.

'And anyway,' he was saying now, 'this news of yours is excellent because if this ship's mate can confirm my suspicions then it will save me a fortune.'

'In what way?'

'Well, the only alternative would be to send someone to Alexandria to check on these advocates. That would cause a long delay and Clarissa would get no peace in the interim. I am convinced that Salik and Twining are in league, solely for monetary gain. Think about it, Felix. Twining was well aware of her situation; he dragged his feet after the death of her husband, and deliberately kept her short of money. His intention was undoubtedly to wear her down. He knew she trusted him and would carry on running things as best she could. He thought Clarissa to be alone in the world, with no relations or friends to care for her, you see. His first objective was clearly to marry her. He had, after all, already proposed to her once. He

234

told her when he proposed this second time that he would be able to devote all of his time to resolving her problems with Salik.' Luc spoke with withering contempt. 'And he would, miraculously, have done so: once she became his wife and her property was safely in his pocket, that is.

'But she had rejected him once and he could not be confident that she would not do so a second time and so he concocted this plan with Salik. Twining already knew that Salik was Sir Michael's son. He would also have recognized in him a greedy, resentful and opportunist personality. A kindred spirit in other words. He would eventually regretfully inform Clarissa that Salik's claim was irrefutable and she would have accepted his word without question: just as she had always done in the past. The only thing he had not reckoned with,' continued Luc, his jaw rigid with determination, 'was me.'

'Yes, I can see your reasoning, but how did Twining manage to make this agreement with Salik so swiftly? He had, after all, only been in town for a week or so prior to Clarissa's arrival. If he had not met Salik before, how could he be sure that he would go along with the scheme, and how did he manage to get such an excellent forgery done so quickly?'

'Those are questions I have yet to answer,

but make no mistake about it, my friend, I shall not rest until I have done so.'

'I have no doubt.' Felix leant back casually in his chair and took an appreciative sip of excellent burgundy. 'But, to go back to your original statement, why does this clipper coming to port save you money?'

Luc hesitated. Felix continued to enjoy his wine and seemed content to let the silence stretch unbroken between them. Finally, making up his mind to be frank, Luc spoke.

'Because if we cannot prove the will to be a forgery by our investigations, the only alternative would be for me, or someone acting on my behalf, to go to Alexandria.'

Felix raised his brow in genuine surprise. 'I had not taken you seriously before, but I must say that your altruism does you credit, Luc.'

Luc accepted his friend's compliment with an impatient wave of his hand. 'But that would not bring Clarissa any lasting peace and so I had decided, knowing that Twining and Salik are not interested in the estates themselves but only in monetary gain, to make them a private offer. To buy them off, in other words.'

Luc sat back and drank his own wine, waiting for the full meaning behind his words to register with Felix. His wait was a short one.

'She is the one then?'

'Yes. I think I have known it almost since the first.'

'And the lady herself, what are her feelings?'

'That is just the problem,' said Luc irascibly. 'Do you not see? I can hardly go pouring my heart out to Clarissa, begging her to name the day and all that rot, when her mind is occupied solely with the loss of her blasted land.'

'But think what she would have to gain by marrying you? As a countess she could easily start afresh elsewhere with her animal husbandry, if she still wished to.'

'Oh, she would wish to all right, that is what makes her so special. Money would not influence her in any way other than against me,' said Luc, with a tight smile. 'She would probably just think that I felt sorry for her, or obliged because of her closeness to my mother, or God alone knows what other reason. How do I know what goes on in a woman's head? That part of their anatomy has never held my attention before.'

Felix smiled roguishly at his friend's apparent distress and earned himself an angry scowl for his trouble.

'Well, well,' said Felix, smiling even more expansively. 'Who would have thought it? The suave Earl of Newbury bested by a woman at last!'

'Felix,' warned Luc with a steely glare, 'if you know what is best for you, you will keep such thoughts to yourself.'

'All right, all right, but allow me my moment of triumph at your expense, I beg of you. I have waited a long time for this opportunity.' He chuckled happily for a while but then stopped abruptly and scowled. 'Oh Lord, have you given a thought for where this will leave me? With you off the field my life will become intolerable. All the matrons will turn their attentions towards me now.'

It was Luc's turn to give an amused chuckle. 'Come on, my friend, why not return to Grosvenor Square with me to see if the ubiquitous Simms has discovered anything further?'

★   ★   ★

Simms had indeed made further discoveries and was waiting impatiently for Luc to return, his usually dour expression for once almost animated.

'What news then, Simms?' demanded Luc, as he and Felix entered the library and helped themselves to brandy. 'Come on, out with it, man. I can see you have made discoveries and

I suspect they are beneficial to our cause.'

Felix and Luc flopped down in front of the fire with their brandy glasses.

'Well, my lords, I am pleased to say that I have discovered Salik's whereabouts. He has been residing in the same lodging house as Twining for some six weeks now.'

'Good God, Simms, are you absolutely certain?'

'Indeed I am, my lord. Jenkins, on my orders, called at the premises in question, asking for lodgings. The landlady stated that there was none available: to which Jenkins replied that a foreign gentleman he had encountered in a tavern had given him to understand otherwise. The landlady said that would be Mr Salik. A charming Egyptian gentleman, according to her, who had been with her for six weeks, but who had sadly moved two days before. His rooms had, however, already been taken.'

'I see,' said Luc reflectively. 'That changes everything does it not, Felix?'

'Indeed, yes.'

'But there is more, my lords. Jenkins is a personable young man of some intelligence and managed, somehow, to take tea with Salik's former landlady, during the course of which he discovered which tavern Salik frequented.'

'Well done Jenkins!'

'Indeed, my lord.'

'I thought Muslims did not touch alcohol?' remarked Felix.

'I doubt there is anything this one will not touch,' responded Luc venomously, 'and I venture to predict the more extreme the pursuit the better. Anyway, this is excellent work,' said Luc, rising to his feet in his enthusiasm. 'Remind me later, Simms, to speak personally to Jenkins.'

'Indeed, my lord.'

'All right, Simms, that will be all for now, but please ask Lady Hartley to step in as soon as she arrives home.'

'I believe their ladyships returned home above half an hour ago, my lord.'

'Then my compliments to Lady Hartley. Ask her if she would be so kind as to spare me a moment?'

Clarissa joined them very shortly thereafter. She had a smile and curtsy for Felix, a guarded, neutral look for Luc.

'How was your afternoon?' Luc asked her.

'The children performed splendidly and your Mrs Stokes plans to make a substantial donation to the orphanage,' said Clarissa devilishly, averting her gaze to hide the hurt that was reflected in her eyes.

Felix roared with laughter. Luc glared at

him and looked distinctly uncomfortable.

'What news, gentlemen?' asked Clarissa, sobering again.

Luc sat her down and told her of the imminent arrival of the clipper from Egypt. He went on to relate Simms' news.

'What does it all mean from our point of view?'

'Well, it is all so much clearer now. How they managed it, I mean. Salik has obviously been in England for far longer than we were given to understand. That gave Twining ample time to arrange the forged will. It also explains why he was so shocked when I appeared. He had supposed you to be alone and unprotected, Clarissa. It also explains why the forger whom we suspect of drawing up the will only disappeared recently: not immediately after doing his work.

'You see, Twining knew you trusted him and did not imagine you would doubt the validity of the will if he assured you it was genuine. It was only when he realized that he had me to deal with that he decided to cover his tracks.'

'Does this now mean that we have sufficient evidence to refute Mr Salik's claim?' asked Clarissa. The hope which flared in her expression and reflected in her luminous eyes, the optimistic note in her voice, tore at Luc's heartstrings and he hated having to set her straight.

'No, m'dear,' he said gently. 'It all helps, but it is, in itself, insufficient to convince any court. Twining is clever enough to come up with a plausible explanation for Salik's early arrival and although it looks suspicious that they lodged in the same building, that could be explained away too as Twining merely being helpful to a stranger in a capital city where he knows no one. No, we need evidence from the mate on that clipper to complete our case.'

'Oh, I see.'

Clarissa hid her despondency well. 'But perhaps evidence of their frequenting that tavern together would be beneficial? What was it called again?'

'The Oak Tavern and no, I think not. We can prove that they lodged in the same dwelling and so frequenting the same tavern would be a natural progression.'

'But if we send someone there they might be able to overhear their conversation and glean something incriminating from it.'

'Possibly, but the risk of discovery is too great,' said Luc, finality in his voice. 'Please, Clarissa,' he continued, as she made to argue further, 'leave this to me. You do not need to concern yourself with the detail.' He patted her shoulder, unaware, in his concern for her, that the gesture came across as dictatorial and patronizing.

Clarissa flinched from his touch and with the briefest of curtsies for Felix left the room. Luc was relieved that she had given up her argument so easily and deferred to his authority. It did not occur to him to wonder why she had not put up more of a fight.

# 12

Clarissa slammed the door to her chamber and let forth with a string of most unladylike but extremely satisfying curses, all aimed at Luc's autocratic attitude and her opinion of it. The most colourful of her cursing though she reserved for him personally. She was infuriated by his dictatorial air; it was anathema to her. Anger surged through her, a raging white fire that was in danger of completely consuming her. It left her breathless and trembling and brought with it an array of emotions which she had never before experienced; all vastly different from the gloomy hopelessness of her recent lethargy.

But, if nothing else, her anger did at least serve to issue a timely reminder that she was still very much able to fight for herself. She had a brain and being a female did not preclude her from using it.

Now that she was able to accept that these people really did mean to try and take what was rightfully hers, did Luc seriously expect her to simply step aside and allow someone else to try and prevent them? And not even be permitted to make suggestions for their apprehension either? It was too much! She had warned Luc when she first arrived that she was nothing like the fragile females of his acquaintance. He clearly had not taken her at her word and Clarissa did not care to be underestimated any more than she was prepared to countenance being ignored.

Flopping onto the sofa she attempted to rein in her temper. In all fairness, Luc was only trying to protect her: that much she understood. The instinct to protect the ladies under his care came as naturally to Luc as breathing. And the ladies in question would expect it of him, leave him to do as he thought best and ask no trying questions. It clearly had not occurred to him to expect any other sort of reaction from her. Clarissa smiled, the steely light of battle in her eyes. His lordship had best prepare himself for a shock. These were *her* lands and no one felt more keenly about the possible loss of them than she did. She could not expect Luc to understand that and she had discovered that it was useless trying to explain. Sometimes actions spoke louder than words; sometimes there was no other way.

Her thoughts turned to the evening ahead: a transference which produced more colourful cursing. For the first time since her arrival in the capital, Luc would not be accompanying her and Aunt Marcia, for they were to attend Lady Bingham's musicale and Luc, like most gentlemen, tended to avoid such events like the plague. Clarissa assured herself that Luc's absence would not cause her any concern; at the same time regretting the lost opportunity to question him further with regard to Salik's machinations. Only Felix's presence this afternoon had prevented her from pursuing the matter then and there. But now, frustratingly, any further opportunity to do so would be lost to her for the rest of the day.

In the event Clarissa and Marcia did not attend the musicale, for they received a note at the eleventh hour to say that Lady Bingham was suddenly indisposed. By then Luc had already gone out for the evening, Clarissa knew not where but probably, she thought cynically, to mend his fences with Emily Stokes. The thought was strangely unsettling and so Clarissa further blackened her mood by dwelling upon the likely loss of her lands instead.

Marcia confessed that she was relieved the evening's entertainment had been cancelled since she had no wish to go out, the afternoon's activities at the orphanage having tired her, and so after a quiet dinner together the ladies retired early.

Clarissa immediately commenced plotting. It was only nine o'clock. She had not expected to have the evening to herself and was convinced that fate had played a part in bringing about this unexpected opportunity. She was not about to waste it and, despite Luc's superior opinion, was convinced that their next step should be to visit The Oak Tavern. And that was precisely what she would do, this very evening. If her good fortune continued, then Twining and Salik would be there and she would, somehow, contrive to get close enough to overhear their conversation.

But she must be cautious. She would obviously need to disguise herself as a man, for even Clarissa knew that only one type of woman went to taverns unaccompanied. Furthermore, if her disguise was not convincing then she would be recognized by her quarry in an instant. She had her breeches that she rode in: they would pass muster, as would her shiny boots. But she had no coat or cravat and surely the clientele at such an establishment would wear more substantial headwear than the single cap which she possessed? It was woefully inadequate for the purpose of restraining her unruly locks at the best of times and could not be trusted to keep them in place for an entire evening.

Clarissa racked her brains, simultaneously curbing her impatience to be gone. She had observed an old greatcoat in the boot room — Luc's perhaps? — and although slightly shabby it would undoubtedly pass muster in The Oak Tavern. The image of Luc's broad shoulders briefly sprang to mind, almost causing her to lose her nerve as she anticipated his likely reaction when he learned of her escapade. The thought of those shoulders served to remind her as well that the coat would be rather too large for her. But that was of no consequence. If she wrapped several layers of sheeting around her upper body before donning her shirt it would fill her out and disguise her shape as well. Smiling at the ingenuity of her plan she proceeded to strip her bed and do exactly that.

In the boot room she found an old muffler which she wrapped around her neck and chin, knowing that if her features were left open to scrutiny her whiskerless face, with its fine, delicate features, would never be taken for that of a man. The greatcoat was only slightly too large, thanks to the layers of sheeting, and she found an old opera hat which would accommodate her hair reasonably well and which she perched on her head at a jaunty angle.

Clarissa was rather pleased with the overall effect and, although dressed far too warmly for the season, hoped that the tavern would be too dim and crowded for anyone to notice her incongruous attire.

Stepping cautiously out of the side door, careful not to be seen by anyone, Clarissa gained Grosvenor Square and walked rapidly away from Luc's house, her heart hammering loudly in her breast. She found a cab without any problems and, before she had a chance to think better of it, gave the cabbie the address of the tavern.

Arriving in Greek Street, Clarissa took several fortifying breaths to calm her nerves, reminded herself of what she hoped to achieve, and pushed open the door of the tavern. Once inside she paused, taking a moment to acclimatize. The room was indeed very full but, fortunately for her, poorly illuminated. There was much noise, raucous laughter and the sound of a poorly tuned piano being badly played. The all pervading odour was of stale ale, staler snuff and even staler bodies.

Clarissa's eyes gradually adjusted to the gloom and she looked about her, relieved to notice that no one appeared to be paying her any special attention. Then she observed a particularly lively crowd of people in one corner of the room and her heart beat a fast, painful tattoo. Her breath stilled as she espied Salik in the middle of that particular crowd holding court, one arm around the waist of a woman whose occupation was obvious — even to Clarissa. Twining stood on the edge of the group, looking as though he would much rather be somewhere else.

Averting her eyes before she drew attention to herself, Clarissa used a gruff voice to purchase a tankard of ale and found a seat close to Salik's group and near to the door, where she could see and hear but hopefully not be seen, and from whence she could make a hasty exit, if it became necessary.

Salik was in high spirits, spending money freely, encouraged by the scantily clad woman on his arm and by several others as well, all of whom were good-naturedly vying for his attention. Twining was endeavouring to call him away but Salik appeared deaf to his pleadings and responded by carelessly push-ing one of the women in his direction.

Clarissa was so intent upon her purpose that it took her sometime to realize a large man had seated himself, uninvited, at her table and was studying her with undisguised interest. It was then, with a feeling of unmitigated horror, she realized her muffler had fallen away from her face and, despite her careful preparations, long strands of her unruly hair had already escaped from beneath the opera hat.

'Well, well, what have we here then?' asked the man in a surprisingly cultured voice, revealing broken teeth and a discoloured tongue as he leered at her speculatively.

Swiftly Clarissa picked up her untouched tankard and hid her features behind it. She turned away from the man, hoping he would be deterred, which, of course, he was not.

'Who are you hiding from then, my dear? What is your name?'

Clarissa, panicking now, continued to pointedly ignore him. Undaunted, he continued to ply her with questions in an increasingly loud voice, which was starting to draw people's attention towards them.

'Are you looking for business, my dear?' he asked. 'Do not be coy now. I am sure a delightful young *man* such as yourself will have no difficulty finding customers to appreciate his — er — assets.'

If Clarissa had previously considered Luc's manner to be in any way insolent, it was nothing to the way in which this man appraised her, making no effort to disguise his intent. She was now seriously frightened, stunned for a moment into inactivity. The man reached across the table and grabbed

251

her wrist — the one holding the tankard — in a tight grasp.

'I am speaking to you, my dear. It is very rude to make no reply. Do not imagine that you can push the price up by pretending disinterest.' He threw a surprisingly large amount of money on the table, his eyes never leaving her face as he smacked his lips in anticipation. 'Shall we go?'

Without thinking about the consequences, Clarissa threw the contents of her tankard into the man's face, followed by the vessel itself, and jumped swiftly to her feet. The man's coarse expletives caused most conversation in the tavern to cease and everyone to look in their direction.

Thanking her lucky stars that she had thought to procure a table close to the door, Clarissa headed blindly towards it, her panic lending added speed to her feet. But the weight of her coat and heavy, ill-fitting boots countered any temporary advantage her fear afforded her. What a fool she had been to come here alone, and to dismiss her cab as well. She was in a highly dangerous situation; she understood that now. The commotion caused by her fight with this mindless oaf was bound to attract Salik's attention and she was sure that at any moment she would be recognized by him. Then what? She shuddered at the very prospect and renewed her futile attempt to escape through the door, now so tantalizingly close.

As she reached for the handle, so the door opened and a strong arm circled her waist. A hand covered her mouth, preventing her from crying out and she was dragged bodily from the tavern. She struggled furiously, to no avail: her actions were not having the slightest effect upon her captor and her last conscious thought was that whoever had her under his control now could, at least, be no worse than Salik — or the brute of a man in the tavern for that matter.

But then, as she was dragged away, struggling and protesting as best she could with that hand clamped over her mouth, she collided against a brick wall: a brick wall that was wearing a superfine coat, blue velvet waistcoat and a pristine cravat, secured with a flawless Ceylon sapphire pin. The wall proved to be a strong masculine chest: a chest she would recognize anywhere — Luc's! Relief flooded through her and she revelled in its sanctuary, never having felt the need of his protection more. Her legs threatened to buckle beneath her as, belatedly, her body reacted to the fright she had received and she struggled to prevent herself from collapsing against Luc.

He threw her none too gently into his waiting carriage, where she fell gratefully into the enveloping comfort and blessed safety of the velvet seat. The carriage moved off immediately and only then did he release his hold on her.

'What in damnation's name do you think you were doing?' His face was set in rigid lines of disapproval. Clarissa had never seen him so angry, never heard him use that glacial tone with her before. She quailed beneath the savageness of his unwavering, basilisk glare.

In spite of her earlier fear though, she was not about to swoon gratefully at his feet like some pathetic wilting violet. She sat straighter on her seat and countered his hostile glare with a haughty expression of her own, putting up her chin for good measure.

'Gaining the information we require to disprove Salik's claims upon my lands, of course,' she responded disdainfully.

'Really!' The one word was laced with enough acerbity to cut through her pose of calm. For the first time ever she was almost afraid of him, but was damned if she would show it.

'Yes, really.'

'And you succeeded, I imagine?'

'Of course! Salik was telling his friends that he shortly expects to inherit a valuable estate from his late father.' She smiled triumphantly.

'Was he indeed?' Luc raised a brow at her, somehow managing to load the gesture with a wealth of sarcasm.

'Yes, and if you had only listened to my suggestions you could have — '

Luc's voice cut her off in mid-rant. 'And this information you went to such lengths to obtain, is that something that we did not know before? Something worth risking your person for, your reputation, your — your . . . ' Luc's voice wavered and, as he appeared to be temporarily unable to speak, Clarissa hastily interceded, anxious to wrest control of the situation.

'Well, no, but . . . ' She hesitated, realizing for the first time that she had indeed learned very little of consequence.

'But what?'

He appeared to have recovered himself, controlled fury once again lacing his tone, and it was that which caused Clarissa to lose her temper.

'Damn it, Luc, I cannot just sit back and wait for you to decide what it is best to do!' She glowered at him, her hostility and resentment rising in direct proportion to her temper. 'They are my lands; it is my future in the balance; all that I hold most dear is about to be lost to me. But you seem to have lost sight of that and all you care about is controlling me.' She scowled defiantly, daring him to contradict her, which, of course, he lost no time in doing.

'I have lost sight of nothing other than the fact that you must learn to do as you are told.'

'Why?' She threw the question at him as a challenge. 'Who appointed you as my keeper? What gives you the right to be so arrogant, condescending, patronizing, autocratic . . . ' She paused for breath and gaining a second wind, continued hurling abuse at him. 'Dictatorial, arrogant . . . '

'You already said that,' he reminded her, sounding amused now, his anger appearing to dissipate as quickly as her own temper bubbled out of control.

'Well, it needed to be said twice. And I cannot just sit idly by whilst these people attempt to defraud me. You cannot ask it of me, Luc.'

Luc moved across and sat beside her. 'Clarissa, you will not be defrauded. I will not allow it to happen. Can you not appreciate that?'

'I know you mean what you say but how can you be so sure?'

'I am entirely sure. You must just trust me, if you possibly can, and take my word for it. If you wish to help you only have to do as I ask and remain patient. What you must not do, however, is put yourself in dangerous situations, such as the one I just rescued you from. If you had been recognized you would have ruined everything. And what would have happened to you then does not bear thinking about.' Luc shuddered and averted his gaze, still offering thanks to all he held most dear that he had arrived in time to save her.

'I was quite safe,' she lied.

'Oh yes, of course you were. I was able to ascertain that much for myself.'

'Oh!' She whirled away from him, attempting to distance herself from the smouldering concern whirling in the depths of his black eyes. 'It is impossible to reason with you.'

Luc, in his turn, mentally relived the events of the evening. For once Felix had not been available to keep him company. He had succeeded in achieving that which everyone had declared to be an impossibility and persuaded the beautiful Angelica Priestley, the new Marchioness Towbridge, to become his mistress. Everyone had been of one mind: it was too soon for her to stray from her much older husband. She was still enjoying the trappings of her new title and wealth too much to put it at risk. But Felix, with his lazy, compelling charm, had proved them all wrong and won a tidy sum on the book at Whites into the bargain. Luc knew he was with his new paramour for the first time this very evening and, chuckling as he imagined the scene, heartily wished him well. He was astonished to discover though that he did not envy him.

At a loose end, he had drifted into Brooks's in search of congenial male company and a good game of cards. But, for some reason he was unable to identify, he had been uneasy and fared badly as a consequence. Admitting defeat, he went home far earlier than could normally be expected and found his household to be in uproar. Caroline had cause to return to Clarissa's chamber after she retired, only to find it vacant, the sheets missing and no explanation as to Clarissa's whereabouts.

It did not take Luc two seconds to guess where she had gone and his blood ran cold at the very thought of what could, even then, be happening to her. He reached the tavern in record time and, careless of whether or not he was recognized by Twining and Salik, made to walk straight in: only to find Clarissa backing out of the door, pursued by a bull of a man who was dripping with ale and had blood flowing from a cut beneath his eye.

'I was safe!' Clarissa insisted indignantly, bringing Luc back to the present. 'I had my disguise.'

'And very effective it was too!'

'It was not my fault that my muffler fell away.'

'And that man who was tormenting you. I suppose he would have just let you be, had you asked him politely enough?'

'I dealt with him.'

'By throwing your ale at him?'

'And the tankard!' Clarissa was convinced that Luc's lips twitched at that, but it was too dim inside the carriage to be sure. 'And besides, I would have managed to get out of the tavern, even without your intervention.'

'And how did you plan to get home? Ladies cannot just walk about unaccompanied, in case you were unaware of the fact.'

'Ah, but I am not a lady, remember?' She indicated her clothing.

'Ah yes, of course!' This time there could be no doubt that he was smiling. 'Clarissa, even that greatcoat is not sufficient to hide a figure such as yours.'

'Ah-hah!' At last she had the better of him and she took a moment to savour her victory. 'I padded myself,' she informed him smugly.

'Did you indeed? Enough to fool that oaf in the tavern?'

'That was only because my muffler slipped.' Why did he always have an answer for everything? 'Anyway, how did you find me?'

'Caroline discovered you were missing.'

'And sent for you, I suppose. I am sorry to have disturbed your evening. Doubtless Mrs Stokes will be furious.'

'I was not with Mrs Stokes.'

'Humph!'

'I repeat,' he said slowly, enunciating every word with slow deliberation, as though speaking to a simpleton. 'I was not with Emily Stokes. Besides, where I was is not the issue: your conduct this evening, however, is. Let us see just how effective your so-called padding is, shall we?'

Without waiting for a response he pushed his old coat off her shoulders and, ignoring her protests, unbuttoned her shirt. The sheeting had slipped to her waist and it was the work of a moment for Luc to remove it. 'We cannot have you returning home like that, can we now?'

Suddenly, she knew not how it happened, she was sitting on his lap. He pulled her towards him and kissed her, hard and passionately, uncaring of her feeble protests. Clarissa could not prevent a gasp of pleasure escaping her and, despite the warning bells that were almost deafening her, she snuggled against him, perversely grateful now for his protective strength.

Luc was rigid with longing for her. He had never wanted anyone as much as he wanted this infuriating, provoking and monstrously disrespectful female and a combination of the waiting and her delightfully evasive, independent spirit was driving him demented. Her thin breeches revealed her charms to him far too graphically, leaving him agonizingly uncomfortable and unsure how far to push his advantage.

'Clarissa,' he whispered, 'you must promise me never to take action again that puts you in danger. You must promise me as well to have nothing to do with Twining and Salik unless I am present. If you behave again as you did this evening then I will put you across my knee and beat you so hard you will be unable to sit down for a week.'

Clarissa gasped. 'You would not dare!'

His only response was an irritatingly superior, somewhat somnolent smile.

Disquieted by his arrogant attitude, Clarissa protested once again. This time he offered her a half smile and continued to speak as mildly as though he were discussing the weather, but Clarissa could detect a steely note of determination in his tone that made her tremble — and not entirely with fear. He was serious!

'My advice to you, m'dear, is that you do not ever put yourself in a position where you are likely to find out.'

'But you cannot.' Clarissa did not intend to let him get away with bullying her. 'I am, after all, not your responsibility.'

'Oh but you are!' Clarissa looked up into a face that had determination etched into its planes; at lips which curled into a wolfish smile. 'And, what is more, you are going to demonstrate to me just how much you regret your impulsive actions this evening.'

He sounded so sure of himself, so much in control, that Clarissa felt a bolt of raw desire shoot through her entire body. Sitting on his lap, so scantily clad, there could be no doubt that he detected it too. His smile broadened into one of smug complacency, as if to confirm her suspicions. He had never appeared to Clarissa to be more dangerous, or more compelling, than he was at that moment. She needed to employ a diversion.

'I will do no such thing!' Her voice sounded half-hearted and unconvincing, even to her own ears. She attempted to put some feeling into it. 'Now, let me be, if you please. I fear I may be about to swoon.' She ran a hand feebly across her brow, unsure how women who swooned carried on but fairly certain she had got it right.

Luc, undeceived, merely chuckled and pulled her more securely onto his knee. 'You are not going to swoon, Clarissa, you are not the type. I doubt that you have ever swooned in your life.' He grinned at her with feigned concern. 'But just in case, I had better keep a firmer hold on you, do you not think?'

Determined as she was not to allow Luc the freedom to do as he pleased, the moment his lips touched hers all caution flew out of the window. She knew she was being pathetically feeble but simply could not help herself; the temptation was just too great and she returned his kiss passionately, hungrily, as though she had no will of her own.

# 13

Clarissa sat with just Mulligan for company the following day. She had slept soundly for the first time since learning of Salik's existence and had dreamt only of Luc: of his self-contained grace, elegant manners and compelling eyes: eyes so full of expressive meaning when they regarded her that a vortex of desire, impossible to ignore, swept her along on a passionate journey into forbidden territory.

It was only when she was alone at night that she could relax her constant guard and admit to the extent of her love for this irritatingly charming dictator. The litany of warnings against such feelings vibrating in her head went unheeded at such times, and she knew that when it came to dreaming of what might have been she was powerless to help herself.

Her mind turned to the scene in the carriage the evening before and to his unmitigated anger at her unilateral behaviour. In retrospect she could scarce blame him. Not that she would ever admit it, mind! But truly she had been terrified and knew that if

Luc had not arrived at the exact moment he did then she would have been unable to fight off her assailant. Even so, had his reaction not been rather extreme, given that she was nothing more to him than a potential conquest? She recalled his threat to beat her and shivered at his audacity. In the cold light of day though what had seemed, at the time, to be a serious threat now appeared as nothing more sinister than another of his arrogant attempts to control her.

As Clarissa continued mulling the matter over she could not have known how close she was to discovering that Luc did not make idle threats. There was a commotion in the hall and the door to the morning room was then flung open, causing Mulligan to look up and growl threateningly.

'In here is she?' asked an arrogant voice.

Clarissa looked up and observed Salik standing on the threshold, hat still rudely on his head and a steely glint of determination in his eye. The butler and Simms hovered behind him, unused to such crass behaviour and wondering how to proceed. They both turned their eyes towards Clarissa, awaiting her orders.

'You cannot go in there!' said Bentley, belatedly finding his voice.

'Rubbish! I merely require a private word

with Lady Hartley. Call these dogs off would you, Lady Hartley.'

'It is all right, Bentley, Simms,' she said in a calm tone, quelling the fear that was creeping into her, 'I will receive Mr Salik.'

Clarissa made the decision reluctantly, having observed the extent of his determination and thinking it best to allow him to say whatever it was he had on his mind and get it over with. Besides, although Aunt Marcia was out making calls and Luc had gone to call upon Felix, to see if there was any news of the vessel from Cairo, she still had Mulligan for protection.

'Very good, my lady,' said Bentley in a dubious manner. 'If your ladyship is quite certain. Just ring if you require me. I will come at once.'

Clarissa kept a restraining hand on Mulligan's collar. Growling, hackles raised, he clearly did not care for Mr Salik. Clarissa decided he was a good judge of character and made a mental note to offer him some extra treats later on.

'God, Clarissa,' said Salik, flinging aside his hat and seating himself without being invited to, 'can you not call that beast off? Dreadful creature!'

Clarissa glared at him. 'Certainly not, Mr Salik. Now, sir, what is the meaning of this intrusion?'

'I see! That is how you wish to proceed. Very well.' Salik smiled at her. Clarissa imagined he was attempting to be charming but the gesture fell woefully short of that mark. 'I wanted to have a private word with you, my dear, away from our respective protectors. I know my father loved you and that you are disappointed not to inherit his property. I just wanted you to know that I have no interest in farming, in sheep or, indeed, in the north of England. Cold, draughty place, as far as I can gather.'

'Indeed!' Clarissa raised a brow, unable to resist feigning surprise. 'How disappointed your father would have been to have heard you say so. He adored his estate.'

'Not as much as he adored Egypt and my mother,' countered Salik, his charming smile giving way to a devious smirk.

'Who is to say it?'

'I say it!'

Salik rose from his seat and moved as close to her as the still growling Mulligan would permit. 'I do not want to be bad friends with you, Clarissa. Twining has told me how much the land means to you and how hard you have worked to make a success of it. I wanted you to know that there will always be a place for you there.' He walked behind her chair, out of range of Mulligan, and placed his hands on her shoulders.

'Unhand me, Mr Salik!'

'Oh, come, come, my dear, there is no need to take that tone. A beautiful lady such as yourself, a lady who has been married no less, surely cannot mistake my meaning? I have no doubt that left to our own devices, and without interference from others, we will be able to come to a mutually beneficial understanding?'

'I doubt that very much.'

His fingers were still on her shoulders but they tensed in response to her dismissive tone; at her very obvious disinclination to look upon him as an equal. But instead of replying, he simply smirked at her and appeared to be considering his next liberty.

Clarissa felt the first stirrings of alarm. She could not reach the bell from her seat. Her only alternative was to release Mulligan. She knew he would fly at Salik in defence of her, but her concern was that Salik might carelessly kick out at the dog. He struck her as being just the sort who would do such a thing. And what if he connected with his bad leg? No, she could not risk that, not after all the suffering that poor Mulligan had already endured. Her only alternative was to try and talk Salik round. They were after all in Luc's house; Salik could not know that Luc was not at home and, indeed, anyone might enter the room at any time.

'Mr Salik, please resume your seat. Perhaps we can discuss this matter like responsible adults.'

But Salik did not move, except to allow his hands to drift a little lower. 'My dear lady, what is there to discuss? I will soon have what you want, whereas you,' he continued, his eyes drifting over her body with a slow insolence, 'certainly already have any number of things that would satisfy me.'

'Mr Salik, please, if you do not — '

The door flew open. Luc stood there, his stance aggressive, the space he occupied too small suddenly to contain his menacing presence.

'What the hell are you doing in my house, Salik?' he demanded to know. Luc's thunderous expression should have been sufficient in itself to intimidate Salik and warn him off but Clarissa could see that he was unmoved by Luc's demeanour. His arrogance was so ingrained, his determination to achieve his end so strong, that he did not have the good sense to back off immediately. Instead he simply offered Luc a conceited smile and moved casually away from Clarissa.

'Merely having a private conversation with my stepmother. No need to concern yourself.

Lady Hartley and I were about to reach a mutually beneficial understanding with regard to her future.'

'I think not, Salik! Now get out before I throw you out. I have issued instructions that you are never again to be admitted to this house. Not,' he added quietly, but in an infinitely more threatening tone, 'that you should have been granted entry on this occasion.'

'By all means!' He picked up his hat, bowed to Clarissa and, giving Mulligan a wide berth, silently left the room.

Luc addressed Clarissa, still in a towering rage. 'What on earth persuaded you to receive him?'

'He barged in without warning, Luc, and I did not know what else to do.'

'Why did you not instruct Bentley to throw him out? What were you thinking?'

'Well, I cannot really say. He just appeared so determined. I thought if I saw him he would go away more quickly. There was so little time to decide.'

Luc regarded her through eyes reduced to mere slits; proof positive of his towering rage. 'And I suppose, in the excitement, you forgot the substance of our conversation in the carriage last evening?' He moved to stand beside her, his face flushed red with anger.

'Do not be ridiculous Luc, you cannot . . . ahhh!'

Luc had moved so quickly that she did not see it coming and before she knew what was happening she was across his knee. He applied his hand to her bottom with considerable force, a force which fortunately for her, was cushioned by the thickness of her skirts and petticoats.

'Clarissa,' he said, his breath coming in short gasps, 'when will you learn to behave yourself and do as you are told?'

'Luc, I am sorry!' She was close to tears, a circumstance so unusual that it brought Luc rapidly back to his senses. He righted her on his lap, his expression softening in response to her obvious distress. He had intended to frighten her into submission and force her to acknowledge the danger in which her recklessness had placed her, not humiliate and demean her.

'I am sorry too, m'dear,' he said, smiling tightly, 'but I have, somehow, to make you understand that the man is dangerous. No good can come out of your receiving him alone.'

'I realize that now. But how did you know he was here?'

'Simms knew where I was and sent word. It's the only thing he did right this morning and might just save him his position. As for Bentley, well, we will have to see.'

'Do not blame them, Luc, I said I would receive Mr Salik.'

'Well you damned well should not have been put in that position and they should have known better than to listen to you anyway.'

Clarissa offered him a shaky smile. 'It was all right. I was in control.' In her anxiety for Simms and Bentley she conveniently forgot just how scared she had felt and attempted to make light of the situation. But there was no denying to herself now that there was something about Salik, a dark, vindictive side to his character, a bitterness which made her truly afraid of him.

'Huh, it did not look like it to me. Damned impudence! Anyway, why did you not set Mulligan at him?'

She hesitated before admitting the truth. 'I thought about it but I was worried that he might kick him.'

'Oh, Clarissa! What am I to do with you?'

He kissed her gently then; all of his anger draining away, before asking the inevitable question. 'Anyway, what did he want?'

'To offer me a roof over my head.'

'At what price? No, do not answer that, I can imagine. The bastard, how dare he! Are you all right? Did he harm you?'

'I am all right, Luc. I will admit though that he did frighten me a little with his vehemence.'

'Oh, Clarissa!' Luc put her slightly away from him and examined her face. 'He frightened you that much but you still put Mulligan's welfare before your own?'

Clarissa shrugged. 'If you had not returned when you did I might have released him after all. Salik is a very bitter man, dangerous too, but he desperately wants people to think well of him and be admitted to society.'

'Huh, some hope! Whatever happens, he will never have a place within the *ton*. I will make sure of that. Now come here and let me make you feel better.'

Clarissa did not need to be invited twice. She moved into the circle of his arms: strong arms that cradled her protectively against him as his lips covered hers. His kiss was possessive, crushing and prolonged. It was also heated and desperate: the passion that always simmered between them begging for release and threatening to spiral out of control. Luc, appearing to recognize the fact, broke the kiss with obvious reluctance.

'That clipper has got to arrive soon. I cannot bear this agony for much longer.'

Clarissa did not need to ask him what he

was referring to. 'We do not have to wait,' she eventually found the courage to say, looking him squarely in the eye.

'Yes, we do!' He smiled gently into her eyes. 'I require your full attention, in order that you may learn your lessons well. You cannot relax and give me that attention, not with everything you have on your mind at present. If that damned boat does not get here soon though, I swear I shall lose what little is left of my sanity.'

Clarissa laughed up at him, enjoying the sight of his handsome face relaxed and gentle once again, at direct variance to his obviously increasing frustration. She had no difficulty in recognizing his expression, or understanding it for what it was, since she did not doubt that her own features were arranged in an identical manner.

'Now,' he said, 'I must leave you again and deal with those two.' He indicated the door to the hall, behind which she knew Simms and Bentley to be awaiting his wrath.

'Oh, Luc, do not be angry with them. It was not their fault.'

'We shall see.'

He gave her another brief kiss and was gone. She could hear his voice bellowing to Simms and Bentley to attend him in the library — immediately.

# 14

Clarissa and Marcia returned home late the following morning, having carried out another exhausting round of social nothingness that had nearly driven Clarissa demented. She knew her godmother meant well but she was finding it harder than ever to endure the constant gossip and speculative glances that were frequently cast in her direction whenever Luc's name was mentioned. Far from noticing Clarissa's plight though, Marcia appeared uncharacteristically oblivious to it. She simply beamed at her in a distracted fashion whenever she attempted to dismiss Luc's attentions as nothing more than brotherly kindness and, unusually for her verbose godmother, had no opinion to offer upon the matter.

Simms approached Clarissa, bowed slightly and handed her a note left for her by Luc. She tore it open impatiently, and read:

*Clarissa*

*I am glad to be able to report news of the Andomino at last. She put into Portsmouth last night. She was indeed caught in the* violent storms that were reported and sustained damage both to her main mast and to her rudder, thus making it impossible for her to navigate as far as the Port of London.

By the time you read this note Felix and I will be well on our way to Portsmouth. I know you will be disappointed not to be with us but you must, surely, see the impossibility of that? Rest assured that we will conclude our business swiftly and return to you by Friday. Try not to worry.

I am confident that any information we obtain will only further our cause and that can only lead, at last, to one conclusion for us. I long for you and will not keep you waiting.

You have my word and my heart.

Luc

Clarissa was so angry at being excluded from the expedition that, at first, she ignored the tumultuous emotions which the second part of Luc's note stirred within her. What could he mean by it? Well, obviously she understood what he meant, but why was he offering his heart as well as everything else? He knew she intended to return to Northumberland and they were unlikely to see one another again. Did he imagine she read anything more into it than that? That was just ridiculous! She was not a young girl, so unsure of herself that she required false promises. She had offered herself to him unreservedly, understood her commitment for exactly what it was and did not have the slightest intention of reneging on her promise.

But Clarissa did not dwell upon his motives. Instead she fought to control the fulminating anger with which Luc's deception left her grappling. He had promised that she could accompany him when he interviewed the mate of the *Andomino*, but once again he had broken his word and arrogantly assumed he knew what was best for her. How dare he take matters into his own hands! She supposed he was attempting to protect her reputation, but he knew well enough that she cared little for such matters. Besides, she could easily have taken Caroline with her and avoided unnecessary censure that way.

Had Aunt Marcia not been observing her so closely she would have stamped her foot in frustration at the very least — or more likely hurled the nearest object through the window — anything to relieve the feelings of utter ineffectiveness which churned within her. Accepting instead that, for the moment at least, she was powerless to do anything about the situation, Clarissa contented herself with resolving to address a few choice words to his lordship when he deigned to return home.

The following morning Clarissa was saved the trouble of pleading off a proposed shopping expedition with Aunt Marcia by the timely arrival of Suzanna. It seemed that she had some business to attend to at the orphanage and wondered if Clarissa would care to accompany her?

'With pleasure, Suzanna!'

'Ah good, Luc thought you most likely would.'

'Luc asked you to take me along?'

'Oh no, nothing like that,' blustered Suzanna vaguely, in a manner so akin to her mother's that Clarissa had to smile in spite of herself. 'He just happened to call with Felix yesterday on their way to Portsmouth and mentioned a meeting at the orphanage which I could attend in his stead. He said you might like to accompany me: to keep it in the family, so to speak.'

'Did he indeed!' What in the name of Hades did Luc think he was about? She was not 'part of the family', but both Marcia and Suzanna were daily treating her more and more as though she was. She mentally added this aspect of his high-handed behaviour to her list of grievances against him.

Friday afternoon brought the dreadful Emily Stokes and her friend Mary to Grosvenor Square to make her promised donation to the orphanage. Suzanna and Louisa happened to be visiting their mother as well and Clarissa could see from their expressions that they too held Mrs Stokes in scant regard. But her donation was indeed a most generous one and the ladies clearly felt that whatever her motives for making it, some gratitude on their part was called for.

Clarissa watched it all with barely contained amusement. Emily was being charming to Luc's mother and sisters and issued an invitation to the 'whole family' to attend a party she was shortly to give. She even inclined her head in Clarissa's direction and included her, unless of course she was to have left the Town by then. Had not Emily heard somewhere that her departure was imminent? It amused Clarissa to observe Emily trying to hide her satisfaction when she confirmed that in all probability that would be the case.

Emily's attention, when not directed towards Luc's mother, was constantly upon the door. Naturally she could not actually ask if Luc was in the house but clearly hoped that he would join them for tea at any moment. Eventually though even she seemed to realize that she had stretched her visit beyond the bounds of politeness and began to speak of leaving. As she rose to do so though the door finally opened to admit Luc and Felix. Emily promptly reseated herself, all thoughts of departure abandoned, and offered him her sweetest smile.

'Mrs Stokes called to make a very generous donation to the orphanage,' explained Aunt Marcia blandly.

'I am sure the children will be more than grateful,' Luc responded neutrally.

'Oh, they are such darling creatures! One could hardly do less.'

'Indeed.'

Luc and Felix helped themselves to tea and, ignoring Emily's continued attempts to monopolize their attention, turned towards Clarissa. In a low tone they advised her that their journey had been a success. The mate was indeed a native of Alexandria and knew the district of Sporting exceedingly well. The street in which the advocate's office was supposedly situated, and at which the will had been drawn up twenty years ago, had burned down more than five years before that. The mate was adamant that the advocate had not recommenced trade at alternative premises. He was entirely sure of his facts for, although only a boy himself at the time, his father had helped to fight the fire and had often spoken with regret about the livelihoods that had been wiped out by the cruel destruction.

Clarissa was so overcome with relief that she exclaimed aloud, clapping her hands in delight, all thoughts of upbraiding Luc for his unilateral behaviour temporarily forgotten. So beside herself was she that she failed to notice Emily Stokes moving about the room, making no attempt to hide the fact that she was listening to their conversation.

'What does all this mean? Are we now in a position to refute the claim?'

'Indeed we are,' agreed Luc. 'At our meeting with Twining on Monday we will make him privy to our knowledge, but before then we must decide what action we intend to take against him and Salik.'

'What are you three conferring about?' demanded Emily, surprising them by soundlessly joining the group. Clarissa looked at her in annoyance, wondering how much she had heard. She had no wish for her affairs to become a matter for public discussion.

'A business matter,' replied Luc succinctly.

'Oh do not speak of stuffy business dealings now,' said Emily airily. 'Let us discuss more pleasant matters. Are you to attend Lady Sinclair's soirée this evening, Luc? I will be delighted to save you a dance.'

'Thank you,' said Luc dismissively, smiling intimately at Clarissa as he spoke, and not caring how rude he sounded, 'but I am unlikely to be there. I have very different plans for this evening.'

Felix, ever the peacemaker, stepped in. 'Were you about to leave, Emily? Allow me to escort you.'

'Thank you, Felix.' And, stony-faced, Emily took her leave, casting a last darkling glance in Luc's direction as she did so.

★ ★ ★

Luc did escort Clarissa and his mother to Lady Sinclair's that evening but ignored Emily Stokes to the point of rudeness. He danced with no one but Clarissa and did not leave her side once throughout the evening. They discussed at great length all that Luc had learned from his visit to Portsmouth and agreed upon their strategy for their visit to Twining on Monday.

In spite of Luc's most earnest entreaties however, Clarissa could not be persuaded to bring charges against Twining and Salik. She knew that word of mouth would be sufficient to damage Twining's business beyond repair and that Salik would have no choice but to return to Egypt empty-handed. She was so deliriously happy that her fears for her future were at an end that she felt she could afford to be magnanimous.

Knowing her as well as he now did, Luc was not surprised by her attitude and anyway, tonight, there was an indefinable air of expectation and anticipation smouldering between them that made it impossible for Luc to concentrate on his reasons in favour of prosecution. Somehow he didn't seem to be able to formulate his arguments with his customary logic. He organized his thoughts carefully enough but the moment he looked at Clarissa's lovely face and drowned helplessly in the depths of her translucent eyes he became lost to all reason. Her expression was expectant, trustful and intimately enticing, causing him to forget exactly what it was he had been planning to say anyway and even why he had deemed it so important to say it in the first place. Instead he simply wanted to hold Clarissa in his arms and kiss those enchanting lips; to punish her for that innocently flirtatious look which he could have sworn she was deliberately slanting at him from beneath her thick, curling lashes.

The evening came to an eventual end and Luc's party journeyed home; the atmosphere within their carriage charged and expectant.

Upon reaching Grosvenor Square, Marcia and Clarissa retired immediately, whilst Luc partook of a final glass of brandy in his library, having bid Clarissa an innocent 'good night' in the vestibule.

Luc savoured his drink in contemplative silence. He prolonged the moment, allowing his household time to settle. He enjoyed the solitude which this nightly ritual afforded him. But tonight it took on a special meaning. Finally he could allow his feelings of anticipation the freedom to run riot. At last their time had arrived and in a few moments he would experience that which he had wanted almost since first setting eyes on Clarissa.

But still he delayed and only when the anticipation became too much to endure did he finally drain his glass and ascend the stairs two at a time.

Luc tapped quietly on Clarissa's door, knowing intuitively that she would be expecting him, which she was. As he entered her chamber his breath caught in his throat. He froze on the spot, temporarily deprived of the ability to move his limbs, captivated instead by the sight that met his eyes. She was propped up in bed, her hair cascading haphazardly about her shoulders, gleaming like a golden halo in the soft candlelight. She somehow managed to look innocent, sensual and provocative all at the same time and Luc knew that if he lived to be one hundred he was unlikely ever to experience another moment like it.

'I knew you would come tonight,' she whispered.

He set his candle down on the small table beside the fire. 'Wild horses could not have kept me away any longer. Come here!'

Without hesitation Clarissa threw back the covers and ran straight across the room into his waiting arms, her functional lawn nightgown billowing about her. Luc caught her to him and kissed her passionately, his hands burying themselves in her lovely hair, just as he had dreamed of doing for so long.

But this would not do! In her haste and inexperience she had plastered herself against him, totally unaware how completely the pressure of her body was arousing him. Luc could not remember the last time he had bedded a virgin. What was more, this one was special, the occasion too important to be rushed. He would take things very slowly and ensure that for Clarissa it was unforgettable. His own needs were of secondary concern: all that mattered was that he gave her pleasure.

'What is this?' he asked with a smile, breaking their kiss and putting her away from him as his fingers ran over the long sleeve of her nightgown.

'The nights are cold in Northumberland,' she said defensively, the slight tremble in her voice displaying the extent of her own nervousness.

'I dare say,' he responded, loosening the tight lace at her neck, 'but they would not be so if you had someone to keep you warm.'

'My dogs sleep with me.'

'Hm, not quite what I had in mind.' He was untying her sleeves now and smiling at her in that slow, sensual manner of his that scattered her senses and made her blind to reason. 'Besides, you should be wearing silk in your bed, if you insist upon wearing anything at all, that is.'

'Oh, very practical!'

'Yes, well, practicality was not what I had in mind either.'

'Luc!' She pulled away from him, her anguished expression a study in uncertainty. 'I am sorry but I cannot do this.' Ignoring his startled expression she pulled her gaping nightgown about her and hugged herself, attempting to control both her shivering and her rising panic. She paced distractedly in front of the fire.

'What is it, Clarissa? What are you doing?'

'Pacing, of course.'

'I can see that, but why?'

'I always pace when I am nervous,' she said, as though that would explain everything.

'There is no need to be nervous, I will give you nothing but pleasure, I can assure you of that.'

'It is not that . . . well, not really.' Pace, pace. 'It is just that, well, no one has ever seen me naked before.' Pace. 'What if I disappoint you?'

Luc offered up a silent laugh, his relief palpable. 'Oh, darling,' he said, catching her by her wrist and pulling her close once again. 'You will not disappoint me, of that I can assure you.'

'But how can you know that? And besides, I do not know what to do or how to respond. It is not actually a subject which forms part of a respectable girl's education you know.'

He chuckled throatily and offered her a broad, infectious grin. 'Fear not, I know exactly what to do!' He was whispering into her hair now, caressing her back with long, practised strokes until he felt her rigid limbs relax slightly against him. 'And as for responding, just do what you feel.'

She seemed completely unable to comprehend his meaning. She could not look at him and hung her head despondently.

'You do trust me, do you not, Clarissa?'

She nodded mutely, her eyes still fastened on the floor.

'Then look up at me and tell me so.'

His gently reassuring, unthreatening tone gradually penetrated her confused mind and at last she found the courage to look up, straight into the most sincere eyes she had ever encountered. 'Yes, Luc, of course I trust you.'

She spoke so quietly that Luc could hardly hear her. But it was enough. He would take control now and she would soon forget all about being nervous.

'Then just relax and allow yourself to feel.' He held out his arms. 'Come here!'

As he folded her against him Clarissa's worries slowly dissipated, all nervousness and hesitation left her and she yearned for that which she did not yet comprehend. Sighing, she returned Luc's kiss, listened as he whispered reassuringly loving words to her and allowed herself to be expertly seduced at the hand of a master.

Afterwards Luc was almost as wide-eyed with surprise as Clarissa. Hardened and cynical, he had never before imagined it would be possible to feel such a fierce and possessive love. He watched her as she lay curled cat-like at his side, dozing, a satiated smile on her lovely face. But sleep was beyond Luc. He lay propped on one elbow watching her, still full of wonder at the indescribable pleasure she had given him. The whole act had become mundane for Luc over recent years but Clarissa had just managed to make sense of it all for him again. He knew, with an unshakeable certainty, that this was the woman he had been seeking for his entire life. Still wrapped in the comforting warmth of heady passion, he vowed never to let her go.

Conscious of his intense gaze, Clarissa opened her eyes, smiled smugly and stretched.

'What are you thinking?' he asked her gently.

'Oh, I do not know really. That I have been waiting for this moment for my entire life perhaps?'

The fact that her thoughts so closely mirrored his did not, somehow, surprise Luc. 'I wonder what I have done to deserve you in my life?'

'I might ask the same question of you. And, you should know, that for the first time in my life I actually feel beautiful.'

'You certainly look it. I think I have been waiting to see you wake up in my bed *en déshabillé* like this since I first met you, silk or no silk.'

'It is not your bed, it is mine.'

This remark earned her yet another kiss. 'Do not be pedantic,' he chided, reluctantly releasing her lips.

'Sorry.'

'So you should be!'

'Thank you for showing me, Luc.' She sounded ridiculously formal, given that she was lying totally naked beside him, but was unsure how else to behave. 'I can return home now secure in the knowledge that I have experienced it all.'

What it the name of Hades was she talking about? Return home? Impossible! Surely she did not imagine that he simply wished to bed her and then rid himself of her? Just what sort of fiend did she take him for? She would become his wife: it was as simple as that. But somehow he knew better than to say so at that moment. Knowing her she would undoubtedly mistake the first proposal he had ever made in his life as an act of chivalry. No, better to wait for the morrow and tackle the subject when they were both fully clothed and as far away from the delightful distractions provided by a bed as possible.

Luc was roused from his reverie by the feel of Clarissa's fingers running across his chest.

'Clarissa!'

'Yes.' Her voice was a study of innocence.

'What are you doing?'

'Playing.'

'That is not wise.'

'Why? Oh, do not worry, I am not the clinging type. I have already told you that I will return home next week and you need never see me again. But since I am here, I might as well take full advantage of the opportunity to broaden my education.'

'That is not what I meant.'

'Oh, is it not? I thought you might consider me to be another Mrs Stokes. But fear not, I will not pursue you after tonight. I gather, however, that you have great stamina. Care to prove it?'

'Clarissa, whatever gave you such a notion?'

'Well, your Mrs Stokes was talking to her friend about your prowess at the orphanage the other day. I think she intended for me to overhear her.'

'Damned woman! But never mind her. Darling, it would not be wise to do it again so soon, much as I would like to.'

'Why not?' Her fingers continued to beat a light tattoo across his chest.

'Well, I suppose . . . ' Luc, still sounding doubtful but unable to resist her, capitulated.

'Where did you learn about such matters anyway, Lady Hartley?' Luc attempted a disapproving tone but it was rather difficult to maintain since Clarissa was continuing to walk her fingers over every inch of his body, conducting an erotic and very thorough survey.

'I might be an innocent but — '

Luc chuckled. 'Not any more!'

'All right, I was an innocent, but I am not deaf. I have heard maids talking.'

'Ah yes, maids. Always a valuable source of information, so I am informed.'

'I have always found them to be so,' confirmed Clarissa conversationally, continuing to concentrate on her task.

Luc shot her a challenging look, rolled onto his back, pulled Clarissa with him and took charge of operations.

# 15

Clarissa woke early but for once did not immediately consider rising. Instead she stretched languidly and smiled to herself as she recalled her activities of the previous evening. In spite of his protests she had persuaded Luc to pleasure her three times. Not that he had been reluctant for his own part: he had made that abundantly clear. He was simply concerned that it would be too much for her, that she was too inexperienced, that he would hurt her, or make her sore. Hurt her? Huh! The whole experience had been a complete revelation and had given her pleasure beyond her wildest dreams. And Luc had been so considerate, so gentle and patient with her. He had taken her skittishness in his stride and soothed away her concerns. She knew she had been fortunate and could not have asked for a more accomplished and proficient lover.

For the first time ever Clarissa felt she was a complete woman and, with an expansive sigh of regret, repented the fact that she would never know that feeling again. But she had spoken no more than the truth when she told Luc she would not cling. She had no intention of behaving like Mrs Stokes, or any of the other ladies she had observed in Luc's company, flirting and blatantly making their availability plainly apparent.

He had looked surprised and disbelieving when she had given him her assurance in that respect and she thought he had been on the verge of contradicting her. *Well, my lord,* she thought to herself now with some satisfaction, *just because other women find you irresistible, there is no need to imagine that I will join their number!*

But somehow Clarissa took neither heart nor comfort from her resolve.

Sternly, she reminded herself that Luc was a rake of the first order and whilst her first opinion of him may have been slightly erroneous, she had still not been far off the mark. She now knew him to be a good, dutiful son; a strong head of the family; a firm and fair landlord. He was also a witty and charming companion. But there was no escaping the fact that he had simply been amusing himself with her: obligingly teaching her that which she had practically begged him to show her. She blushed at the thought of her forwardness, whilst simultaneously revelling in the bolt of desire that streaked through her at the recollection of his experienced hands exploring her body so expertly; of his wickedly enticing, meaningful smile; of black eyes burning passionately into hers.

She shivered but banished all carnal thoughts resolutely, refusing to become just one more woman following a long line of predecessors, sighing for the want of his attentions. Instead she focused upon his dictatorial attitude, his presumption that she would follow his dictate without question when dealing with the matter of her lands. This thought helped her to regain control and she was able to smile brightly at Caroline, who chose that particular moment to enter her room.

'What, still a-bed, my lady?' she remarked with surprise. 'It is almost nine o'clock.'

'Good morning, Caroline.'

'It is a fine day, my lady.' Caroline pulled back the curtains to admit a flood of sunlight and looked at Clarissa with something approaching suspicion. 'And you look remarkably well this morning, if you do not mind my saying so.'

'I do not mind in the least, Caroline. And I should look well, do you not think? After all, my problems are at an end and we shall soon be able to return home. The prospect delights me.'

'Hm, is that what is making you look so bonny, I wonder?'

'Of course, Caroline, what else could it be?'

'What indeed, my lady?'

As Clarissa seated herself before her glass and pondered upon her reflection she could see for herself just why Caroline was looking at her in such a strange manner. Indeed, Clarissa could scarce believe what she was seeing with her own eyes. Considering that Luc had not left her chamber until shortly after five o'clock, and given how little sleep she had achieved before that, she had to admit that her complexion bore a bloom this morning, the likes of which she could never before recall seeing upon it. Her eyes sparkled with the pure joy of life and her lips — still delightfully swollen as a result of Luc's prolonged kisses — seemed to be turned upwards in a permanent smile.

Caroline was uncharacteristically quiet as she brushed Clarissa's hair but she too seemed to be afflicted with an overwhelming urge to smile broadly today.

Clarissa was about to go down to breakfast when there was a knock upon her door. Caroline answered it and returned to Clarissa bearing a wrapped parcel.

'This was just delivered for you, my lady.'

'Indeed, I wonder what it could be?'

Clarissa opened the parcel and blushed scarlet to the roots of her hair as she extracted two exquisite silk nightgowns.

'Been shopping again have we, my lady?'

'What, no, of course . . . oh, I mean yes, Caroline, yes, indeed I have! You know, I feel so dowdy in this elegant house, wearing my old lawn nightgowns. Besides, they are so threadbare. I thought I would take the opportunity to replace them whilst I am here.'

Aware that she was babbling — a sure sign to someone who knew her as well as Caroline did that she was lying — Clarissa fell silent. But far from contradicting her mistress Caroline merely contented herself with a *quite so, my lady* and a knowing smile. She did not even make any mention of her mistress's blush. Caroline surely knew Clarissa too well to believe for one moment that she had wasted the ludicrous amount of money that these garments must have cost just for the purpose of sleeping in them? Caroline must know very well also that Clarissa would freeze to death in such flimsy night attire when she returned to Northumberland.

But Clarissa was temporarily too confused to gather her wits sufficiently about her and Caroline would just have to think what she wished. Luc was clearly responsible for the gift. But how had he managed it so soon?

Perhaps he kept a ready store of such items to hand to bestow upon his conquests? Far from feeling insulted, the idea amused her and she found herself smiling once again. Still, she would kill Luc for embarrassing her thus in front of her maid.

She fingered the beautiful, gossamer thin silk dreamily, imagining how luxurious it would feel when worn next to her naked skin and regretted, for a moment, the fact that Luc would never see her thus attired.

Clarissa entered the breakfast parlour a short time later to find Luc there alone. He rose to greet Clarissa and held out her usual chair, the one next to his. His greeting was as formal as always, since servants were present, but there could be no mistaking the devilish glint in his eye.

'Good morning, Lady Hartley, I trust you slept well.'

'Thank you, my lord, I find that I had a most memorable night's repose.'

'I am very satisfied to hear you say it. You certainly look exceedingly well this morning. Lady Sinclair's gathering must have agreed with you, I think?'

'Something about last evening's activities certainly agreed with me,' she responded, a hint of mischief creeping into her already vivacious expression.

'You must enjoy new experiences, I think?'

'Indeed, I enjoyed everything that I experienced yesterday.'

'And your appetite has returned, I am glad to observe,' remarked Luc, indicating the enormous serving of breakfast that Clarissa had helped herself to.

'I find that my appetite for all things is undergoing a marked revival.'

'No doubt due to the excellent news regarding your estates?'

'Undoubtedly.'

The footman left the room to replenish a dish, leaving only Bentley standing a discreet distance away from the table.

'Luc! Those nightgowns, what do you think you are playing at?'

'Do you not like them?'

'It is not that. It is just that . . . well, Caroline saw me open them.' Clarissa blushed again, unaware how desirable it made her appear. It was a long time since Luc had dealt with a woman who still blushed. 'She must know I did not purchase them and guess that you are responsible.' She glared at him, acutely embarrassed.

'Ah yes, I dare say.' He sat back in his chair, looking exceedingly smug, just as Marcia entered the room.

'Wear one of them for me tonight,'

whispered Luc, standing to greet his mother.

'Tonight?' she whispered back. 'What are you talking about?' There would be no tonight. Had she not made that clear to him? But Luc's attention was now entirely focused upon his mother and he appeared not to hear her.

A short time later Clarissa was seated in Luc's curricle, with just Mulligan between them and one footman up behind. Marcia had decreed that they should all go to Richmond Park for a picnic, only to remember at the last minute that she was engaged elsewhere but insisting that Luc and Clarissa go anyway.

Arriving at Richmond the footman busied himself unloading the picnic, whilst Luc, Clarissa and a delighted Mulligan strolled the park. The dog gambolled about with his lopsided gait, chasing the sticks that Luc threw for him and making them laugh with his clumsy attempts to round up the ducks that were resting on the bank of the river.

'Come on, m'dear,' said Luc, taking her arm and whistling to Mulligan. 'Let us enjoy our luncheon.'

They did so, mostly in silence, but Clarissa was aware of a tension between them caused, she knew, partly by her refusal to meet Luc's eye. She ate his meat, feeding morsels to the hovering Mulligan, and drank the cool, crisp champagne that he poured for her into a crystal flute. She made absent responses to his remarks but, far from being closer to him after their night of passion, she felt now as though he were a stranger once again.

Clarissa wondered whether she was subconsciously preparing herself for the pain of separation? And it would be a painful experience; she knew that now. Her feelings would be a thousand times removed from those she had anticipated the occasion would engender just a few short weeks ago. Far from turning her back on Luc for the final time with a feeling of relief at never having to see him again she accepted now that their parting would be nothing less than a brutal agony for her.

'Clarissa?'

'Oh, I am sorry, Luc, did you say something?'

'Actually,' he said with a smile, 'I said the same thing three times.'

'I am sorry, what did you say?'

'I asked whether you would care for more champagne? Not the most engrossing question I confess but one that requires a response nevertheless.' He was smiling indulgently at her and Clarissa heartily wished he would not do so. Just the sight of his irresistible lips curving gently upwards, the softening of his expression as he consumed her features with eyes that clearly wanted, was sufficient to set her heart racing and her mind to already regret the loss of him.

'Thank you, but no more for me.'

'Then will you not eat a little more? You have taken but little.'

'No, Luc, thank you. I ate a large breakfast.'

'Indeed you did.' That smile again. Clarissa was unable to meet it with equanimity and looked away, confused and unsettled. 'Hoskins,' he said to the footman, 'you may clear away.'

Hoskins left them sitting on a rug beneath an accommodating oak tree. The silence, the aching stillness, lengthened between them and Clarissa, conscious that she should make an effort to converse with him, searched her mind for a suitable subject. They had already discussed at length the course which their interview with Twining and Salik would take on Monday and there was little more that could be said upon that subject. Relating her plans for her return to Northumberland would bring up the unspoken matter of her departure, so that was not possible either. The orphanage? That was surely safe ground? Clarissa opened her mouth to speak but Luc pre-empted her by taking her gloved hand in his and, mindless of the public place they were in, turning it over and kissing the inside of her wrist softly.

'Now, Lady Hartley,' he said, employing a gentle tone of authority. 'why do you not tell me what has been on your mind the entire morning?'

'What do you mean?' she responded, deliberately evasive.

'You know what I mean.'

'Luc, I do not . . . '

'Clarissa, the one thing I have always been able to rely upon you for is plain speaking. Tell me what troubles you, my love.'

'I just . . . well, it is just that I am feeling somewhat confused.'

'By what happened between us last night?'

'Partly.'

'But, in the broad light of day, you have not come to regret it?'

'No, of course not.'

Luc studied her in silence, unnerving her and prompting her to speak again.

'All right, yes, perhaps just a little. You see, I thought we had agreed that I would not cling.' She rose abstractedly to her feet. 'That one night was all it would be but now you are openly sending me intimate gifts and implying that you wish to come to me again. I

303

do not understand why that should be.'

'You do not?' He appeared incredulous.

'Luc, I am grateful to you for what you taught me last night. Nothing could have prepared me for the reality of it all and I will always treasure the memory.' She closed her eyes briefly and hugged herself. 'But I do not wish to be something with which you amuse yourself until you become tired of that game. I have no wish to follow in Emily Stokes's footsteps, or any of your other paramours for that matter.'

'And is that what you think I am doing, merely amusing myself at your expense?' Luc spoke mildly, but there was no mistaking the curling disdain beneath his words.

'Is that not what all gentlemen do? It is certainly the impression I have been left with since coming to the capital.'

'But I thought we had got beyond that? I was of the opinion that we meant more to one another than that.'

'What else could we possibly mean?'

Rising to his feet also, Luc caught hold of Clarissa's wrist, bringing her to a halt in front of him. 'Do I have to spell it out? I thought you realized: I wish you to marry me.'

'What?' Clarissa sank unceremoniously down onto the blanket, her utter surprise at his declaration robbing her legs of their ability to support her. Luc resumed his seat beside her and took her hand.

'Does the idea dismay you as much as that?' he asked quietly.

'The idea has completely flummoxed me, Luc, if you want to know the truth. I had no notion that you felt that way.'

'What, you consider that I behaved as I did last night with a chaste lady of quality just for sport?' There was a sharpness to his tone, an edge which clearly indicated what he thought of such disreputable behaviour.

Clarissa sighed, grappling for the right words and wondering at her sudden awkwardness of expression. 'Luc,' she said, in what she hoped was a conciliatory tone, 'no one but you knew the true nature of my marriage. As far as the world at large is concerned I am an experienced widow and therefore viewable as fair game, I believe is the expression, much the same as Mrs Stokes.'

'Good God, Clarissa, do not dare to compare yourself to that woman!'

His vehemence startled and discomforted Clarissa. 'Perhaps we should return home?'

'Not until we have resolved the situation between us. Clarissa, I am sorry, my love, I have handled this badly. Allow me to start again and tell you of my true feelings for you.

'When you first arrived I must confess that I anticipated little pleasure from your visit. But as soon as I realized how unique you are, how different to the hordes of women I meet daily, I started to take more of an interest in you. And at that first ball we attended together, when you told me in no uncertain terms just exactly what you thought of society in general and me in particular, my interest was truly piqued. To be honest, women tend to fawn over me, as you have no doubt observed,' he added with a self-depreciating smile, 'and no one has ever dared to speak to me quite so frankly before.'

'Luc, I — '

Luc held up a hand and prevented her from continuing. 'Hear me out, Clarissa, please. When I realized how much interest you had in the orphanage, how much Mulligan likes you and how envious other women were of you, I realized that I had, at long last, met someone truly unique. I had met the lady I have been waiting for my entire life.' He paused to smile softly at her before demanding accusingly, 'What took you so long to find me?

'When you described your work in Northumberland with such evident passion,' he continued, 'and demonstrated your determination to continue with it no matter what obstacles were placed in your path, I confess that I felt an admiration for your spirit that I have never before entertained for anyone. Your resolve to marry a man old enough to be your father just so that you could carry on with that work was something that no one could fail to admire. And I found, to my astonishment, that I could not bear to have you think badly of me. That is why I broke my rule and took you to the orphanage. I knew you would understand what I am trying to achieve there and I was right, I think?'

'Yes, Luc, but — '

'I think it was when I saw you with Rosie cuddled on your lap that I first resolved to make you mine. I could not get the image out of my head of you holding our own children thus.'

'But, Luc, I cannot marry you.'

'Shush, let me finish. I wanted to tell you before now: in fact I thought you might have already guessed. I wanted to come to your bed, to court you and make love to you, to pay homage to your beauty and purity. But then the business with Salik came up and I knew we had to resolve that first. I considered that if I proposed to you then you might think I was doing so as an act of kindness, because of your connection to my mother, or some other such nonsense. No, I could not risk that! I needed you to be in full possession of your lands and to be able to consider my proposal as an equal. But now, my love, you are in that position and I want you for my wife. I want you to spend the rest of your life at my side. What do you say?'

Clarissa met his impassioned gaze, which seemed to reach out and enfold her like a tender caress: heartfelt, all-encompassing and passionate. She did not doubt the depth of his feeling and understood that unquestionably he spoke from the heart. His expression was a combination of fear, hope and expectancy as he awaited her answer. She had never once known him to be unsure of himself before today and fought to control a shudder as she made to reply, knowing that her words would appear to him as heartless and ungrateful.

'Luc.' She reached up and gently pushed a lock of hair away from his face. He caught her fingers in a vice-like hold and kissed each one in turn. 'I truly had no idea you felt that way.'

'I know. That is part of the attraction.'

'But I cannot marry you.'

'Why not?'

'Because we live in such different worlds. I could not fit into yours any more than you could into mine.'

'What makes you so sure of that?'

'My life is in the north. My passion is my sheep. I have no time for the *ton* and the ways of society — I find it meaningless and it would make me miserable. But you were born to it and have a right to expect your wife to share in it with you; to shine as a society hostess. I could never imagine myself in that position and neither would I wish to be.'

'No! I have been tired of the *ton* for a long time now. That is why I exploit it and use the profits I make to do some good. The orphanage. It amuses me to think of all those foppish characters paying out good money in order to support the urchins we take in. Good God, can you imagine how some of them would react if they ever found out?' They shared a complicit smile at the thought. 'But, I had decided even before you came into my life that I would spend considerably less time in the capital from now on.'

'What will you do?'

'Go to Berkshire and concentrate on my horses. We could share our time between the two estates. I am well aware how important your farming is to you and you have my word that I would not interfere and you would still enjoy the freedom to continue with your work as you see fit. We need spend very little time in the capital.'

'Oh, Luc!'

Luc stood again and pulled Clarissa to her feet. 'Why is the idea so abhorrent to you?'

'It is not that, Luc, it is just that I had not considered getting married again.'

'Not even to me?' He offered her a beguiling smile, one which made her heart lurch and her resolve wobble.

'No, believe it or not, the idea had not crossed my mind.'

'But even though I have told you how I feel, you are still not prepared to consider it?' His voice was tight, his expression too closely guarded for her to interpret his desperate feeling of angst.

'It is such a surprise.'

'Clarissa, look me in the eye and tell me that you do not love me. If you can do that then I will walk away from you and we will not discuss the matter again.' Luc placed his index finger beneath her chin and tilted her face towards him, forcing her to meet his impassioned gaze.

She could not do it. She was incapable of concealing her feelings, incapable of disguising the deep oneness she felt with him, and looked away.

'I thought so!' His exclamation was triumphant.

'You must allow me time to consider the

matter, Luc. It has all been so sudden.'

'Naturally.'

They headed together towards the waiting curricle. Clarissa sensed Luc's satisfaction at having extracted her promise to consider his proposal as acutely as she sensed his frustration at being unable to kiss her in such a public place. But, as he handed her into the curricle, he flashed a predatory grin at her. 'And whilst you are considering the matter?' His meaning was unmistakable.

Clarissa met his gaze boldly and held it. Sighing, she knew she could not resist what he was offering her: that whatever decision she came to with regard to marriage she would give in to temptation and spend a second night with him. 'I will wear one of my new nightgowns for you tonight.'

Luc's smile at winning that particular battle was a wicked signal of intent. It lit up his whole face and made him look so impossibly handsome that Clarissa was forced to avert her gaze lest he recognize the naked, aching sense of longing she felt for him and was unable to conceal.

★　★　★

Luc found Clarissa to be true to her word. When he entered her chamber that evening she was sitting propped up in her bed once again, her beautiful hair spilling across her pillows. But this time she was wearing his gift, an enigmatic smile of welcome — and nothing else. He paused for a moment, taking in the sight of her, so different from the hesitant and vulnerable creature she had been only twenty-four hours earlier.

'Let me see!' he commanded, when he was finally able to find his voice.

Clarissa rose from her bed but slowly this time and walked towards him at an unhurried pace, the soft silk adhering to the warmth of her body and offering Luc a timely reminder of the delights which were in store for him. One short day had made a world of difference to her. She had developed the confidence to display her new found sensuality: she had lost all anxiety and was proud to display herself before him.

'Remarkable,' he opined, as he ran one hand gently down her back and pulled her towards him. 'Just perfect.'

Tonight Luc was determined to take even more time and demonstrate to Clarissa just what pleasures she could expect on a daily basis if she agreed to marry him. He spent an age caressing every inch of her body before he even began to remove the nightgown. By the time he did so Clarissa was in a fervour of desire, her passions stirred to the point of madness. Luc was enjoying prolonging the moment and gauging her reactions — until that is Clarissa allowed her impatience to bubble over and took matters into her own hands, causing him to draw in his breath sharply.

'Two can play at that game,' she warned him teasingly.

'You are a fast learner, my lady.

'I had a good teacher, my lord.'

'Indeed you did.'

But she had made her point and, gathering her in his arms, Luc carried her to the bed.

Afterwards she lay in his arms, satiated and smiling.

'When we are married I shall not have to think of returning to my own chamber, as I am doing at this moment.'

'I have not agreed to marry you, Luc.'

'Not yet,' he conceded, 'but you will soon enough.'

'And what, may I ask, makes you so sure of that?'

'Because you enjoy what we have just done too much,' he said, running a finger gently across her cheek, a gesture which produced a passionate shudder as fire flooded through her veins. 'See! And because, having denied yourself such pleasures for so long, I cannot see you giving them up again so easily.'

'There are other gentlemen,' Clarissa informed him with a defiant tilt of her chin.

'Hm, yes indeed there are.' Luc kissed the end of her nose. 'But none of them would be able to make you feel as I do,' he added, sure of himself and his ability to gratify her. 'Besides, I cannot see you taking a lover when you return to Northumberland just to indulge your new found passions. That sort of behaviour is not within your character.'

'You have it all figured out, I see. But why, pray, should I wish to subject myself to a husband's tyranny when I have enjoyed the freedom to do as I please for so long?'

'Tyrannical, am I?' He made to turn her over and spank her in punishment.

Squealing, Clarissa squirmed out of his arms and his reach, laughter engulfing her. 'You most certainly are!'

'You love me, Clarissa,' said Luc confidently, pulling her against him, 'even if you cannot yet bring yourself to admit as much. But I think it only fair to warn you, I want you for my wife and I am not accustomed to being disappointed. I always get what I want eventually.'

'And what about what I want?' she asked him flirtatiously.

'Ah yes, about that.'

And rolling over her, he bent once more to kiss her.

# 16

On Sunday morning Clarissa and Marcia attended church. Luc remained in his library, attempting to devise irrefutable arguments to convince Clarissa to marry him. She was making noises about returning to Northumberland next week, after matters with Twining had been settled. Well, he was damned if he would allow her to go without him. He was not prepared to part with her so soon after finding her and once she acknowledged what she already knew in her heart — that she loved him and was his — then she would go nowhere without him. How to convince her though, that was the rub?

Perhaps her unbridled enthusiasm for activities between the sheets was the answer? Maybe if he refrained from visiting her at night and satisfying her belatedly awakened desires it would bring home to her just what pleasures she would be giving up by not marrying him? Pleasure seemed such a hopelessly inadequate word to describe what it was that she brought to him. She was perfection: everything he had given up hope of ever finding in a woman. She gave herself to him without reservation, entirely and joyously. She made no attempt to hide the pleasure that she took from his attentions either. Well, that was common enough amongst his bedfellows, he admitted to himself modestly, but the difference with Clarissa was that she expected nothing in return.

Luc's married paramours required gifts, the widows such as Emily Stokes wanted marriage. But Clarissa it seemed wanted nothing but the gratification he could offer her. She was a shamelessly eager pupil, who appeared to suffer not at all from remorse or embarrassment, in spite of the way in which she surrendered to him with such unbridled enthusiasm. Luc could not live without her and vowed to pursue her with single-minded determination, confident that she would eventually submit to his indomitable will.

Luc's mother had become less and less subtle with regard to his continued unmarried state over recent years and Luc knew that the point she was trying to make was a valid one. He was thirty years old and knew it was high time he settled down and sired an heir. Two years his junior, Simon had been married for three years and already had two children. All three of his sisters were married, leaving only his youngest brother, still at Oxford, single.

Luc took his mother and sisters' ribbing on the matter of his marriage prospects in good stead. This was partly because he knew it was their way of expressing their rightful concerns at his dilatory attitude towards matrimony but also because he was aware how much pleasure they took in gossiping and speculating about such matters. He was the head of their family and they had a right to expect him to behave in the prescribed manner and ensure the continuation of the line. All of a sudden Luc was in a tearing hurry to oblige them.

He had been reluctant to follow the example of many of his contemporaries and settle down with a lady whom he did not love or respect, simply to beget an heir. Luc required a partner with whom he could share more than just a bed. His wife must be lively, intelligent, willing to share his passion for country living and, above all, someone who was not given to obsequiousness. He had seen more than enough of that trait to last him a lifetime. But now, just when he had given up all hope of finding her, she had breezed, quite without warning, into his life. And of one thing he was determined: she would not leave it again until she had agreed to become his wife.

Luc was roused from his reverie by a knock at his door. It was unusual for him to be interrupted on a Sunday morning. Most of the staff were at church and few would be around at this hour. Knowing it must be a matter of some import to warrant such an intrusion, Luc bade his caller enter. Simms did so, an agitated expression gracing his normally dispassionate features.

'Forgive the intrusion, my lord, but Fielding is here from the orphanage and desires an immediate word with you.'

'Show him in, Simms, and remain with us. There must be something seriously amiss for him to call in this manner.'

Fielding must have been hovering in the hallway for Simms merely opened the door wider and beckoned and he joined them in an instant.

'Forgive me, my lord, but I fear I bring bad tidings. Rosie has disappeared!'

'What?' Luc rose from his seat, a look of consternation on his face. 'How can that possibly be?'

'Well, my lord, my wife and the helpers took the children to chapel this morning as usual. Rosie, and Annie of course, were amongst their number but when they formed up outside the chapel at the end of the service Rosie simply was not there. We thought at first she had perhaps just wandered away from the group but a thorough search failed to discover her and now, having questioned the children, it seems she did not even enter the chapel with the rest of the group in the first place.'

'How in God's name did that happen?'

'We are at a loss to explain it, my lord.'

'Did anything unusual happen on the way to chapel, Fielding? Any strangers taking a special interest in the children?'

Fielding, comprehending Luc's meaning, paled. 'Not that anyone can recall, my lord. But then, as you are aware, the streets are always crowded — even on a Sunday.'

'So she has been gone for more than two hours?'

'Yes, my lord. My wife, as you can imagine, is in a dreadful state.'

'I can, indeed, imagine.'

'She blames herself for not checking they all entered the chapel safely but really, my lord, I have told her she should not think thus. After all, where can the children go, other than back onto the streets from which they were rescued and I think you know as well as I that they would, all of them, rather die than endure that fate: Rosie perhaps most of all.'

'Indeed, Fielding.' Luc resumed his seat, attempting to control his rising panic and think logically. 'Reassure your wife as best you can. You are correct when you say that no blame attaches to her. Now, what steps have you taken to look for Rosie?'

'Every available adult from the institution is combing the streets for a sign of her and asking everyone they meet if they have seen a little girl clutching a rag doll — so far without success.'

'All right, Fielding, I will come back with you and see what is best to be done.'

'Very good, my lord.' Fielding looked relieved to be absolved of responsibility.

'What of me, my lord, what assistance can I offer?' asked Simms.

'Remain here, Simms, just in case word of her is received. And as soon as the staff return from church send some men to ask questions in the vicinity of the orphanage. It is possible that she has been taken by force and someone may have noticed something.'

'That thought had occurred to me, my lord. But by whom?'

'A good question,' agreed Luc grimly. 'Perhaps one of the customers from the inn at which Rosie was previously held?'

'God forbid!' exclaimed Simms.

'The men have my permission to offer generous gratuities in return for reliable information, Simms.'

'I will so inform them, my lord.'

'Oh and, Simms,' said Luc, turning back from the doorway, 'send someone round to Park Street with my compliments to Lord Western and ask him if he would join me at the orphanage.'

'Very good, my lord.'

Luc hurried from the room, his first concern being, of course, for Rosie's welfare: his second for Clarissa when she heard that the little girl she had come to love so much was wandering alone and unprotected in some of the roughest streets of the capital.

★  ★  ★

Clarissa and Marcia returned from church. Marcia was, as always, chattering nineteen to the dozen but Clarissa barely heard her for her head was still hopelessly full of memories of her second night with Luc. It had been even more fulfilling than the first evening. She felt a warm glow and a sweet, rushing spasm of desire incubating within her. A paroxysm of pleasure was now her most constant companion, hovering at close quarters, ready to entice her into its heady embrace the moment she relaxed her guard.

But then she considered his marriage proposal and sobered immediately. It had come as a complete surprise, was the very last thing she had been expecting and she knew not what to do about it.

Luc commanded such presence. The moment he entered a room he effortlessly dominated it and everyone in it naturally deferred to his authority. Could such a man really want her as a wife and even if he did, could she keep him happy for very long? She doubted that. Her tastes were too simple. Her life lacked the sophistication of his and despite what he said, she felt sure he would soon tire of rusticating in the country. He would require good society, would inevitably feel the need to surround himself with fashionable people and hanker for amusing diversions: she would not and inevitably they would drift apart.

She doubted that Luc had ever proposed to a lady before because, from what she had seen, no one else would be likely to refuse him. And did she intend to refuse him herself? Could she resist him, now that he appeared so determined to have her and, in all honesty, did she actually want to? He had sounded sincere when he assured her he would not interfere with her operation in

Northumberland; but was he? He had, after all, promised to work with her to unmask Twining and Salik but had then blithely gone his own way without reference to her. A little voice inside her head told her he had been trying to protect her and save her from her own impetuous behaviour. When she recalled her disastrous trip to that tavern she conceded that he had a point. But still, where did that leave her? Could she ever believe his assurances again?

And what of other women? Clarissa had seen for herself just how prepared they were to throw themselves at him — the married ones especially — and was it not common practice for married men of his class to routinely take a mistress? The very idea of it appalled her and she knew she would never be able to sit quietly by, as so many fashionable wives apparently did, and turn a blind eye to the situation. But if they were separated for long periods — he in London and she in the north — surely it would become inevitable? Just look at Felix. She had seen the way he behaved with the beautiful Angelica Priestley, and the lady had only been married for a year!

Clarissa just did not know what to do. But what she did know was that she loved Luc in a single-minded and passionate way that, a few short weeks ago, she would never have believed possible. But she had never admitted as much: he had simply assumed that it was so. Such arrogance! And what was more, he had never actually told her that he was in love with her.

Clarissa was becoming agitated now, working herself up into a high dudgeon and inventing difficulties in her vivid imagination that might never exist. She decided that instead of prevaricating further she would just have to take the direct approach and do a little plain speaking of her own. At the next opportunity she would confront him with her anxieties and see what he had to say for himself.

Happier now she had decided upon a course of action, Clarissa glanced up to see Bentley hovering before her.

'This was recently delivered for you, my lady.' He proffered a silver salver bearing a bulky package.

'Thank you, Bentley.'

Clarissa took the package to her chamber, thinking it to be another of Luc's outrageous gifts and not wishing to display her embarrassment in front of the servants. Reaching her room she tore away the paper and gasped in alarm. Annie fell out and landed at Clarissa's feet with a dull thud.

Bending to retrieve the doll, Clarissa clasped it towards her, knowing full well that Rosie was in some sort of terrible danger, for she would never voluntarily surrender Annie. Falling to her knees, she searched frantically through the wrapping, desperate for a clue as to the identity of the sender. There was a note, she belatedly realized, tucked into the doll's clothing.

*Lady Hartley — she read — there is a closed conveyance in the street across from your house. Enter it immediately. The driver knows where to take you. If you do not come immediately you will never see the owner of the doll again. Tell no one of your plans.*

The note was signed: *A Wellwisher.*

Without thinking twice, Clarissa flew back down the stairs as though her life depended upon it, still clutching Annie. Ignoring a startled Simms, who was at that moment crossing the hall, she snatched up her pelisse and bonnet and fled into the street.

'Where are you going, my lady?' Simms called after her, his normal *savoir-faire* attitude replaced by a distinct note of alarm. But if she heard him Clarissa made no reply and Simms watched in frustration, and with a growing sense of unease, as she entered the waiting carriage.

Knowing that his lordship would be furious at her sudden departure, doubtless blaming him for not preventing it, Simms asked Bentley if he knew where she had gone in such a tearing hurry. Bentley informed him of the parcel that had been delivered for her but knew not what it contained and could shed no further light upon the matter. They were joined at that moment by Caroline, clutching brown paper, string and the note, all of which she had found on the floor in Clarissa's chamber, demanding to know where Lady Hartley had gone. Simms read the note and cursed in a manner that even his master would not have been able to better. Caroline had never known the stately Simms ever to appear the slightest bit flustered, or to use anything other than the most fastidiously correct language, and that worried her for Clarissa's safety more than anything else.

Snapping his fingers in the direction of a hovering footman, Simms ordered Luc's gig to be readied and brought to the front door immediately. He knew that he must go to the orphanage himself and deliver the intelligence of Lady Hartley's abrupt disappearance to his master and that there was not a moment to lose.

* * *

Clarissa's journey was short: less than ten minutes before the carriage came to a halt. She had no idea where she was. The blinds were closed tight and, full of concern for Rosie, she spared no thought for herself. She was certain now that something awful had happened to the little girl for whom she entertained such affection and was determined to rescue her from it. She could only imagine her terror at being separated from her familiar surroundings, and more especially from Annie. Clarissa simply had to get to her: to hold her and reassure her. Not for one moment did she consider her own safety. Nothing could happen to a lady of quality in the middle of London in broad daylight but a small, unprotected child . . . well, that was altogether another matter.

The carriage came to a halt and Clarissa was assisted from it by a man she did not recognize. He ushered her into a building, but so preoccupied was she that it took her a moment to recognize that she was at Mr Twining's office. Only then did she experience the first stirrings of apprehension.

Whatever was happening it involved her and she suspected that Rosie was merely being used as a pawn. The man with her opened Twining's door and pushed her into the room, his rough treatment of her only adding to her growing sense of foreboding.

'Ah, Lady Hartley, there you are at last!' exclaimed Salik, bowing before her. Even in her distressed state Clarissa could not fail to observe how inferior his bow appeared, now that she was so accustomed to Luc's elegant proficiency in that regard. 'How pleased I am that you could join us so promptly.'

Rosie was across the room, her tiny form almost swamped by the size of the chair in which she sat, arms wrapped round herself as she rocked back and forth, eyes staring vacantly into space. Seemingly unnoticed by the child, tears were streaming steadily down her terrified face. Twining's clerk, Simpson, stood impassively beside her, indifferent to her terror. It was the sight of him, as much as anything else, that moved Clarissa to a ferocious anger which she could scarce control. She was uncomfortably aware that Rosie had removed herself to some other plane, somewhere pleasant where nothing could touch her: doubtless the method she had unconsciously adopted to survive the rigours of life before she was removed to the safety of the orphanage. It was a situation Clarissa was outraged to see her being forced to endure and made her both incautious and mindless of her own danger.

Upon seeing Clarissa, Rosie jerked abruptly back to the present and cried out in relief. Ignoring Simpson's attempts to stop her she flew across the room into Clarissa's arms, sobbing her little heart out.

'There, there, darling, all is well now. I am here and so is Annie!' Clarissa gave Rosie her doll, but continued to hold her in a close embrace, stroking her shaking back and infusing her own warmth into her in an attempt to stop her from trembling quite so violently. She whispered gently to her and told her how brave she was. But Rosie was not about to cease her wailing. She was terrified and Clarissa glared furiously at Salik and Twining. 'If you have harmed her in any way I shall not be held responsible for my actions!' she blazed.

'Fear not, my lady,' said Twining, his manner irritatingly ingratiating. 'Not one hair on her head has been touched.'

'You had better be telling the truth or you will live to regret it, you just mark my words. And what exactly do you think you are playing at, Mr Twining? I would have expected better of you?' Clarissa scowled at her attorney, who seemed unable to make her any sort of answer and visibly shrank beneath the violent force of her anger. He shuffled away and sat behind his desk, looking thoroughly miserable.

'Never mind the child,' said Salik, extracting her forcibly from Clarissa's arms and ignoring her renewed wails of protest. 'Keep her over there, Simpson, and for God's sake, keep her quiet!'

'It is all right, darling, take Annie and sit over there again for a moment. We will be leaving shortly.'

Slightly mollified, Rosie spoke for the first time. 'Where is Uncle Luc?'

'He will be here soon, darling, and then we shall all be able to go home.' Clarissa tried to sound confident but her anger was rapidly giving way to apprehension. Twining she could have dealt with, but she was already fairly certain that this situation was not of his making. One look at the ruthlessly determined expression on Salik's face was enough to remind her that he would be altogether a different proposition.

'That I doubt,' said Salik smoothly. 'Now, why do you not take a seat, Lady Hartley, and we can discuss our reasons for bringing you here.'

It was not a question and Clarissa knew

that if for no reason other than Rosie's sake she must comply. She perched herself on the edge of a stiff, upright chair, and stifling her panic as best she could, turned the full force of her irate glare upon the smirking Salik.

'Now, sir, perhaps you will have the goodness to explain this outrage?'

# 17

Luc and Felix directed an increasingly frantic search for Rosie from the office at the orphanage. Luc reassured a very distressed Mrs Fielding that no blame attached to her but that he needed her to remain steadfast and organize activities for the rest of the children to distract their attention away from Rosie's plight. One of the disadvantages of encouraging such a closeness amongst the children, Luc was now discovering, was that when one of them was in trouble it affected them all. He had arrived to find them uncharacteristically subdued, huddled together in small groups and speaking in whispers. Luc could only hope that some imaginative recreation would restore them to their normal, and suddenly very desirable, boisterous state.

Luc sent out his men in teams to search an ever widening area and to question anyone who might have seen anything at all but so far their efforts had proved to be fruitless. It was as though Rosie had simply disappeared from the face of the earth and Luc was now convinced that she had been deliberately abducted. It appeared that a closed and unmarked carriage had hurtled along the street whilst the children were crossing it, moving at such a fast pace that they had been forced to scatter in all directions to avoid being run over. All of the children could clearly recall Rosie being amongst their number prior to that but no one had seen her since.

'It is no good, Felix,' conceded Luke wearily, as yet another of his men reported back negatively. 'I am convinced that she has been taken and that it has something to do with that carriage.'

'Yes, but who do you imagine might be responsible? Surely not one of that bastard of a landlord's former customers?'

'Unlikely. If one of those scapegraces wanted another child why go to the trouble of trying to abduct one as well protected as Rosie? You know as well as I how easily they could find another elsewhere.'

'True enough. Do you imagine that Rosie was simply taken by chance then? An opportunistic abduction?'

'Possibly. It would be extremely difficult to target one particular child amongst so many with any likelihood of success.'

'Unless you drive a carriage fast through the middle of them and specifically watch the child you are interested in.'

'Exactly! And if that child was known to always to carry a rag doll, that would surely make her easier to identify?'

'Which would mean it was Rosie that they specifically wanted. But why?'

'That, my friend, is a very good question.'

Luc and Felix fell silent, searching their minds for an adequate explanation. Luc was finding it increasingly difficult to hide his frustration, his mounting concern and his anger. Rosie had been under his indirect protection. That made this outrage personal. He was aware also that for every hour she remained missing, she could be taken further and further away from the capital and could, even now, be facing heaven alone knew what horrors.

Luc smashed his fist against the desk, but it did little to relieve his feelings of impotence. Why Rosie, for God's sake, and why now? The fact that she was a particular favourite of his made her disappearance all the more difficult to rationalize.

He shuddered as well when he contemplated Clarissa's horrified reaction when she learned of Rosie's disappearance. But the prospect of her distress at least had the effect of snapping Luc out of his inertia. His befuddled brain cleared and he found himself able to think lucidly again. With the return of his rationality, the ghost of a suspicion occurred to him: a suspicion which should have been obvious to him long before now. He sat a little straighter and attempted to put it into words.

'Whoever took Rosie,' he said slowly to Felix, 'did so, I believe, because they knew of my particular affection for her.'

'So you think whoever took her did so to revenge themselves against you for some reason. But who would even contemplate doing such a vile thing? Who would use a little girl merely to get back at you?'

'You have a penchant for good questions today, Felix.'

'Whom have you upset of late?'

'Humph, care to take your pick?'

A commotion outside the office caused both gentlemen to look up. The door opened to reveal Simms, dishevelled and out of breath.

'Good God, Simms, whatever is the matter?'

'Forgive me, my lord, but I almost lamed your horse getting here as quickly as I could!' He clasped a hand to his chest and bent himself double as he attempted to regain both his breath and his composure.

'Calm down, Simms, and tell me what has occurred to distress you so.' Luc was really concerned now. For Simms to move in anything other than the most dignified of manners was rare, but for him to appear with his apparel askance was quite simply unheard of.

'It is Lady Hartley, my lord.'

Luc jumped to his feet, as agitated now as Simms. 'Is she harmed? What is it, man? What has happened to her? Tell me!' He grasped Simms's shoulder and almost shook it out of its socket.

'Luc!'

Felix's voice brought Luc back to his senses and he released his hold on his valet. 'Tell me at once!' Luc clasped his hands behind his back to conceal the fact that they were shaking.

'Bentley informs me that a package was delivered for her ladyship just before her return from church, my lord. Bentley gave it to her as soon as she returned home and she took it to her chamber to open. Shortly thereafter she came flying back down the stairs, rushed out into the street and climbed straight into a closed carriage which was waiting there and which drove off immediately she was inside.'

'Dear God, no!' Luc fell back down into his seat, clutching his head in his hands.

'I did try to prevent her, my lord, but she

was deaf to my pleadings.'

'If she was intent upon her purpose then I can imagine that she would have been. Have you any idea what made her go off like that?'

'Caroline found this note on her chamber floor, my lord.'

'What? Why did you not say so before?' Luc snatched the note from Simms's hand and read it rapidly. 'But I still do not understand. Why would this make her go tearing off? An anonymous note?' Too agitated to read it properly, he handed it to Felix, more concerned and mystified than ever.

'Look, Luc, the note mentions a doll.'

'Indeed, my lords, Lady Hartley was clutching the contents of the package when she made her flight. It was a rag doll.'

'Rosie!' agreed Luc and Felix in unison.

'Well, that answers your question, Felix. It must be Twining and Salik who have Rosie and they are using her as bait to tempt Clarissa there.'

'But how can they have known that she was at home without you?'

'They must have watched me dash off to the orphanage when Rosie was reported missing. It seems I have played right into their hands.'

'Maybe, but how would they know of

Clarissa's attachment to Rosie? Your connection to this place is not common knowledge: much less Rosie's particular appeal.'

'They have obviously been watching us and I was too preoccupied to notice.' He thumped his fist into the palm of his other hand and swore profusely. 'We were so busy watching them that we did not think they could be returning the favour.' Luc snorted disdainfully. 'And I thought I was being so artful.'

'But even if that is so, Luc, for what purpose would they want to lure Clarissa away from home?' One look at Luc's expression was sufficient to make Felix regret his question.

'I can only hope, Felix,' responded Luc as he gathered up his hat and gloves, 'that they have somehow gained intelligence of our discoveries in Portsmouth and in their desperation think to persuade Clarissa out of her lands by threatening harm to Rosie. Come, my friend, there is no time to lose.'

'But where will they have taken them?'

'To Twining's office in Lincoln's Inn, of course.'

'Are you sure? Why not to his lodgings?'

'Because Lincoln's Inn will be deserted on a Sunday, whereas the residents of his lodging house are all likely to be at home. Remember that nosy landlady we discovered? Any distressed sounds from children or women,' said Luc, his jaw tightening in anger, 'would undoubtedly draw her attention. Come, we are bound for Lincoln's Inn, there is not a moment to spare. Are you with me?'

'Of course!' Felix picked up his own hat.

'Simms!'

'My lord?'

'Inform Mrs Fielding that Rosie is found and will shortly be restored to her. Call off the men's search and send them home. You are to return to Grosvenor Square immediately and reassure the household. Do not reveal any more than is absolutely necessary. I do not wish Lady Deverill to be any more distressed by these unfortunate events than she undoubtedly already is.'

'Very good, my lord, but . . . ' Simms hesitated, unwilling to criticize his master but fearful for his safety, found the courage to go on, 'would it not be better if I, and some of the men, were to accompany you?'

'Oh no, Simms,' said Luc, smiling tightly. 'Lord Western and I can handle Salik and Twining. In fact, I have been waiting for just such opportunity.'

★  ★  ★

Clarissa looked about her with what she hoped would pass for an imperious and detached air. The reality of her situation was fast coming home to her. She was here, in the middle of Lincoln's Inn, on a Sunday morning. She was certain that there would be no one else about. Twining and Salik had selected the timing for this abduction with obvious care. She had left no word of where she was going or, indeed, why she had departed Grosvenor Square so precipitately.

She could appreciate now the full extent of her folly in entering a strange carriage alone. Luc's reaction, when he heard of it, did not bear thinking about. But, in her own defence, she could honestly say that seeing the doll had been a real shock that had temporarily deprived her of the ability to think rationally. Instead, her only concern had been for Rosie's undoubted plight. No thought regarding her own safety had so much as crossed her mind, not even for one minute. But now, as she looked about her and her wits were restored to her, she had ample opportunity to appreciate the full extent of her foolhardiness.

There was Simpson, across the room from her, his face still expressionless as he stood guard over a sobbing Rosie. Clarissa observed for the first time his blank, hostile eyes, the cruel twist to his lips, and did not have the slightest doubt that he would do whatever Twining or Salik asked of him, without emotion or pity. The very thought made her shudder inwardly but she disguised the fact as best she could. Showing any weaknesses before her captors would, she instinctively knew, be a grave miscalculation.

Every instinct Clarissa possessed told her that if she was to survive this situation, she must somehow find a way to gain the upper hand and, to do that, she must remain defiant and make full use of the advantages at her disposal. But what were those advantages? She obviously could not overpower her strong and determined captors; she had no weapon about her and was in no position to call for help. So where did that leave her? Think Clarissa, think!

Focusing her mind on her dilemma, Clarissa came to the conclusion that her only weapons were her femininity, her elevated position within society and her wits, which were undoubtedly sharper than those of her captors. Not much when faced with three ruthless men, but Clarissa did not have the slightest doubt that if she and Rosie were to prevail then she must, somehow, make full use of them.

Mr Twining was standing behind his desk observing her closely, his expression now

341

under closer guard and difficult for Clarissa to fathom. She thought she detected regret there and something else too: apprehension perhaps? But she got the feeling that any power he might have once possessed had long since been wrested from him. He was no longer the main player in this drama and it was Salik, brutal and determined, who was the driving force.

She turned her attention to her stepson. He was standing at her side, leering malevolently. What should have been a reasonably handsome face was twisted and made ugly by bitterness and resentment. Clarissa suspected that, even in these dire circumstances, he was attempting to play the part of the gentleman he so desperately wanted to become. She almost laughed aloud at the thought, despite her plight. Gentlemen were born not created and even if he did, somehow, manage to swindle her out of her fortune, Clarissa knew that mere money alone would never in itself be sufficient reason for Salik to be accepted into good society. If nothing else, her time in the *ton* and the endless mornings spent in the company of the grand dames, had taught her at least that much. This realization bolstered her spirit and gave her fresh hope.

Clarissa reminded herself that she, at least, was a lady. All right then, she would use that circumstance to her advantage. She did not know yet quite how she would go about it but one thing she did know was that she must, under no circumstances, reveal to Salik the full extent of her fear. It could prove to be fatal. She was used to men trying to bully and cheat her over business matters in Northumberland. They seemed unable to comprehend that a mere woman could make a success of farming and came to the erroneous conclusion that she must have more money than sense and therefore be ripe for the taking. They had though, to a man, eventually discovered just how misguided they were.

Clarissa thought longingly of Luc. She was fairly sure that he had not been at home when she and Aunt Marcia returned from church. She did not need to be able to actually see him in order to detect his presence: somehow she had just known that he had not been there. Despite the large number of people living under his roof, the house somehow felt empty without his compelling and all powerful presence. She wondered, somewhat desperately, where he had gone and when he could reasonably be expected to return.

Then, the faintest glimmer of hope surfaced as she recalled Simms's anguished cries ringing in her ears when she made her anxious flight from the house. She recalled how he had behaved when Salik had called, uninvited, at Grosvenor Square. Simms always knew where his master was and Clarissa suspected that Luc had charged him with keeping an eye on her. The thought had previously annoyed her — but not anymore.

The note. Of course! She had dropped it on the floor of her chamber in alarm. Surely Caroline would have found it long before now and passed it on to Simms? That being the case, Simms would have wasted no time in getting word to Luc. But no, that was no good either. The note did not say where she was going and she did not think that anyone had seen her with Annie, so how would Luc know where to look for her? Clarissa's spirits plummeted, along with her fleeting hopes, as she realized afresh that she was on her own. Luc would be frantic with worry by now but how could he possibly know to start looking for her here?

Unless? Unless he remained calm and took the time to reason the matter through? Who else in London, other than Twining and Salik, would be desperate enough to attempt to kidnap her? The more she considered the matter, the more obvious it appeared and she could only wonder at her own denseness in not seeing it earlier. Yes, that surely must be the case. Luc would fathom it out and come to her rescue. All he needed was time and somehow she must find a way to gain it for him. Dissimulation, prevarication and circumvention, delaying tactics in other words, were most definitely called for.

'Well, my lady,' said Salik pleasantly, 'at last we find ourselves able to discuss the business that lies unsettled between us but this time without unwarranted intervention from uninvolved strangers.'

'Indeed, yes, Mr Salik,' she responded, sitting ramrod straight and bestowing a friendly smile upon the odious man. This surprised Salik, who had doubtless expected a continuation of her earlier contempt and she could tell that it had left him wondering how to react to such unexpected civility. Clarissa silently congratulated herself and vowed to continue in like vein. It would be difficult for him to react violently when faced with the genteel manners that he so obviously admired. Her suspicions were confirmed when Salik continued to look at her in silent confusion. Clarissa grabbed at the advantage she had created. 'But before we do so, perhaps we could take some tea? The church service this morning was especially tedious and the interior of the church impossibly arid.'

Clarissa made the suggestion of tea as

though it was the most reasonable course of action in the world, leaving Salik little room to dissemble. Hiding her anxiety, she offered him a sunny smile and, after what seemed like an eternity, he returned it with an ingratiating grin of his own.

'But of course, ma'am.' He made her a slight bow. 'Simpson!' He snapped his fingers imperiously. 'See to it at once!'

'But what about the child?' Rosie, who had fallen silent, obligingly commenced screaming once again.

'Why do you not let her come and sit with me until tea has been cleared away?' suggested Clarissa amiably. 'I am sure I will be able to quieten her.' Clarissa held Salik's gaze. Since reaching the conclusion that he was the person whom she should humour she had spoken to no one else, other than Rosie.

'By all means.'

Rosie, at a signal from Clarissa, scampered across the room. Clarissa lifted her onto her lap and cuddled her, holding her trembling body tightly against her own. So far, so good. Salik had done everything she had asked of him without question. And now it would take time for Simpson to make the tea and she would ensure that when it was finally served she and Rosie took an eternity to drink it. That could buy them as much as half an

346

hour, which could prove decisive for Luc. If Salik had the temerity to try and rush them, then Clarissa would just have to try and charm him into submission. She suspected that he was susceptible to flattery and, given the precariousness of their situation, she was not above playing upon that fact to gain them the time they needed.

Racking her brains, Clarissa kept up a constant stream of conversation as they awaited the arrival of the tea. The problem which confronted her though was that there were so many subjects it would be infinitely better not to mention. Northumberland was out of the question: as was her animal husbandry. Anything to do with Luc was likely to inflame Salik's volatile temper, and asking him about his life in Egypt would only bring to mind the subject of his father.

Eventually Clarissa took a leaf out of her godmother's book and chatted animatedly, passing on snippets of society gossip, giving the impression that she thought Salik would know the people involved. Amazingly, he appeared pleased that she would consider conversing thus with him and took a great interest in the news she imparted, often interrupting her to clarify names and relationships. He appeared particularly pleased when she mentioned the names of some of the most prominent people in Town. For the first time ever Clarissa was grateful to Marcia for her ability to chatter about nothing, at the same time making it sound both salacious and entertaining. She was sure that never before had this trait been put to better use. She dug deep within her memory and extracted every last vestige of juicy gossip she had bothered to take in, not hesitating to improvise and embellish remorselessly.

She told him of their visit to the opera the previous week and the activity in a box opposite their own. Suzanna had explained to her that it was occupied by Harriette Wilson, a famous courtesan and former leader of the *demi-monde*.

'She was with Henry Brougham, the lawyer and inventor of the carriage, which bears his name, you understand.' At a nod from Salik, Clarissa continued. 'Mrs Wilson, it would appear, had been under the protection of Lord Worcester at one time. Lord Worcester, as you will know, Mr Salik, is the Duke of Beaufort's heir. Anyway, it seems Worcester's association with Harriette ended badly when he did not pay her the annuity he had promised her. She gained her revenge by publishing his letters, which naturally caused all manner of scandal. Brougham, you will recall, unsuccessfully defended Mrs Clarke, the Duke of York's former mistress, against libel and is a great friend of Mrs Wilson's.'

'This is a most fascinating account, Lady Hartley,' said Salik, with oily sincerity and a twisted smile, when Clarissa's words slowed. 'Pray continue.'

'Indeed, I was just getting to the best part. Beware of courtesans with wit and a scorching pen is the moral of the story, would you not agree, Mr Salik? It seems that Mrs Wilson was constantly short of funds, not knowing the meaning of economy, if you understand me. She wrote of her dealings with other gentlemen but offered them the opportunity to purchase their way out of her publications. Many did so but it seems that one of her long time lovers, Arthur Wellesley, told her to 'publish and be damned!' Just goes to show that you cannot intimidate a great soldier, I suppose.

'Anyway, I digress. Where was I? Oh yes, about the opera. Well, the most entertaining part about it all, Mr Salik, was that the Beauforts were in the box directly opposite and had to spend the entire evening facing Mrs Wilson. It was too delicious!' Clarissa gave a convincing parody of the laughter she had heard that evening, as people admired Mrs Wilson's nerve, laughed at Worcester's discomfort and generally enjoyed the situation enormously.

Clarissa had thought at the time she was possibly the only person present who enjoyed the drama being performed on the stage more than the one being enacted in the auditorium.

'Poor Lord Worcester looked as though he was about to have apoplexy. Mind you, I felt sorry for his little wife. After all, it was hardly her fault. And as for the duke, well . . . his face was scarlet but, to give him his due, he sat it out. He is clearly a gentleman not given to intimidation and stubbornly refused to leave until the end of the performance. It was really too amusing.'

Salik sat beside her, laughing and encouraging her to say more. When she finally ran out of gossip she changed the subject to himself — a topic she had always found men more than happy to expand upon — this one clearly being no exception. He appeared content to respond to her polite enquiries in a tone as amiable as her own. She observed him obliquely as he visibly relaxed in her company, arrogantly considering, she imagined, that his charm had brought about the change in her.

She discovered that he liked what he had seen of England, excepting for the climate, which he found to be damp and depressing. Salik was of the opinion that he was suited to a life in England and did not doubt he would fit in splendidly. Clarissa's heart sank as she learned of his intention to remain. It could only mean one thing: he intended, by whatever means necessary, to procure his father's lands for himself.

A crashing of tea cups and the eventual rattling of a tray being carried alerted Clarissa to the fact that the refreshments were being brought into the office.

'Ah good!' she exclaimed brightly. 'I cannot tell you how welcome this will be, Mr Salik. How kind of you to suggest it. I have had nothing since breakfast.'

'Then please pour for us,' he responded, with a suggestively intimate smile, which made Clarissa's insides crawl. But the refined tone of voice he had adopted strengthened her resolve. She had not heard him speak thus on any other occasion. He was obviously attempting to ingratiate himself with her and imitate her upper-class accent, a realization which gave Clarissa encouragement. All the same, the strain was starting to tell upon her. Her head was thumping with a tense headache: her brain less and less equal to the task of coming up with further ideas for procrastination. If Luc was coming he had better make it soon.

Clarissa handed round cups of tea and smiled at the little girl curled on her lap.

'Come along, Rosie darling, will you not drink a little tea?'

'I want to go home!' Tears were suspiciously close. Clarissa could hardly blame the poor little scrap; she felt like crying with frustration too.

'Soon, darling, I promise you. Now just drink a little for me, like a good girl. Do you think Annie would like some tea too?'

Salik stood up, his tone of voice and mood having undergone a sudden reversal. 'Come, come, Lady Hartley!' His gentlemanly façade had abruptly been replaced with an impatient yet fiercely determined expression. 'Do not imagine I cannot see what you are about. This amusing little charade on your part, although vastly entertaining, will do you no good. No one knows where you are and no one will come to your rescue so you would do well to put the idea out of your head and focus your attention on me instead.'

'I am at a loss to understand you, sir.' Clarissa hid her concern with difficulty and sipped daintily at her tea. She was alarmed by the sudden change in him, at his violent mood swing. She knew not what had prompted it and was no longer quite so confident that she could handle the situation.

'Do not take me for a fool, my lady.'

'Salik!' Twining spoke for the first time.

'Where are your manners?'

Salik laughed aloud and turned to look at Twining, a mixture of anger and contempt flashing from his eyes. 'You English astound me. You stab one another in the back without a second thought, casually dally with one another's wives and take any number of other liberties, but if one dares to be impertinent, or, God forbid, if one should forget to offer tea, it is as though the world will end.'

'There is always room in this world for good manners, Mr Salik,' remarked Clarissa with wilful condescension, unable to help herself from deliberately agitating Salik.

'Perhaps, but enough of this I say!' He swung round impatiently. 'Simpson, clear this mess away and we will get down to business.'

Clarissa sat in silence. Her ploy had indeed gained her half an hour but she was unsure now if it would do her any good. It was obvious that Salik would not stand any further delays and anyway, Clarissa no longer felt quite so confident about Luc's imminent arrival. Supposing he was out for the entire day and Simms did not know where he was? But she steadfastly dismissed that notion, refusing to entertain such defeatist thoughts. If she and Rosie were to survive this exceedingly perilous situation — a situation which was being controlled by a dangerously unbalanced individual — then she needed to remain alert and keep her wits about her. She consoled herself with the thought that Salik would eventually make a mistake and when he did she would be poised to regain the advantage. Wallowing in self-pity would achieve nothing.

Simpson returned to the room and looked expectantly at Salik.

'Take the child back across the room,' he ordered.

Simpson attempted to grab Rosie by the wrist. She howled and spat at him like a wild cat and clung to Clarissa.

'Allow me,' said Clarissa calmly. Without waiting for a response, she carried Rosie across the room and sat her gently back on her chair. Ignoring Simpson, she knelt down and whispered words of encouragement to her: assured her that they would soon be going home and that she must be a brave little girl until they did. It appeared to work. Rosie hugged Annie close to her thin little chest and sat in silence, once again rocking vacantly back and forth.

'Now, Mr Salik,' said Clarissa, calmly resuming her seat. 'What did you wish to discuss with me that necessitated such dramatic measures to get me here alone on a Sunday morning?'

'Do not play the innocent with me, Clarissa.' He leered at her. 'You know very well what this is about.'

'Indeed, sir, you are quite mistaken.'

'All right then, my dear, we will play it your way. I know all about your friends' little trip to Portsmouth and what they discovered there. Unfortunate that, but no matter.' His pleasant tone of voice turned without warning into a petulant whine: a child deprived of a favourite toy and determined to throw a tantrum. 'If Deverill had not interfered everything would have been settled by now!' He fisted his hand and crashed it against the wall. 'Those are my lands and I intend to have them.'

'On the contrary, Mr Salik, they are nothing to do with you and no magistrate in this land is likely to uphold a fraudulent will.'

The calm confidence in Clarissa's tone, her casually dismissive attitude towards his claims, appeared to anger him even more. 'Of course they are mine! My father loved me; I am his only son: I am entitled to them.'

'You are entitled to nothing, Mr Salik,' responded Clarissa dismissively. 'I did not even know of your existence before Mr Twining drew my attention to it. If your father really had intended you to inherit, do you not think he might have taken the trouble to mention the fact to me?'

'Perhaps he did?'

'Are you questioning my integrity, sir?'

'Are you questioning mine?'

'Yes!' The time for appeasement was past.

A deathly silence fell upon the room. Salik's face darkened with rage and his breathing became laboured and ragged. His temper was reflected in his thunderous expression as he stood over her, clenching his fists threateningly.

'Oh dear, Mr Salik, if you are aspiring to become a gentleman you really must learn to control your temper in front of a lady.' Clarissa looked up at him, her countenance as calm and serene as her quietly spoken words: a complete contrast to his tumultuous anger. She knew it was dangerous to deliberately bait him thus, but she did not care for bullies and was not about to give in to this one as easily as he might imagine.

But once again his reaction surprised her. Her calm words and dignified demeanour appeared to strike a cord with him. He took a deep breath and made a huge effort to control his temper.

'My apologies, Clarissa, I forgot myself for a moment.' He made her a slight, apologetic bow. 'But no matter, this is what I propose. You continue to work the land as before on my behalf and I will not interfere.'

'And that is it?' enquired Clarissa incredulously. 'We can prove that you are a fraudster, a cheat and a liar but you still consider that I will countenance some sort of partnership with you?'

'You appear to be forgetting one small factor,' he countered smoothly, nodding in the direction of Rosie, who was still rocking herself gently, crying quietly and staring vacantly into space.

'Mr Salik, really! I credited you with more intelligence than that. You can hardly keep the child captive forever and as soon as you release her I will tell the world what you have done.'

'Of course I can keep the child! Who is to miss her? She has no family and the institution in which she lives will not have the time or resources to search for her. She will soon be forgotten. Perhaps I will keep her for myself,' he said, in a mildly considering tone, 'or then again I could sell her on.'

'You fiend!'

'The decision lies entirely with you, Lady Hartley.' It was Salik now whose voice was calm with reason.

Clarissa looked at him contemptuously. She was now convinced that he was evil — and extremely dangerous — for she did not have the slightest doubt that he held Rosie's life in as scant regard as he intimated.

'You seem to have overlooked the fact that I have powerful connections, Mr Salik,' she said at last, pulling herself up to her full height. 'Connections who know of your intended fraud and can prove it in an instant.'

'It is only fraud, Clarissa, if I attempt to steal the land from you. If you sign the document that I have prepared, surrendering the lands to me voluntarily, then there will be no crime to answer for.'

'Except blackmail, intimidation and kidnapping,' she countered sarcastically. But this only produced a charming smile from Salik.

'Except for those trifling matters,' he agreed casually.

'Even if I did sign the document I could prove later than it was done under duress. I think the courts would be more than sympathetic to my plight.'

'Not if you read the wording of my document. You see, you have discovered how much my father loved me and knew he intended for me to have the lands but he was too unwell to draw up the necessary document before he died. Twining here was privy to his wishes, is that not so?'

Twining simply nodded his head, fidgeted in his chair and looked more uncomfortable and miserable than ever.

'And naturally,' continued Salik, 'having met me, you were overcome with remorse at not abiding by your beloved husband's wishes and decided you could not live with yourself unless you set matters straight.'

'You will never get away with it!' Clarissa expostulated, far less sure of herself now.

Salik was cunning and resourceful and appeared to have thought it all through very carefully, leaving Clarissa feeling unsure about how to extract herself from this mess without further risk to Rosie.

'You have not asked where you fit into my plans, Clarissa,' continued Salik pleasantly. 'No matter, I will tell you anyway. You, my dear, will continue to look after the sheep that you adore so much. But I cannot possibly permit you to ride all over the place, all day long: astride your horse no less! Charming though you doubtless look, it would never do.' At Clarissa's astounded expression he merely smiled. 'Oh, I know all about your activities, my dear, never fear. No, you will direct others according to your wishes, maintain the estates' accounts and honour me with the rest of your time.

'Naturally,' he continued conversationally, 'you will warm my bed. I might even decide to marry you, if you please me sufficiently.'

He nodded significantly in the direction of her body. 'Not that you could fail in that respect but, who knows, I might tire of you after a while. you might find my demands a little more insistent than my late, lamented father's, but I dare say you will grow accustomed to them in due time and even come to enjoy them. Oh, and naturally, I will expect you to show your appreciation and obedience towards me at all times.'

'Mr Salik,' said Clarissa, her voice resonating with a combination of anger and disgust, 'let us be clear about one matter: regardless of the future of *my* lands I will never, understand me, *never*, be intimate in any way whatsoever with you. Do we understand one another, sir?'

'Clarissa.' Salik walked up behind her and slid his hand over her shoulder, allowing it to come to rest on her breast. 'If you know what is good for you, you will do exactly as you are told. And believe me, my dear, you will enjoy it. You will enjoy it, you will thank me and you will beg me for more. Now, do you understand me, madam?' His fingers closed around her breast, hard and possessively. 'Ah, yes!' he sighed, closing his eyes briefly. 'I think you will be able to give me everything I was hoping for.'

Clarissa gritted her teeth, guessing that if

she showed the revulsion she was feeling it would merely serve to spur him on.

'Unhand me, sir!' she commanded, with as much authority as she could muster, when she could bare his insolence no longer. But he merely smiled at her and clamped his fingers even more savagely about her flesh.

# 18

Arriving in record time at Lincoln's Inn, Luc and Felix were rewarded with the sight of a closed carriage standing outside Twining's office: confirmation that Luc's deductive powers had not deserted him.

'They are here! That must be their carriage. You were right, Luc.'

'Indeed! Fortunately for us Salik is not blessed with much originality of thought.'

'How do we proceed now?'

'I think the time for caution is long past. Any delay on our part could result in harm being done to Rosie or Clarissa, or both. Let us get in there.'

'Lead on!'

The outer door to the office was bolted from the inside, causing Luc to slap his thigh in frustration. He should have anticipated that and come prepared.

'That bolt appears to be sturdy. What do we do now?'

Luc's attention was focused upon a small window, to the right of the door. 'Do you remember that time at school when we managed to get ourselves locked in the cricket pavilion?'

'Y-yes, and I recall we eventually managed to escape without detection, but I do not remember how?'

'We forced the window.'

'Of course! Are you carrying your dagger, Luc?'

Luc shook his head, frustrated by his loss of incisiveness. 'Naturally!'

Armed with Luc's dagger it was the work of a moment for them to force the window open. Felix, being slightly the smaller of the two, crawled silently through and opened the main door to Luc. They stood motionless in the outer office and heard voices emanating from Twining's office. Luc squared his shoulders.

'As I said outside, the time for stealth is past. Are you ready, my friend?'

Felix nodded, his demeanour as grim as Luc's.

Luc took a deep breath and kicked the office door open. It slammed against the wall with a satisfying crash and caused everyone in the room to look towards it.

'My lord!' Clarissa half rose from her chair but was forced back down again by Salik's hand, once again on her shoulder. 'There you are at last,' she continued brightly. 'What kept you for so long? Rosie and I have been most anxious.'

'My apologies for the delay, Clarissa,' he responded in like vein, 'I trust you have not been too inconvenienced by it?' He moved calmly towards her.

'Stay where you are, Deverill!' commanded Salik.

'Or what?'

Salik inclined his head in Rosie's direction. Simpson was now forcibly restraining her from rushing towards Luc and Felix. 'Or just one of Simpson's hands will break her little neck with ease. It is the sort of thing he enjoys doing.'

Simpson gave the ghost of a smile and moved his hand casually in the direction of Rosie's neck.

'Do that, Salik,' said Luc, his voice low and unmistakably threatening, 'and there will not be a rock large enough for you to crawl beneath.'

'Huh, do not dare to threaten me with your attitude of superiority. I have the upper hand now. I am in control here.'

Luc shrugged. 'It sounds as though you are unsure about that and need to convince yourself,' he remarked languidly.

Salik moved away from Clarissa and addressed the newcomers, refusing to rise to Luc's bait, switching his attitude instead to that of English gentleman. 'Since you are here

I have no objection to sharing with you the agreement that I have just reached with Lady Hartley. She will sign over to me all that is mine by rights and in return she will be permitted to continue with her work on the land.'

'Nonsense!'

Luc's casual dismissal of Salik's plans appeared to enrage the Egyptian. He turned on his heel and faced the room, his face puce with anger, desperation and an air of madness about his wild eyes. 'Nonsense, is it? Well, let me tell you that I am ten times the man you will ever be! My father loved me and intended that I should inherit all that was rightfully mine.'

'Then why did he not make that provision?' enquired Luc, even more calmly.

'Because he died before he was able to do so.'

'And why did he not bring you to England and recognize you as his heir.'

Salik faltered for the first time since Luc's arrival. His face slowly drained of all colour. 'Because of the ridiculous rules governing your society,' he snapped, his previous confidence no longer in evidence. 'I am as good as any of you but could I be accepted as your equal? Oh no, I am not the son of an English lady, neither am I legitimate and that would never do.' His voice oozed sarcasm. 'But now, the time has finally come for my revenge.' He whirled round, a look of delirium in his eye. 'I will have what is rightfully mine. I will bring my mother over here to live as she should have been living for all these years and Clarissa can now dance attendance upon her.'

'Give it up, Salik.' Twining, forgotten by them all, spoke so unexpectedly that everyone started with surprise.

'You spineless cretin!' Salik looked as though he might strike him. 'This was all your idea but the moment difficulties arose you wanted to give it up.'

'You planned the whole thing, didn't you, Twining?' suggested Luc, his tone one of indifference.

'Yes he did.' Salik answered for him.

'You knew of Salik's existence and you knew that was what Sir Michael was sending money to Egypt for.'

'Yes.'

'Why?' asked Clarissa, anguish in her voice. 'Why would you do that to me, Mr Twining? I trusted you.'

He hung his head, unable to bear Clarissa's perplexed scrutiny.

'You needed protection,' he eventually muttered. 'I could think of no other way to persuade you to let me look after you.'

Luc snorted disgustedly.

'He approached me with the plan shortly after my father's death,' explained Salik, with a shrug. 'I received a letter from him inviting me to London and enclosing the fare. When I arrived he suggested the whole scheme to me. He knew where we could get a will drawn up, but he needed me to ensure that the Arabic was correct and that we had not overlooked anything obvious. We thought, of course, that Lady Hartley was alone and unprotected,' he added accusingly, too preoccupied to notice the dangerous tightening of Luc's jaw. 'Needless to say, he was to profit from the scheme as well, but only if his preferred line did not work. You wanted her to marry you, I think?' Twining looked at Salik in apparent surprise but remained sullenly silent. 'You made the mistake of taking me for a fool as well, Twining. But as soon as I met the beautiful Clarissa and saw the way you looked at her I knew that must have been your primary objective. But you were not certain of success, were you, and needed an alternative plan to fall back upon? That was where I came in. And in spite of everything that has gone wrong, we will still succeed. Things have gone too far now for us to withdraw.

'You see, we have friends in strange places it appears, who were happy to warn us of your discoveries in Portsmouth and that gave us time to plan this delightful little gathering today.' Salik picked up a letter from Twining's desk, the obvious source of their intelligence. Luc frowned. He had seen paper of that type before. It was good quality, thick cream and embossed with a distinctive border in gold script. 'And now, just as you arrived I was informing my dear stepmother of the details of our agreement. She will reside with me in Northumberland, manage the estates on my behalf and supply me with very diverting company.' Salik's hand moved to Clarissa's breast once again. Luc could take no more and went to lunge at Salik, who simply laughed and pulled Clarissa in front of him.

'Stay where you are, Deverill!' he warned. 'Now, where were we? Oh yes, regarding the pleasures in store for me.'

Once again, without warning, his mood swung from pleasantly relaxed to a towering rage: this time seemingly occasioned by Clarissa's contemptuous glare. Luc had no doubt that he was severely unbalanced, his resentful and spiteful character being long formed at the feet of a weak and devoted mother, who was powerless to temper his excesses.

'You will learn to respect and obey me, my lady. I should warn you that I enjoy inflicting pain and will not hesitate to do so if you force me into it.'

Clarissa was wearing her blue striped muslin gown. Salik placed his hand on the bodice and ripped so violently that he exposed her chemise, camisole and half of her breasts. Clarissa stood motionless, a cold look of contempt in her eye, which appeared to both excite and infuriate Salik. He grabbed Clarissa by her wrist and attempted to force her to her knees in front of him. 'Damn your superiority, madam, I demand that you show me the respect I deserve!'

Rosie, forgotten by them all, still sat in her chair. Simpson, intrigued by Salik's treatment of Clarissa and very obviously aroused by it as well, smirked sadistically and absently removed his restraining hand from Rosie's shoulder.

'N-o-ooo!' Rosie screamed like a banshee and, evading Simpson's belated efforts to catch her, dashed across the room, hurling herself forcefully at Salik. Everyone looked at her in surprise. Salik, momentarily frozen with shock and indecision, hastily released Clarissa and pushed her sharply away from him in order to deal with the approaching child. It was just the diversion that Luc had been waiting for and he hesitated not at all. In two strides he reached Salik and laid him out cold with one well aimed blow to his miserable jaw. Felix, sensing Twining would be no problem, dealt with the unprepared Simpson in a similar way.

Relieved beyond belief that everything had been concluded so successfully, Luc looked towards Clarissa, ready to pick her up and take her home. But instead, what he saw caused him to gasp in dismay and his heart to miss a beat. It was as though time had been suspended and Luc could not, for a moment, believe what he was seeing with his own eyes. Clarissa had hit her head on the corner of Twining's desk when Salik pushed her so roughly aside. She lay on the floor in a dead faint, a pool of blood beneath her head. She was not moving and, as far as an anguished Luc could ascertain, was not even breathing.

# 19

Clarissa opened her eyes cautiously, only to close them again immediately. The pain in her head was unbearable, a rhythmic pounding at her temple, which was even harder to endure with open eyes. But closing them was no good either: it simply made the room spin. She needed to know where she was and what was happening to her. Steeling herself for a fresh bout of pain she cautiously forced her eyelids upwards for a second time. Everything appeared fuzzy and she still had no idea where she was. Feeling cautiously about her she discovered she was lying on a couch of some sort and someone was holding something welcomingly cool against her forehead. The room was warm and she could hear the gentle murmur of concerned voices about her.

'Ah, thank the Lord!' said a voice that sounded like Aunt Marcia's. 'I think she is coming round at last. Clarissa dear, are you all right?'

Clarissa looked about her, managing to focus a little better this time. Her gaze collided with two pairs of concerned-looking eyes: both of which were at the same level as her own. One pair undoubtedly belonged to Rosie, who was sitting cross-legged on the floor and staring at her steadily, a worried frown creasing her brow. The second pair lived in a black shaggy head, from which a long pink tongue protruded. Mulligan. What were Rosie and Mulligan doing sitting so closely together? Mulligan was an unpredictable dog. Surely it was not safe to leave him alone with a small, unwary child?

'Where am I?' she asked in a distant voice, which sounded most unlike her own. In response the figure she now realized she had been unconsciously searching for all along came into focus and, bending down beside Rosie, took her hand.

'You are home now at Grosvenor Square, Clarissa, and quite safe.' Luc smiled at her, that meltingly gentle, heart rending smile he appeared to reserve just for her. 'How do you feel?'

'My head is pounding.'

'It will soon heal, my love.' Caroline's voice came from above her head. It was clearly she who was responsible for the cold compress.

'What happened?'

'Can you not remember?' asked Luc, concerned that her memory did not appear to be returning along with her consciousness.

372

'Not really,' admitted Clarissa. 'But why is Rosie here? I am delighted to see her of course but . . . wait a minute, was there not something amiss with Rosie?' She frowned. Something was nagging at the back of her mind but she gave up attempting to recall what it was. Thinking required too much effort and was simply too painful. 'And why is Mulligan so close to Rosie? Is that safe, do you suppose?'

'Mulligan and Rosie have taken an inexplicable liking to each other and appear to be inseparable. As things stand at this moment it would take a braver man than I am to attempt to come between them.' Rosie placed her hand lovingly on Mulligan's head and cooed at him, as though to lend proof to Luc's words. Mulligan responded by pushing his head gently against her arm, seeking more attention, which Rosie seemed only too happy to bestow.

'Do you think you can sit up a little, my lady, and take some tea?' asked Caroline, all concern. 'I am sure it will make you feel better.'

Cautiously, Clarissa eased herself into a sitting position, efficiently assisted by Caroline. The room swam alarmingly at first and Clarissa grabbed at the arm of the couch for support but after a moment it all settled down again and she was able to look about her properly.

She was in the drawing-room of Luc's house. As well as the people she had already recognized, she was surprised to find Felix there as well and, even more surprisingly, Simms. As soon as she was sitting steadily, Rosie climbed onto the couch and snuggled her small body as close to Clarissa as she could manage. Lifting one arm, Clarissa smoothed back her hair and held her close. Mulligan meanwhile, dropped his shaggy head into her lap and gazed up at her with slave-like devotion.

'As you can see,' said Luc with a smile, knowing better than to suggest Rosie remove herself, 'we are all delighted to have you safely back with us.'

Clarissa sipped gratefully at a scalding cup of tea, under the watchful gaze of everyone else in the room. Finishing her second cup, she put it aside and demanded to know what had been going on. 'I remember now much of what occurred in Mr Twining's office but do not recall how I come to be at home.'

Seeing that Clarissa was not about to be denied, Luc addressed Caroline. 'Did I understand aright? Has cook just finished the baking?'

'I believe that to be the case, my lord,' she

answered with the sweetest of smiles.

'Then perhaps, Caroline, you would take Rosie and Mulligan into the kitchen to see if cook requires any assistance tasting the cakes.'

'Certainly, my lord. Come along little one,' she added with an encouraging smile, holding out her hand, 'I am sure cook will be grateful for your help.'

'Lady Hartley will not go to sleep again if I leave her?' asked Rosie anxiously.

'Do not worry, darling, I will be here when you get back.'

'Well, all right then,' agreed Rosie reluctantly after a lengthy pause, during which she appeared to be ponderously considering her options. The prospect of warm cakes straight from the oven finally winning out over her desire to remain with Clarissa, Rosie slipped her hand trustingly into Caroline's and they left the room together, Mulligan limping along at their heels.

Luc took up the position that Rosie had vacated at Clarissa's side and took her hand in his. If Marcia thought this improper she certainly did not say as much. Instead she simply beamed encouragement in the direction of her son. But Luc was blind to his mother's devices. Instead he was trying to decide how much to reveal to Clarissa of the events which occurred after she was pushed to the floor. One thing he knew he would never adequately be able to explain was the anguish, the gut-wrenching desolation, that had overtaken him when he had seen her lying on the floor and had thought her to be dead. There was a huge gash to her head, caused when she hit the corner of Twining's desk and her body had appeared lifeless. The sight of it had left him momentarily frozen with sheer terror: his mind overloaded with shock and raw, mind-numbing pain.

Felix had taken control. Salik and Simpson were both unconscious as well and Twining was proving to be no problem at all. Instead he was effusive with his protestations of innocence. He had not intended that matters should reach this sad impasse: he had been against the abductions all along but Salik would not listen to reason and had intimidated him into compliance.

Luc, busy attending to Clarissa, had merely glowered at him, disdain and withering contempt winning the battle to grace his features, and resisted the overwhelming desire to land a well aimed blow to his miserable face as well, but only with the greatest of difficulty. Clarissa was breathing, thank the Lord! That was all that mattered to him. Her head wound did not appear to be as serious as he had at first feared and, as his powers of reasoning returned, so he recalled that head wounds were notorious for bleeding profusely. He managed to staunch the flow of blood, his mind all the while considering what to do next. Should he risk moving Clarissa? And what of the three men who had perpetrated this act of savagery? He should have permitted Simms to send for the Runners after all. Luc was uncharacteristically indecisive.

Felix, with a sobbing Rosie cradled in his arms, touched his friend's shoulder. 'I think we should bind the hands of these three and lock them in the store room here,' he said emphatically. 'We can have the Runners here to take them in charge soon, but in the meantime I think we should get Clarissa and Rosie home to Grosvenor Square. Urgently, Luc,' he added, when Luc showed no signs of hearing him. The pressure of Felix's hand on his shoulder increased and Luc belatedly came to his senses.

'You are right, of course,' he agreed, jumping into action.

Having bound the fugitives, Luc draped his coat around Clarissa and carried her to his waiting curricle. Felix locked the store-room door and joined him in the conveyance, Rosie still firmly cradled in his arms.

Marcia, together with Caroline and Simms,

were waiting anxiously in the drawing-room for news, all disparity in rank forgotten at this time of crisis. Both women exclaimed in horror as they observed Luc's grim face and the seemingly lifeless body of Clarissa clutched in his arms.

But then Caroline took control. A bed of sorts was made up for Clarissa on a couch, close to the fire in the drawing-room — Marcia having decreed it would be warmer there as the fire would not yet be alight in her chamber. A footman was despatched to summon the apothecary. Upon examining his patient the medical man proclaimed that Clarissa, apart from the nasty cut just above her hairline and a severe concussion, did not appear to have suffered any permanent damage. The relief in the room was palpable. Luc concentrated all of his efforts on shutting out the abject agonies and feelings of self-recrimination which continued to plague him as he watched part of Clarissa's beautiful hair being cut away so that her wound could be properly cleaned and dressed. But then he remonstrated with himself. One small tress was of no consequence when measured against the fact that his future wife was alive, safe from harm and recovering her senses.

'What do you remember, sweetheart?' Luc asked her.

'Well, I am not sure.' She frowned with the effort it took her to cast her mind back to the events of the morning and winced at the stinging pain that ensued, leaving her feeling dizzy and disorientated. 'The last clear memory I have is of Salik losing his temper and grabbing hold of me.'

Luc's jaw tightened into a rigid line, his brow creased in anger, as he too recalled the incident and the feeling of complete impotence that had enveloped him. He slid a protective arm around Clarissa's shoulders.

'Yes, he tried to force you to your knees and I was powerless to do anything about it.' Luc clenched and unclenched the hand that rested on her shoulder. He stopped speaking and stared off into the distance, fighting an inner battle to bring his turbulent emotions under control. Alive to his torment, Clarissa reached across and took his hand. 'But Rosie felt no such reservations,' continued Luc, finding his voice again. 'She broke away from Simpson and ran at Salik, screaming her head off, surprising and distracting everyone.'

'Of course! I remember that now. But what happened afterwards?'

'Well, that gave me the opportunity I had been hoping for and I landed a hefty blow to Salik's head,' he said, with evident satisfaction.

'Good for you!'

'Yes, but unfortunately, when Rosie ran towards Salik, he pushed you out of the way. Your head hit the side of Twining's desk, which knocked you out. I thought he had killed you, Clarissa,' said Luc, his voice naked with emotion as he experienced, for the thousandth time, the cold fingers of fear that had paralysed him.

'Humph, it would take more than the likes of him to do away with me,' snorted Clarissa derisively. 'But how brave of Rosie. What made her behave thus, I wonder?'

Luc hesitated. 'That is partly why I sent her from the room. You see, Clarissa, we have no clear idea of what she endured before coming to the orphanage, but when she arrived she had considerable scarring to both wrists. We think the innkeeper, with whom she lived, punished any misdemeanours on her part by chaining her to a wall.'

'Oh dear God, the poor mite!'

'Yes, as you say. But be that as it may, we had been wondering how much she remembered about her previous life, as she has never once referred to it. Now we know. You see, m'dear, Salik grabbed you by your wrist too as he tried to force you down. It must have struck a chord with her. You know how much she admires you and she simply acted with

380

the instincts of a child. You represent security in her eyes and she wanted to protect you.'

'And possibly saved our lives into the bargain. What incredible bravery!'

'Indeed.'

'What I do not understand, Luc,' said Felix, 'is how they knew of your connection with Rosie in the first place.'

'Salik said something before you arrived about having followed us there on a couple of occasions,' said Clarissa. 'You will recall, Luc, that whenever we arrived all the children were pleased to see us but it was always Rosie who ran to us first.'

'Yes, that is true.'

'I have a question too, Luc,' said Clarissa into the silence that had fallen. 'Who was it who gave them prior notice of your discoveries in Portsmouth? Surely, no one else knew of them?'

'I can answer that one as well.' Luc's expression was grim. 'I recognized the paper when Salik held up the letter he had received. I have received several on that stationery myself: it is very distinctive. Emily Stokes!'

'What? Surely not?' gasped Marcia and Clarissa together. Felix's face drained of all colour and he looked uncomfortable.

'I am afraid so. I think when she was here on Friday and saw the three of us talking so animatedly, she finally realized that she was never going to achieve her objectives with me,' said Luc, with brutal frankness. 'I should have waited to tell you our news until after she had left, Clarissa.'

'Do not blame yourself, Luc,' said Clarissa, touching his hand again. 'You could not have anticipated her actions. And besides, I was too anxious to know what you had discovered to allow you to delay.'

'Maybe.' He smiled at her again gently, his eyes alight with love. 'And I was so anxious to put your mind at rest, and so pleased with our discoveries, that for once I dispensed with caution. I should have known better.'

'But how did she know so much?' asked Clarissa.

'Do you not remember? She was eaves-dropping quite blatantly. She must have gathered at least something of what we were saying. She certainly knew we had been to Portsmouth. Did she question you about it when you escorted her home, Felix?'

'Well, yes, and I am sorry to say that I told her one or two general things. I was simply making conversation, trying to mend bridges,' he said apologetically. 'I did not see any harm in it.'

'Why should you have?' Luc asked his friend.

'She asked me who the mysterious Mr Twining was that she had heard us discussing. I told her he was Clarissa's man of business, attending to her estate. That seemed to settle her curiosity and we then spoke of other matters.'

'But that would have been enough,' observed Luc. 'It would be the work of a moment to have one of her servants find his direction. His profession would naturally place him in Lincoln's Inn and that made it simple for her to carry out her spiteful act of revenge.'

Felix appeared devastated and hung his head. Clarissa smiled at him softly and took the opportunity to thank him for the part he had played in effecting their rescue.

'But you have not told me how you came to find me at Twining's office,' she continued, encompassing both Luc and Felix with her eyes as she spoke.

Luc explained Simms's role in that respect and the deductions they had made as a result.

'Of course! I am sorry, Simms, that I dashed off like that. I can see now that I should, at least, have appraised you of my intentions.'

'It might perhaps have been a wiser course of action, my lady,' agreed Simms, with a slight bow and the merest suggestion of a rare smile.

'Anyway, once I got there and realized what peril Rosie and I were in, I decided that you would definitely find us sooner or later and that the only thing I could do in the meantime was to procrastinate.' She went on to make the gentlemen laugh: telling them how she forced Salik to serve them with tea and then made polite conversation, as though being abducted was an everyday occurrence.

Luc shook his head in a mixture of wonder and admiration. 'You are impossible!'

Clarissa smiled back at him impishly and basked in the warmth of his admiration.

'And she should rest properly now as well,' put in Marcia. 'She has been though a great deal, the poor lamb.'

'Of course, Mother, you are right, as always.'

And before Clarissa could object Luc had swept her effortlessly into his arms once again and carried her up to her chamber, where he reluctantly left her to the tender ministrations of Caroline.

★ ★ ★

Luc put his head round the door again during the middle of the evening: a hopeful expression on his face. The scene that greeted him was one of orderly calm and sweet domesticity. Clarissa was fast asleep, her breathing sound and even. And so was Rosie, curled tightly against Clarissa's side, her small head resting on the same pillow as Clarissa's, their hair entwined. Mulligan was stretched out in front of the fire, large head resting on his equally large paws, eyes half closed. Caroline sat serenely in a chair by the fire, sewing in her lap.

'As you can see, my lord, all is well.'

'Indeed.' Luc felt ridiculously disappointed that Clarissa was obviously so soundly asleep. He had so much wanted to spend just half an hour talking with her, holding her hand and reassuring himself that she really would be all right.

'It would be as well to leave her be, my lord,' suggested Caroline gently.

'Yes, of course. But has she eaten?'

'Heartily!' said Caroline, causing them both to smile affectionately.

'How does Rosie come to be here in this room?'

'I could not get her to settle in the nursery alone. After all, the poor mite has never slept anywhere alone before: much less in an enormous room such as that. She would not settle unless I remained with her and obviously I needed to be here for her ladyship. This seemed to me to be the ideal solution.'

'And you were right, as always. Come now, Mulligan,' he continued, 'let us leave these ladies to their rest.'

Mulligan rose, with evident reluctance, from his warm fireside position and trotted towards his master. Luc's throaty chuckle filled the room, even though the door was already half closed behind him.

'So I've lost you to her as well have I, old boy?'

Caroline gave a satisfied smile, sniffing to clear eyes suddenly moist with tears. As she heard Luc address this remark to his dog any doubts she might have entertained about Clarissa ever finding a man truly worthy of her had finally been dispelled.

# 20

Clarissa was assured by the doctor the following morning that her concussion was fast receding, that her wound was not infected and would heal in due time. Only then did Caroline reluctantly relax her vigilant guard and permit her patient to leave her bed for a few hours.

Clarissa headed straight for the library. Well rested and with a clear head she was no longer prepared to delay the conversation which she knew she must have with Luc. She had decided that if he still wished to marry her then he must give her better reasons for his aspirations than heretofore. He must also tell her, without any prompting on her part, that he truly loved her and, just as importantly, he must promise to remain faithful only to her. If he could convince her of his sincerity in both those regards then she would willingly accept him.

Squaring her shoulders she tapped on the library door, feeling resolute and purposeful and yet also ridiculously nervous. If he was unable to give her the answers she sought then she was determined to make good her plan to return home immediately and banish from her mind for ever any thoughts of what might have been.

As she entered the library she was encouraged by the surprised and delighted expression on Luc's face, which served to both lift her spirits and strengthen her resolve.

'Clarissa! How are you feeling? Should you be out of bed, m'dear?' His concern for her welfare was all too obvious as he stepped across the room to greet her and, taking her hand, led her to the sofa in front of the fire. 'Now sit down at once and tell me what the doctor had to say?'

'Oh, Luc, do stop fussing so! He has given me permission to get up for a few hours. Had it not been so I would never have managed to get past Caroline, I do assure you.'

Luc smiled down at her. 'Yes, that I can believe! But how do you feel?'

'Better thank you and well rested. But, Luc, we need to talk.'

'We do indeed, sweetheart, but surely it must wait until you are fully recovered?'

'No, Luc,' she responded with renewed determination, 'now.'

'Oh dear, this sounds serious,' he said lightly. 'Are you sure you are well enough?'

'There is nothing wrong with my mind,'

she countered irascibly.

'All right, all right!' Luc held up his hands in mock surrender and grinned boyishly at her, but Clarissa was in no mood to fall victim to his seductive charm and would not return his smile.

'Luc, you asked me to marry you. Why?'

'Why?' He appeared confused by her question.

'Yes, why?'

'Well, for the reasons that I have already outlined. My admiration for you . . . and respect.' He faltered slightly, wondering what it was that she wished to hear and then reached for her, preferring to demonstrate his feelings in the way that came as second nature to him. But she put up her hands to ward him off, intent upon maintaining the distance between them. If he so much as touched her . . .

'No, Luc, I need to hear your reasons.' If he touched her she would relent, she just knew it. She was equally aware that if she met his all-seeing, penetrating gaze; if she allowed herself to be drawn in by his mesmerizing, ethereal eyes; she would be deaf to her inner voice of reason. Steadfastly she averted her gaze, concentrating her eyes in apparent fascination upon the rug at her feet, and awaited his response.

Stillness submerged the moment but Clarissa would not break the silence between them. She was determined that the next move should be his. Seeming to realize it, Luc spoke to her in a gentle, guileless tone.

'I want you to be the mother of my children.'

'And so you want to marry me just to beget an heir. Is that it?' She was not quite convincing in her disapproval — and she knew it.

'Of course not, Clarissa, what a thing to suggest. Surely you understand . . . '

An untimely knock at the door cut him off in mid flow. Exasperated, Luc bade his caller enter. Simms stepped into the room, looked surprised to see Clarissa there and, with an apologetic smile, enquired as to her health.

'I am much recovered, I thank you, Simms.'

'That is excellent news, my lady.'

'What is it, Simms?' barked Luc.

'Your pardon for the intrusion, my lord, but this letter was just delivered by express from Newbury. I thought it might be of some importance.'

'Thank you, Simms.'

Clarissa watched Luc as he opened his letter and scanned its contents. As he did so his whole demeanour changed. His jaw set in an angry line, something locked in the stern planes of his face and his expression became increasingly sombre as he continued to read.

'Start packing, Simms, we leave for Newbury immediately!'

'Very good, my lord.'

Simms silently left the room, not the slightest bit ruffled by this unexpected departure in their routine.

'Your pardon, Clarissa,' said Luc, his severe expression turning into a meltingly gentle look of regret as he regarded her once again, 'but we must postpone this discussion until my return. I shall not be gone above a week but this business cannot be delayed and there is no time for us to talk properly now.'

He pulled her to her feet and into his arms, closing them carefully about her, mindful of her delicate condition. His full, sensual mouth descended towards hers and he kissed her so gently but with such controlled passion that it sent a dizzying sensation of desire spiralling through her entire body, scattering her already turbulent emotions into even great disarray.

'You should return to your chamber and rest, m'dear,' he told her as he broke their kiss. 'Oh, damn this business, why now?' he added with an exasperated sigh, as he bent to kiss her one last time.

Clarissa left him and followed his advice. Even this short interview with him had tired her and she felt the need for repose. When she awoke several hours later she did not need to be told that Luc had already departed the house. She felt strangely vulnerable and alone somehow — which, she told herself, was ridiculous. But there was no escaping the fact that the house seemed eerily quiet and empty without his energetic and forceful presence, the lack of which it was obviously impossible for her to detect from within the confines of her own chamber but which she was still convinced she could sense.

In an attempt to seek diversion, Clarissa entered Luc's library in search of something to read. The room still bore signs of both his occupation of it and of his hurried departure. Papers had not yet been tidied away and the letter he had received, causing him such consternation and precipitating his abrupt flight to Newbury, still lay on his desk. Overcome with curiosity Clarissa could not resist the opportunity to peep at its contents — only to immediately wish that she had not done so.

It was penned in a lady's hand and begged Luc's immediate assistance, as the worst had happened and his correspondent, Beatrice Higgins, was afraid for herself. The letter was respectful and stopped short of requesting

Luc's actual physical presence. Clarissa wondered, just for a moment, who this Beatrice could be and what problems she could possibly have that caused Luc so much anger and had the power to cause him to drop everything and run to her aid.

Then she decided that if she was being so dense she must still be concussed. The brutal reality hit her then, reverberating around her brain like thunder. Obviously Beatrice was yet another of his mistresses. Presumably gentlemen with Luc's advantages in life had them conveniently stashed away close to all of their residences? Perhaps Beatrice's husband had discovered their dalliance, or someone inappropriate had found out the true nature of their relationship and was attempting to cause trouble. It surely must be something of that ilk to cause Luc to go dashing off so abruptly?

Realizing that Luc must have very strong feelings for the lady, if he was willing to obey her siren call so readily, drained her soul and a sheer physical pain, the likes of which she had never come close to experiencing before, ripped through her like a sabre. Clarissa felt as though her heart was withering within her breast and dying. Until that moment she had not realized just how much he meant to her and this confirmation of his duplicity twisted and tore at her insides, leaving her gasping for breath. The anguish and desolation she experienced at that moment caused her legs to buckle beneath her. She sat upon the sofa and, clutching her head in her hands, let out an agonized wail: the pain was simply too severe to be endured in silence or to be contained within her.

But letting it out did little to relieve her turbulent despair and finally she gave in and sobbed wretchedly until she had no tears left to cry.

Gathering herself together as best she could, Clarissa returned to her room and attempted to sleep. If Caroline saw her tear-stained face then explanations she did not care to make would be demanded. She excused herself from dining with Aunt Marcia, using her illness as a legitimate excuse, and merely picked at the delicious food which was sent to her room. As she did so her emotions underwent a marked change. Crying had rid her of the brief sentimentality she had permitted herself to entertain in respect of Luc and had replaced it with a slow, burning anger which she wrapped around her like a cloak, guarding her raw emotions and ensuring she did not again weaken and weep for something that could never be.

She fed her anger by dwelling upon Luc's motives. It was all so obvious now. Of course he would not change! He would continue to live his life just as he always had and she had played into his hands by assuring him that she disliked the capital and everything to do with good society. Obviously, that was just what he was looking for in a wife. He required someone from the right background in order to bear his children but who would be content to rusticate in the country and not interfere or ask awkward questions about the way he lived his life. He would marry her, ensure she was carrying his child and abandon her in Northumberland whilst he continued to live his life in any way he saw fit. What a widgeon she had been to almost fall for it. And, of course, he would keep his word not to interfere with her operation in Northumberland. After all, how could he countermand her orders when he was obviously intending to be elsewhere, indulging his extraordinary passions with one mistress or another?

The next morning, composed and determined, Clarissa informed an astonished Caroline that they would return to Northumberland the following day and to commence the preparations. Caroline tried to dissuade her mistress but had seen that look of intransigence before and knew she would be deaf to the voice of reason. What had happened to bring about this sudden change in her, that was what Caroline was burning to ask and, more to the point, what about his lordship? But Caroline could sense that something of immense import had occurred. She could see that Clarissa was mortified and, fearful of her volatile temper, for once did not have the courage to question her motives.

Aunt Marcia was far less circumspect. Clarissa was not yet well enough to undertake such an arduous journey. Surely she could wait another week or two? What was the rush? Clarissa kissed her, thanked her again and again for her kindness but was obdurate and would not be dissuaded from her purpose.

The following morning she entered her carriage to commence her journey: her heart — what was left of it — a leaden weight, dragging her into the depths of despair. But her face was set in grim lines of determination: her mind was made up and there would be no turning back.

As soon as she had waved her god-daughter away, Marcia removed to the morning-room, penned a hurried note to her son and summoned Bentley, instructing him that it should be sent to Newbury immediately.

# 21

Luc sat in the drawing-room at Deverill Hall, having successfully concluded his business on behalf of his old friend, Beatrice Higgins, far more swiftly and effectively than he had imagined would be possible. He would remain one more day in Newbury and deal with a few pressing matters his steward had brought to his attention and then return to London — and Clarissa.

It was at the end of the long day with his steward that his mother's note arrived: together with another. He read his mother's missive first and frowned in bewilderment. What in the name of Hades had caused Clarissa to run off like that and why had his mother not attempted to prevent her? She was surely not fit enough to undertake such an arduous journey; especially in that old rattletrap of hers? And, more to the point, what of the unsettled business between them? Luc was at a loss to understand her behaviour, and not a little perplexed by it.

Placing his concerns on one side for a moment he turned his attention to his second letter, instantly recognizing Felix's hand. It

397

appeared that Lord Eversham had been particularly keen to speak with Clarissa at a ball two nights previously and upon being informed of her return to Northumberland had dropped everything, with the season still in full swing, and headed for his own estate in that county.

Luc was now seriously concerned. He had noticed before that of all her suitors, Clarissa only appeared to have time for Eversham. Surely though she had not made an agreement with him? Had she done so, Luc was certain that she would have claimed a prior commitment when he proposed to her. She was, after all, straightforward in her dealings with him and not given to dissembling.

A surge of jealousy so fierce it caused him acute physical pain swept through Luc. Just the thought of that fortune-hunter getting anywhere near his beloved was enough to turn his blood cold. But it was not in Luc's nature to sit by inactive and wallow in self-pity. There was only one place now that he wished to be and, calling to the long-suffering Simms, told him to pack again and prepare their fastest travelling chaise: they were bound for Northumberland at first light.

They reached their destination in record

time thanks to Luc's grim determination and to the quality of his horses and conveyance. He checked into the best inn in Morpeth and headed straight for Greenacres. Caroline greeted him, showing both pleasure and very obvious relief at his unexpected arrival and informed him that Clarissa and her steward were on the far north-east border of the estate. A dry stone wall had collapsed and some of her best sheep had barged through the gap, trapping themselves on a dangerous precipice. Luc had no difficulty imagining Clarissa, still recovering from both her injuries and a tediously long journey, at the centre of this dangerous rescue mission and sighed in exasperation. Would she never learn?

'And she is out there attempting to get them back, with no thought for her own safety, I suppose?'

'Indeed, yes, I fear so. I did try to prevent her but she has not been herself since leaving London, my lord, and there is no reasoning with her.'

'I dare say not!' Luc was already remounting his horse and heading in the direction Caroline indicated, his head full of just what he intended to do to his headstrong, rebellious and passionately idealistic future wife when he finally got his hands on her.

Luc found the broken wall easily enough and heard a familiar voice echoing quietly from the other side of it. Three men were standing together, peering cautiously in the direction of that voice. Seeing Luc approaching, four motley dogs looked up and trotted across to investigate. Clarissa's menagerie presumably? But Luc hardly saw them — or the magnificent falcon perched on a low branch just above his head — his only concern was for Clarissa.

The men saw him and looked up. One of them, better dressed than the others and obviously the steward, stepped forward. Luc introduced himself and asked what was going on.

'Broken wall,' said Masters, stating the obvious. 'Blossom there,' he continued, indicating a large and elderly-looking sheep balanced precariously on the precipice, 'obviously went through to see what was what. Curious creatures are sheep and some of the others followed. We got the rest of them back safely but Blossom is stuck.'

'And you permitted Lady Hartley to go after her alone?'

'She would not have it any other way. We tried to dissuade her but she was deaf to reason. Right fond of Blossom is Lady Hartley and she reckons she can persuade her from the edge by talking to her.'

'I am sure she does!' agreed Luc, rolling his eyes in exasperation.

He walked across to the wall and called to Clarissa gently. She looked up at the sound of his voice, an astonished expression on her face. Luc was convinced that just for a moment he could detect a fleeting look of exquisite pleasure as well, but she quickly organized her features into an annoyingly neutral expression of greeting and he was no longer able to gauge her true feelings.

'What are you doing here?' she asked accusingly.

'I might ask the same thing of you?'

'Rescuing Blossom, of course.'

'Have you any idea how dangerous it is on that precipice?' Loose rocks, dislodged by Clarissa, tumbled down the couloir into the valley a hundred feet below, causing Luc's heart to miss a beat. Only the knowledge that the ground would surely give way under his weight if he went across to remove her bodily from danger prevented him from actually doing so.

'That is why I came out here myself,' she responded with perfect equilibrium. 'I am lighter than any of the men.'

'Come back here to safety at once,' he instructed, silently cursing her wilfulness.

With a resentful toss of her head, Clarissa complied. There was something about Luc in his present mood that did not brook argument. Ignoring his outstretched hand she stepped deftly over the broken wall and took up a position at his side.

'And what are we supposed to do about poor Blossom now?' she asked challengingly, hands on hips, the light in her luminous eyes bellicose.

'Just leave it to us.'

'Humph, such hubris!' She folded her arms and glowered at him. Luc responded to her aggressive stance by grinning, his smile broad and infectious. He was where he most wanted to be, her rebellious attitude did not concern him in the least and he would now earn her gratitude by rescuing her damned sheep for her.

Luc conferred with Masters, who confirmed that Blossom was placid and unlikely to panic. Climbing the broken wall, rope in hand, Luc stood on the edge of the solid ground and expertly lassoed Blossom. Two men came up behind him and together they hauled the sheep back to safety. Clarissa was upon her as soon as she had been lifted back across the wall, cuddling her and generally making a fuss of the totally unperturbed animal. Luc stood where he was, content now to bide his time and drink in the sight of Clarissa's shapely legs encased in their sturdy breeches.

Eventually satisfied that Blossom had suffered no injuries, Clarissa rejoined Luc. 'Thank you,' she said succinctly.

'You are welcome,' he responded, with equal verbal economy, waiting for her to meet his eye.

'What are you doing here, Luc?' she eventually asked of him.

'I could ask the same question of you.'

'I live here, remember?'

'H-hm, excuse me, m'lady, but I think you should see this.' Luc and Clarissa followed Masters to a point further along the wall. 'I have been having a bit of a look round. Could not understand why that wall should suddenly collapse. It was in good repair when I last checked it a week or two ago. This is a quiet part of the estate. No one would come out here without a reason but look at this.' Masters pointed to an area that had been trampled by hoofs. There were also fresh droppings. 'None of us have been out here for over a week,' he added, 'and I have looked at that section of wall too. It did not fall by accident.'

'Sabotage!' cried Clarissa, horrified. 'But why?'

'I could not say, my lady.'

'When I think what could have happened to Blossom and the others. Anyone who knows anything about sheep would appreciate that their innate sense of curiosity would make them want to see what was through that gap.'

'And so someone wishes you harm, Clarissa,' said Luc, joining in the conversation at last. 'Any idea who?'

'None whatsoever.' She hesitated. 'Not unless it is someone working for Salik.'

'Unlikely. Why would he want to risk damaging what he considers to be his own land? But I agree with Masters, this damage is deliberate. I also think that whoever did it will wish to know how successful he was.'

'They will come back, you mean?' said Clarissa, the glint of battle returning to her eye.

'Most assuredly. With your permission?' He raised a brow at Clarissa and she nodded her consent. 'Masters, post two men here out of sight and report back to the house as soon as anyone is seen. You say this part of the estate is remote and not used by passers-by so anyone coming here can only have one purpose.'

'Exactly so, my lord.'

'Come, Clarissa, you should be resting.'

And ignoring her scowl at his proprietorial behaviour he placed his hands on her waist and lifted her bodily onto her horse.

'How do you feel?' he asked her as they rode, side by side, back to Greenacres. Her face was pale and drawn, there were dark circles under her eyes and her head wound was still covered by a dressing, from the sides of which multi-coloured bruising spiralled outwards in an ugly mosaic.

Clarissa bit back the stinging retort which sprang to her lips and made do with a *perfectly well, thank you*. Luc wisely refrained from making any further comment, suppressed the grin that sprang to his lips and they completed their ride in a strained silence.

Once inside the house, Luc took control once again, much to Clarissa's chagrin, and closed the drawing-room door firmly behind them: first having told a beaming Caroline that they did not wish to be disturbed.

Clarissa took up a seat beside the fire, her dogs all vying for the position closest to her. She looked at them steadfastly, at an arrangement of flowers on a side table, out of the window — anywhere but at the powerful, self-contained figure of Luc looming danger-ously above her. He appeared perfectly at ease now, his irritation of earlier behind him, and content to allow the uneasy silence prevailing between them to continue. The atmosphere was intense, charged with anticipation, and some other inexplicable something. Eventually Clarissa could stand it no more and, looking up briefly, spoke.

'Why have you come, Luc?'

'Why? I should have thought that was obvious. We have incomplete business, if you recall.' His tone was mild.

'Huh!'

'And what does that mean?'

'I should have supposed, my lord, that my departure would have put paid to all that nonsense and saved you this long trip north into the bargain.'

'Would you indeed? Is that how you normally respond to a proposal of marriage, by running away from it?'

'When that proposal is intended as a marriage of convenience then yes, sir, I do!' She put up her chin, daring him to contradict her words.

'What do you mean, Clarissa?' He bent towards her and looked intensely at her face. She had not anticipated such minute scrutiny and was too slow to hide the hurt and anguish that suffused her features.

Standing to avoid his unwavering perusal, she paced the room. Did he take her to be that much of a simpleton? Surely he did not still expect her to meekly agree to his proposal? Too angry to prevent it, the question which she had sworn to herself she would never ask him, slipped unbidden from between her clenched lips.

'Why did you go to Newbury, Luc?'

Comprehension dawned then in a blinding flash and Luc could only curse his laggardly brain for not realizing the truth much earlier. She often went to his library in search of reading material — he had given her leave to do so — she must have seen that letter from Beatrice. Relief followed quickly on the heels of understanding and he smiled at her: a slow, glittering smile of intent.

'Beatrice Higgins and I are old friends,' he remarked languidly.

'I dare say, but what is that to me?'

'A great deal. I would expect my friends to become my wife's friends also.'

'What!' Clarissa could not believe her ears. He still expected her to marry him, in spite of everything she had discovered, and to be friendly towards his mistress as well! Just what did he take her for? 'Of all the presumptuous, arrogant, opinionated . . . ' Clarissa paused for a moment and took a deep breath. What was the point of railing against him and losing her composure into the bargain? She fought a brief battle to bring her temper back within her control and addressed him once again. 'I think you had better leave my house, sir.' She turned away from him.

'What has upset you so, my love?' he asked innocently, unable to prevent himself from teasing her a little more. 'Do you not wish to know more of poor Beatrice's troubles?'

The pathos in his tone — feigned surely? — made her look up at him sharply. 'Why do you make sport of me, sir?' She forced herself to speak with a discouraging indifference she did not feel.

'Because, my darling, it is very difficult not to when you behave thus. If you wished to know who Beatrice is why did you not simply ask my mother?'

'Your mother! Do not tell me that she condones your liaisons with these women . . . these women of, of . . . '

'Of the educational class?' offered Luc helpfully.

Clarissa stared at him, too angry and confused to speak but, somewhere deep within her, she was starting to feel as though she had made some sort of terrible mistake. The delirious feelings of ridiculous hope that accompanied this suspicion brought colour flooding to her face and tiny tentacles of desire — never far from the surface in her confrontations with Luc — stirred enthusiastically into life.

Taking pity on her, Luc placed his hands on her shoulders and gently guided her back to her chair. 'Clarissa,' he said softly, looking straight into her beautiful, wary eyes, 'Beatrice was my sisters' governess.'

'What?'

'Indeed, yes. When she retired she moved to a small cottage in the village rather than accepting the tied cottage in the grounds which we offered her. She had some money of her own, you see, left to her by her late husband but about a year ago a relative of her husband's returned from overseas and contacted her. He has, rather as Salik has with you, been trying to wheedle money out of her ever since and recently resorted to quite violent methods. I thought I had resolved the matter before I left Newbury but it seems he thought he could try intimidating the old lady again, safe in the knowledge that I was in London for the season and assuming that Beatrice did not have the authority to report to me there.' Luc paused for emphasis, his expression hard and icy. 'Well, he has discovered just how wrong he was and will not be troubling Beatrice again.'

'Oh!' It was all Clarissa could think of to

say. Colour flooded her cheeks for a second time as she realized the enormity of her mistake, whilst relief caused every muscle in her body to slacken. She expelled the breath she did not realize she had been holding, not having understood until that moment just how much it mattered to her that Luc should not be the heartless philanderer she had recently supposed him to be.

Luc smiled at her. 'Indeed, oh! And so now, do you suppose, we could continue with our much postponed discussion about my proposal of marriage to you? You wished to know why I had proposed and well — '

Once again the conversation was not to be, for there was an urgent tapping at the door. Caroline entered, looking suitably apologetic. 'Your pardon, I know you did not wish to be disturbed but Masters is here on business he insists is of the utmost urgency.'

'The wall, I suppose. Send him in, Caroline,' said Clarissa, pleased for a reprieve from Luc's intensity and for the opportunity to rearrange her turbulent thoughts.

'You were correct, my lord,' said Masters, without preamble. 'Someone did indeed come to inspect the wall and far quicker than I would have expected.' Clarissa hid her irritation at her steward for automatically addressing Luc. Did absolutely everyone naturally defer to his authority?

'Do you know who they were, Masters?'

'Indeed, my lord, they were two grooms in Lord Eversham's livery.'

Clarissa let out a gasp of horror.

'Thank you, Masters, I expected as much.'

'My lord.' Masters made a slight bow and left the room.

Clarissa recovered from this second revelation in five minutes with surprising alacrity. 'You suspected Lord Eversham of causing the sabotage?'

'Indeed! After all he did leave London in pursuit of you.'

'Nonsense! He informed me that he left several days before me, being as bored as I was with the proceedings. He stayed with friends *en route*, delaying his return and had no idea until he got back to Northumberland that I was also here. When he discovered that I was, he kindly came to call.'

'Clarissa, he left town two days after you did.'

'What? He could not have done! It is not possible.'

'Well, I can assure you that he did.'

Clarissa was stunned, stunned and furious to discover that once again she had been taken in by a plausible story. Eversham had called upon her three days after her return and they had ridden her estate together. He has spoken to her of farming and other country matters of mutual interest and she had enjoyed his congenial, undemanding company — at first. He had called again the following day and they had taken tea together. Somehow he had managed to stay to dinner as well. When she thought about it now Clarissa was not sure how that had come about, but quickly realized that it had been a mistake because yesterday afternoon he had called once more and proposed to her. She had known before he finished speaking that she would reject him but when, for the first time in their relationship, he patronized her — implying that the hard work she so enjoyed was not a suitable occupation for a lady, she could not be expected to understand its complexities, etc — making her sound like a mindless scatterbrain, it had been all she could do to remain civil in her rejection of his suit.

Before she could respond to Luc, they were interrupted yet again by Caroline informing her mistress, with a tight lipped look of disapproval, that Lord Eversham had come to call.

'Receive him, Clarissa,' urged Luc, slipping into the adjoining room and leaving the door slightly ajar.

Eversham strode into the room, a confident look of superiority on his face. 'My dear.' He bowed over Clarissa's hand and kissed it lingeringly. 'I have just heard the frightful news about your wall. Such a shame! I do trust that no sheep were lost.'

'Thank you, my lord, no. We managed to save them all.'

'You did? Excellent!' He paused and feigned horror. 'But surely, my dear, you did not attempt to rescue them yourself? My God, when I think of the danger you put yourself in. Surely your men did not allow it?'

'I am mistress here, Lord Eversham. My men take their orders from me.'

'Yes, of course, but, my dear, all this upset just goes to prove how right I have been all along in my advice to you. Farming is no occupation for a lady. That precipice is so dangerous I — '

'Excuse me, my lord, but how did you know that a precipice was involved?'

He looked momentarily nonplussed. 'Well, my dear, because you said so.'

'No, sir, I did not.'

'Well, then, I must have assumed it to be the case for I know the stretch in question slightly. Did we not ride that way together the other day?'

'No, sir.'

'Then one of your men must have told one of mine.' He looked relieved to have thought of it. 'Yes, that must be what it is.'

'Or perhaps, when you ordered your men to break down that particular stretch of wall?' suggested Luc, strolling casually into the room.

'You!' All the colour left Eversham's face.

'As you see.'

'What . . . I mean, Lady Hartley, surely you left London because you wanted to distance yourself from . . . ' His voice dwindled away beneath Luc's basilisk glare and Clarissa's continuing silence.

'You were saying, Eversham,' said Luc conversationally, moving to stand beside Clarissa.

'Well, I . . . I mean I just called to commiserate with Lady Hartley. I did not know you had a visitor, my dear, I will take my leave for now.'

'Just one thing, Eversham,' said Luc in a glacial tone, 'so that we understand each other right well. If anything, anything at all, goes amiss with Lady Hartley's land, or her livestock, in the future, I shall know it is you who are responsible and you will have me to answer to. Are we perfectly clear on that?'

'You dare to threaten me, sir?'

'Indeed I do,' concurred Luc mildly.

'Well really, really, I . . . ' He backed out of the room, still blustering wildly but knowing he was beaten.

Clarissa and Luc watched him go in momentary silence, before their eyes locked and they burst into spontaneous laughter.

'Thank you, Luc, you appear to have rescued me yet again.'

'My pleasure.' He moved towards the door and locked it.

'What are you doing?'

'Well, it appears impossible for us to have a conversation without interruption.'

'Yes but — '

'And I am tired of interruption,' he said, taking a meaningful pace towards her, his expression determined. 'I was about to tell you why I wish to marry you, Clarissa. Was that not what you wished to know?'

'Yes, but it is no longer of concern.'

'Because you have decided to marry me anyway?' he suggested, smiling expansively with anticipated victory. 'I knew you would see things my way eventually.'

'Certainly not!' Really, the conceit of the man.

'Then perhaps I had better explain my reasons. I want to marry you because you are different from the ladies I invariably meet. You are intelligent, entertaining, lively, beautiful and,' he hesitated, and offered her that heart-rending smile of his, the one that robbed her of the ability to think lucidly, 'as well as wanting you to mother my children I want to marry you because I cannot imagine being separated from you ever again. It is simply too painful to be endured. You cannot imagine the torture I went through when I received my mother's note informing me of your departure — and Eversham's. In short, Clarissa, I love you and cannot live without you. Will you consent to be my wife?'

Clarissa looked at him through tear-filled eyes, willing her resolve not to break down now. 'Not unless you can convince me there will be no other lady in your life except for me. I know it is customary for gentleman such as yourself to take mistresses but, Luc, I should warn you that you would not find me at all accommodating in that regard. I would not be willing to tolerate any form of duplicity; no matter how discreet.'

'You have no cause for concern on that score. Do you really imagine I would ever yearn for any type of solace that you could not provide?'

'It is my understanding that these things happen as a matter of course.'

'I have sown all of my wild oats, my love, and am ready to settle down with just you.

You have my word on that.'

Clarissa regarded him in silence for a long time. His gaze did not once waver and she felt herself floundering somewhere in the depths of his piercing black eyes, now so full of entreaty, so sincere. Just for a moment Clarissa feared for her sanity. Could this Adonis standing before her really be offering her his all? It hardly seemed credible: yet it was apparently true. She would be mad to refuse him but how could she be sure that he would keep his word?

Sighing, frustrated by her weakness, bubbling over with a happiness that refused to be suppressed, Clarissa lifted her eyes to his and smiled. She would not decline his proposal, she knew that now. She wanted him with every fibre of her being and no longer had the strength or willpower to pretend otherwise. Whatever problems lay ahead, they would somehow resolve them together.

One final realization clinched this decision for Clarissa, persuading her that following her heart and accepting him was the only thing she could do. If she meant as little to him as she had so recently thought, then why had he followed her all the way to Northumberland? Could it be that he really did actually love her? He had, after all, finally said the words: words she had long since despaired of ever hearing fall from his lips. Her heart soared and threatened to overflow: too small suddenly to contain all the feelings of elation and surging happiness that were laying siege to it.

'If I ever find out that you have taken a mistress, Luc, then I will not answer for the consequences. If that situation ever arose I would not be held responsible for my actions.' In spite of her best efforts she was unable to maintain her stern expression and it gradually gave way to a radiant smile of unmitigated joy. 'You would do well to heed my warning, my lord.'

A glimmer of hope took up residence in Luc's eyes. 'Can I take it that you are saying yes?' He could not yet trust himself to believe the very obvious truth. She must say it.

'Yes, Luc, I would very much like to marry you, please.'

We do hope that you have enjoyed reading this large print book.

Did you know that all of our titles are available for purchase?

We publish a wide range of high quality large print books including:
**Romances, Mysteries, Classics**
**General Fiction**
**Non Fiction and Westerns**

Special interest titles available in large print are:
**The Little Oxford Dictionary**
**Music Book**
**Song Book**
**Hymn Book**
**Service Book**

Also available from us courtesy of Oxford University Press:
**Young Readers' Dictionary**
**(large print edition)**
**Young Readers' Thesaurus**
**(large print edition)**

For further information or a free brochure, please contact us at:
**Ulverscroft Large Print Books Ltd.,**
**The Green, Bradgate Road, Anstey,**
**Leicester, LE7 7FU, England.**
**Tel:** (00 44) **0116 236 4325**
**Fax:** (00 44) **0116 234 0205**

*Other titles published by*
*The House of Ulverscroft:*

## THE UNCONVENTIONAL MISS WALTERS

### Fenella-Jane Miller

Eleanor Walters is obliged, by the terms of her aunt's will, to marry a man she dislikes: the irascible, but attractive, Lord Leo Upminster . . . Leo finds Eleanor's unconventional behaviour infuriating, her beauty irresistible and their agreement not to consummate the union increasingly impossible. It is only when he allows his frustration and jealousy to drive her away that he realizes what he has lost . . . Meanwhile, in her self-imposed exile on a neglected country estate, Eleanor becomes embroiled in riots and treachery. In a desperate race, can Leo save both her life and their marriage?

# PERFIDY AND PERFECTION

## Kate Allan

In the English village of Middleton, at the time of Jane Austen, the rector's daughter, Sophy Grantchester, keeps a shameful secret: she's a novelist. Seeking inspiration for her next book, she finds it in the form of her rakish cousin, Lord Hart. She writes him into her story, and — unwittingly — into her heart. To his surprise he falls for his poor and proper cousin — but she cannot be a wife. For surely no man would tolerate her novel writing . . . However, determined to win her, Lord Hart resorts to devious means. But Sophy could have told him that trickery is no recipe for success in love.

# DANCE FOR A DIAMOND

## Melinda Hammond

It's 1815, and Antonia Venn describes herself as a very average sort of female: a poor little dab of a girl, and certainly nothing to win the heart of a man of fortune or fashion. So in a bid for independence, and at a time when the waltz was born, she decides to open a dancing school in Bath, despite the misgivings of her family. And it is here that she takes on the beautiful Isabella Burstock as a pupil. However, this decision puts Antonia on a collision course with the young heiress's autocratic brother . . .

# FREE SPIRIT

## Coral Leend

Reaching port in his battered sailing barque after a brutal journey around Cape Horn, Madoc Morgan is keen to see Nia La Velle, the woman he loves. Nia, his former tomboy playmate with gypsy blood, is now an educated lady. Nia hides her enduring love for Madoc and un-wittingly sparks off a turbulent family feud between Madoc, his brother Robert and his fiancée Lucy, who also has feelings for Madoc. As jealousies ride high, how can Madoc end the feud that is tearing them all apart?

# THE ADVENTURESS

## Ann Barker

Florence Browne lives in poverty with her miserly father, but seeking adventure, she goes to Bath under the assumed name Lady Firenza Le Grey. But there, she meets a man calling himself Sir Vittorio Le Grey, who accuses her of being an adventuress. When her previous suitor, Gilbert Stapleton, visits Bath, Florence is plagued by doubts. Is Sir Vittorio the wicked Italian he appears to be? Are Mr Stapleton's professions of love sincere? And how can she accept an offer of marriage from anyone while she is still living a lie?